The Invasive Species

FRANKIE BOW

Hawaiian Heritage Press

DEDICATION

To my endemic and our two little hybrids.

CONTENTS

ACKNOWLEDGMENTS

I could not have written this without the tireless support of my family. Thank you.

CHAPTER ONE

"Careful!" I yelled.

"I'm always careful, Molly." Emma accelerated around the battered Subaru that had been impeding our progress and veered back into our lane just in time to avoid going head-on into the lifted black truck hurtling toward us from the opposite direction.

"Geez," Emma declared. "People need to learn how to drive."

We were headed through a thickly forested section of unincorporated Kuewa, down to the Farm Lots subdivision to meet Art Lam. I was excited and a little apprehensive about conducting our first interview with a prominent farmer. Like most of the business owners I had met in Mahina, Art was outspoken and prickly.

The jungle around us looked deceptively calm. Only the top branches of the green canopy overhead flailed and tossed.

"I thought they said the hurricane was supposed to pass us by," I said. "I hope we don't get blown off the road. Donnie was worried about us driving down. If anything bad happens, he's going to be all, 'I told you so.' Oh, he said to watch out for the antis."

"You mean the eco-loonies? Pfft. What are they gonna do to us? All rickety, frail vegans, those guys."

"I was a vegan for a few months in grad school. It didn't make me rickety and frail. It made me fat and grouchy."

"Oh, but Molly. Didn't you tell Donnie this was for our grant?"

"He was impressed by my being a co-investigator on a federal grant until he realized it was going to mean extra work for me and no extra money. He was like, 'Oh, so you'll be even busier than usual, which means I'll get to see you less. You'll be more stressed-out when I do see you, and we won't have any more money coming in. Tell me again why I should be happy about this?'"

"What did you say?"

"The only way I could explain it was, 'This is who I am. This is what I do.'"

"Right on," Emma said.

"I told him, 'I ask questions. I find answers, and I help to advance knowledge. Even when it means driving through a hurricane to interview a grumpy farmer.'"

A blast of wind jolted Emma's car and spattered her windshield with droplets. Emma swore and switched on the wipers.

"Having a grant keeps you mobile," Emma said. "It looks good on your CV in case you want to go somewhere else. Especially in your discipline. I mean, how many business communication professors have grants?"

"I would never mention staying mobile to Donnie. He's already paranoid about it. I don't know why. He's afraid maybe deep down I'm planning to leave Mahina and move back to the mainland."

"It's a pretty common fear. It's the reason it takes us a while to warm up to you people."

"You people?"

"Malihini. Mainland transplants. Immigrants. Invasive species. You move here. You make friends. You decide you can't hack it here, and you end up leaving us."

"I'm not going anywhere. Did you just call me an invasive species?"

"So what then? He's gonna give you a hard time about the grant?"

"No. He said he still didn't understand why I was doing it, but the most important thing was to have a happy wife. Happy wife, happy life."

"He actually said, 'Happy wife, happy life?'"

"I know. It sounds kind of condescending. But I don't mind so much. It means he and I have congruent goals, right? I can work with that. Are you sure we're going the right way? This road isn't even two lanes wide anymore."

"Speaking of invasive species," Emma said. "All

this stuff that's crowding us on the sides of the road? This is all strawberry guava. And those trees overhead? Those are Albizia. They're a menace."

"The tall ones making a canopy over the road? They look nice."

"They grow fast, and they're top-heavy, but they have a shallow root system. So they're the first thing to fall over in a high wind."

"Good to know since we're driving down a road lined with them on a windy morning."

"I think I saw a couple on your property," Emma said.

"Oh, Albizia. I knew the name sounded familiar. Donnie's been after me to get those taken out. But if I do that, my carport and the whole front of my house won't have any shade."

"How long have you been married now?" Emma snorted. "You're still living in your own separate houses?"

"Separate houses are the key to marital peace."

"I bet that's not what Donnie thinks. Well, here we are. Art Lam's place should be up ahead."

"Emma, what happened over there? Did the wind do that?"

Emma slowed the car and pulled over to the side of the road, where the patchy asphalt disappeared into the jungle. She got out, and I scooted over the center console to exit on her side. We approached the damaged area of the orchard. It looked uglier the closer we got.

"That's not wind," Emma said. "Those look like

clean cuts."

I pulled up my tablet and started to snap photographs. I could see the hacked up vegetation used to be a papaya grove. The chopped trees lay askew, their clusters of bulbous fruit still intact.

"They left all of the papayas," I said. "What was the point?"

"Not theft. Vandalism."

I continued to snap pictures, turning in a slow circle. Even with the cloud cover, it was too bright for me to see what was on the screen. I'd have to trust I was getting what I wanted. Whoever was responsible for the destruction had started at the side of the road, and made a small incursion into the papaya grove. Further in, the trees stood intact. Maybe the vandals got scared, or caught, before they could finish the job.

"Does this have to do with the biotech debate?" I asked Emma. "Are these papayas transgenic?"

"Probably. Pretty much all the commercially grown papayas in this state are. And have been, since the late 1990s. Funny how everyone's getting upset about it now. Where were we supposed to meet Art?"

"In the house. I wonder if he knows about this."

"Molly. Over here."

I turned toward her, still taking pictures. To give the users an analog experience, the tablet's designers had built in reassuring shutter-click and film-advance noises. Click, whir. Click, whir. Click—I lowered the tablet slowly.

Emma and I stared at a boot. Which was on the end of a leg. Which had been separated, recently and rather violently, from its owner.

CHAPTER TWO

We sprinted down the road toward Art Lam's farmhouse, the only building visible on the stretch of narrow road. "Farmhouse" was probably too grandiose name for it. The building was a single-story kit home with battered sand-colored siding and a rust-splotched white metal roof.

Emma and I knocked and rang the doorbell, then tried the front door. It didn't budge.

"It's locked," I said stupidly.

"Of course it's locked," Emma scoffed. "Where do you think we are, Mayberry?"

"I can't get a signal here." I pressed buttons on my cell phone, finally shaking it in frustration, as if that would force the recalcitrant device to see things my way. Water droplets plopped onto my face and bare arms, and I noted, in a sort of detached way, I felt cold.

"*My* carrier doesn't even pretend to get reception

way out here. Maybe we should go back and wait by the car till someone drives by and flag them down."

"Out here? No way. I don't want to end up with my head in someone's freezer."

"Maybe there's a phone in the house," Emma said. "I'm gonna look for a way in. What? You get any better ideas?"

Emma disappeared around the corner of the house. I didn't like the prospect of breaking and entering, but our only other option was to leave the scene without calling anyone, and that didn't seem right either. I set off after Emma. On the side of the house, access to the two small windows was blocked by heaps of black plastic plant pots and macadamia nut husks. (A byproduct of local mac nut production, the husks apparently make a wonderful mulch for phosphorus-depleted soil. I'd learned all about it in my gardening club.)

"Hey, Emma," I called. "Maybe we should just drive back up to town until we get a signal—"

A vitreous crash interrupted me.

"Got it," Emma yelled. I ran around to the back of the house to see Emma's stubby leg disappearing through a window.

"Emma, what did you do?"

She poked her head back out.

"It was stuck. I hadda break it. Go back around to the front."

"Where did you learn how to do that?" I followed Emma into the house. It smelled like cigarettes, pine cleaner, and stale coffee.

"Those jalousie windows are way too flimsy. An' you leave a paint bucket right under the window, you're just asking to get broken into. Hello?" Emma called out.

We crossed the living room en route to the kitchen.

"Hello?" I echoed. No answer. The house was empty, as far as we could tell.

We finally found a phone, a wall-mounted, rotary dial model.

Emma picked up the receiver and listened, then dialed.

The nine took an excruciatingly long time to ease back to its home position. The two ones, which followed, went much faster.

"Hello?" Emma said. "Eh, we get one emergency. Nah, too late. Address?"

I scrambled to dig through my bag in search of the address, with no success.

"We're down at Art Lam's place," Emma said. "You know Art Lam, right? So there's a dead body. No, I didn't ID him. Actually, I don't know. We're not sure it's a whole body."

I made a face, and Emma shrugged as if to say, "Sorry."

"We didn't take a close look," she continued. "Yes. Yes, I do. No, I'm not. Okay, we'll wait."

Emma replaced the receiver.

"They'll be here as soon as they can."

"Looks like the eco-loonies mean business," I said. We were silent for a moment, contemplating

Art Lam's green and gold shag carpet.

"All right," Emma said. "Let's get those panes back in the window before the cops get here. As far as they know, we found the door unlocked. Right?"

CHAPTER THREE

By the time the emergency responders showed up, Emma and I were back in her car, quietly watching raindrops streak across the windows. Detective Ka`imi Medeiros rapped on the driver's side window and signaled us to get out.

Detective Medeiros was a big man. Fortunately, he was equipped with a big umbrella. The three of us stood sheltered from the rain as a uniformed officer and a paramedic, both gloved, poked through the hacked-up papaya trees. Then they stopped. The officer took a photo, and the paramedic crouched down to do something. I turned away, not wanting to see what happened next.

"Professor Barda." Detective Medeiros scowled at me.

"Detective."

"You're a long way from home."

Ka`imi Medeiros and I had become acquainted

the previous summer when a houseguest of mine met a nasty end. Medeiros has known my husband, Donnie, since second grade or thereabouts. Somehow, the familiarity wasn't translating to any kind of warmth on his part. It was almost as if he believed Emma and I were responsible for the grisly scene in front of us. Our explanation, that we were conducting research, didn't seem to thaw him.

"Who knew you were coming down here to interview Art Lam?" Medeiros asked.

"Our Institutional Research Board has a copy of our scheduled interviews," I said.

"Art could've told someone," Emma added.

"Do you know if Art Lam had any enemies?"

"Based on today's events, my guess would be yes," Emma said. "Who'd want to kill a papaya farmer, though?"

"Until we ID the remains," Medeiros cautioned, "we can't make any assumptions as to the identity of the victim."

"Art Lam wasn't in his hou—" I began, cutting it short when I felt Emma's foot treading firmly on mine.

"Officer, we need to get back to campus." Emma stepped toward her car. "Will this take long?"

"Just a few more questions," Medeiros said.

Emma sighed.

After a good hour of relentless and, in my opinion, needlessly repetitive interviewing, I had to say something.

"Detective, my class starts in half an hour."

"If you're late to class because of a murder investigation," Medeiros said, "I'm sure your students will forgive you."

"Not her accounting majors," Emma said.

"She's right, Detective."

Medeiros sighed.

"Okay, go. But don't leave the island. We're going to want to talk to you again."

On the drive back, the wind intensified, bouncing branches around and pummeling Emma's little car.

"What a morning. And now I get to teach for three solid hours."

"Seriously?" Emma said. "What idiot gave you *that* schedule?"

"Well, I'm the interim department chair. So apparently I'm the idiot."

"Oh. I almost forgot. What are we gonna put in our notes for today's interview?"

"Shoot, I don't know. Remember what Medeiros said? They're not even sure it was Art Lam."

"Yeah, hard to recognize him without his head."

"Emma!"

"Sorry."

"I don't want to talk about it anymore. Do you mind?"

"Fine. Hey, so how's it going with your never-shuts-up student? You have him today, right?"

"Oh, Lars Suzuki. I don't know what his deal is. Maybe he has some kind of condition."

"Look it up," Emma said.

I turned on my phone. "Still no signal. We'll have

to wait till we're closer to town. Lars is probably waiting for me at my office already, ready to walk me to class and talk my ear off."

"He does that every time?" Emma asked.

"Pretty much. He seems like a nice kid. He's just so *up*. He wears me out. Like an energetic puppy. He would be great to have at a dinner party, though. You'd never lack for conversation."

When Emma and I got to campus, I took a deep breath and switched to teacher mode, readying myself for an afternoon of what Arlie Hochschild calls "emotional labor." I had to be upbeat for my students. It wasn't their fault I'd almost tripped over a dismembered body earlier. They didn't have to know how I yearned to drive straight home, take a hot shower, climb into my fluffy spa bathrobe, and wait out the storm with a lightweight mystery and a big glass of red wine.

Lars Suzuki was waiting for me at my office door. On the way to the classroom, he trotted beside me, talking without a break about his other classes, his approach to the assignments in my class, and his newest job, an internship in our fundraising office. To hear him tell it, Lars had a lot of different jobs. I supposed he managed to talk himself into them, and then talk himself right out of them again soon after.

Lars was one of those college kids who, at the age of twenty or so, still looked like a boy. He was just over five feet and slight. He wore his straight black hair about an inch long, exactly the right length to stick out from his head in a radial pattern like Nancy in the old comic strip. I smiled and nodded at appropriate intervals as we walked together, relieved I didn't have to talk.

We reached the classroom building, a stained concrete block with a red metal roof. I found the room I was looking for and pushed open the swinging door. Lars followed me inside without hesitation, his nonstop chatter echoing off the green tiles.

"Lars," I said. "This is the ladies' room."

He backed out and examined the area around the door. His face fell as he spotted the word "Ladies" stenciled in black paint on the concrete wall.

"I'll see you in class," I called out to him.

"Okay, Professor," he called back. "See you in class."

By the time my last class let out, I had a dull ache in my stomach. I hadn't eaten all day, which only happens if I am very upset. I didn't stop at my office. Instead, I went straight out to the parking lot, threw my laptop bag into the passenger seat of my 1959 Thunderbird, buckled in, and started driving. I should have stopped at the grocery store to stock up on coffee, but I didn't do that either. As my two-and-a-quarter inch whitewall tires (just like in the original Thunderbird ads) splashed through muddy puddles and my vacuum motors struggled to push the wipers across the windshield, all I could think about was how much I wanted to be home and done with this horrible, horrible day. Driving up to the wrecked papaya orchard, and then spotting the single boot…all day I'd been struggling to push the image out of my head.

I concentrated on the immediate future: I'd steer my car into the shelter of my narrow carport, run inside, and pour myself a glass of wine. Maybe a hot bath next, but first things first. Then I'd send a text to Donnie inviting him to stop by after he was done at the Drive-Inn. Things would look better once I got home, and Donnie was with me.

My optimism, as it turns out, was premature.

CHAPTER FOUR

The toppled tree had taken out a side window and a good chunk of my new copper gutter on the way down, landing on my carport hard enough to crush the metal roof into a V-shape. It was almost as if the Albizia had sacrificed itself deliberately, just to ruin my day.

It was just getting dark. Donnie would still be at work. I backed into the street and started driving the few blocks down toward the Bayfront, to Donnie's Drive-Inn. Through the tangle of power lines strung across the narrow street, I could see a sliver of the bay. The water reflected the sky, a moody, churning gray.

Donnie walked out to meet me the moment I pulled into the parking lot. When I saw him, I immediately felt better. Tall and well-built, his neat black hair touched with gray at the temples, my husband was awfully easy on the eyes. He didn't go to the gym and didn't need to. He spent all day moving heavy things around: fifty-pound bags of rice, pallets of frozen hamburger patties, and the painted red picnic benches, which had to be upended and hosed down every night.

I climbed out of the driver's seat into Donnie's embrace and began to sob into his Donnie's Drive-Inn polo shirt.

"Donnie," I blubbered. "It's a mess. It's…I don't know if anyone can fix it."

"It's okay. I have a whole stack of clean shirts in the office."

I looked up to see his handsome face clouded with worry. He produced a clean tissue from somewhere and handed it to me.

"Oh, your shirt. Sorry about that. No, when I went home just now... You know how it's been so windy today? Well, one of my trees—"

"I saw. One of your Albizias fell over."

"You saw?"

Donnie pulled me close. Wearing my platforms, I was exactly the right height for my nose to lodge in his armpit. I closed my eyes and inhaled his spicy-clean deodorant smell.

"I went by your place this afternoon to check for damage," he said. "I called Konishi Construction right away."

I pulled my head free.

"You already called?"

"Just for an estimate," he said quickly. "Don't worry. I didn't make any decisions for you. I know you don't like people making decisions for you."

"No, no, it's good. It's great. Thank you. I thought I was going to have to find someone myself. So I guess I'll move to your place now. For however long it takes to fix the damage, anyway. I hope it's okay."

"Of course. Stay as long as you want." He kissed the top of my head. "I have to get back. See you at home tonight. You going to be all right?"

"Sure. I'll be fine."

I watched Donnie walk away, his red polo shirt straining over his strong shoulders and his smooth, golden biceps. I supposed there were worse things than moving in with my handsome husband for a little while.

I drove the short distance back to my house and went inside. Branches protruded into the house through the window. The floor underneath was covered with water, leaves, and broken glass. I swept up as much of the mess as I could, then pulled some clean towels from the linen closet and wiped the floor until it was merely damp. That was as good as it would get. In Mahina's humid climate, nothing ever gets completely dry.

I checked my computer for new email messages. The only one that required an immediate reply was from the Student Retention Office. Linda (they all seem to be named Linda) was asking me to consider making the required readings in my Intro course optional. I could just imagine how her bright idea would go over with those students who actually had bought the textbook and course packet when class started two months earlier, and completed the assigned work.

Linda had also attached a list of students who "needed" to be excused from an upcoming writing assignment. These exemptions, she explained, were based on results from the new Foundation-funded software connected to our Learning Management System and designed to track student progress in real time. We hadn't yet achieved the administrators' dream of replacing the faculty with software, but we were getting closer.

I wrote back, politely telling Linda the suggested changes were not possible at this time, what with the semester already half over, and thanking her for keeping me "in the loop." The university's legal department (blessings upon every one of them) had ruled that because of academic freedom, the Student Retention Office couldn't *require* us to dumb down our classes, although they were free to *ask* us to do so. This verdict had been greeted with wailing and gnashing of teeth on the part of the administration, and much rejoicing by the faculty.

I made sure my reply was sent, packed up my computer, and retrieved my overnight bag from the wrecked carport. I went to my bedroom and collected a week's worth of outfits, a few items of jewelry, my makeup bag, my special comb for curly hair, and my Alice Mongoose sleep shirt. I took one last look around before I left, to make sure I wasn't forgetting anything. It was both liberating and discouraging to realize how little I had worth stealing.

It may have seemed unusual for a happily married couple to live apart, but when Donnie and I got married, each of us already had a house. Donnie's was a spacious ranch model on three acres. He'd had it redone by a famous interior designer from Honolulu, known for his spare and elegant aesthetic. It had a professional kitchen with a gas range, which was unusual on this island. (The utility wasn't about to dig through volcanic rock to install gas lines, so if you wanted to cook on a flame you had to arrange to get propane delivered. For a serious cook like Donnie, it was worth it.)

My 1920s plantation house was far more modest than Donnie's place. But it was conveniently located in town, just a few blocks from Donnie's Drive-Inn and a short drive from campus. I'd redone the plumbing, added ceiling fans, refinished the hardwood floors, and overall gotten it just the way I liked it. The drawback—and it was a big one—was the single bathroom. Donnie and I had considered selling our respective properties and buying something together, but so far, it hadn't worked out.

Donnie's house was about a twenty-minute drive out of town when the traffic was good. And on this day, the traffic not good. The wind had knocked a tree onto power lines, pulling down two utility poles onto the main highway. The utility's repair crew was taking up the right lane, forcing all traffic into single file. Eventually I made it through the bottleneck and turned off onto Donnie's street.

Donnie's backyard was surrounded by a chain link fence, a necessity back when Donnie's son Davison used to keep a pack of hunting dogs. I still held my mainland prejudice against chain link fences. Donnie didn't understand why I would have a grudge against something so practical, but chain link fences made me think of the neighborhood near where I went to grad school: Windblown trash, weedy vacant lots, and ominous graffiti. Shopping carts piled with junk, next to mounds of dirty blankets, which, on closer inspection, turned out to be human beings *way* down on their luck. To me, a chain link fence said "skid row." To Donnie, it was simply a practical choice. It wouldn't rust in the rain or get knocked over by rambunctious Rottweilers.

I parked on the street, found the key, threw my overnight bag over my shoulder, and went inside. The interior, as usual, was immaculate. The chalk-white walls of the living room were hung with paintings from a couple of local artists he'd just started collecting. A carved koa wood bowl, patterned with sections cut so thin they were translucent, glowed on the coffee table. The centerpiece of the room was a low-slung Ettore Sottsass sofa in gunmetal leather with black seat cushions. I liked the sofa. It almost made up for the chain link fence.

I took my clothes down the hallway to the master bedroom, unloaded them onto the platform bed, and opened the closet. To the right of Donnie's perfectly pressed black slacks and his crisp aloha shirts and Donnie's Drive-Inn red polo shirts hung two of my dresses. I scooted the polo shirts aside to make more room and hung up the clothes I'd brought from home: a charcoal Lilli Ann jacket with black piping; wide-leg sailor trousers; a black pencil skirt; a few white blouses, both short sleeved and long.

Donnie could talk all he wanted about my moving in so we could live like a real married couple. As long as I wasn't getting any more than a linear foot of closet space, I'd always feel like a guest in his house.

I heard the front door open.

"Molly?"

"Donnie?" I slid the closet shut and hurried out to the living room. "You're home early. Everything okay?"

"Ka`imi Medeiros stopped by the Drive-Inn. He told me what happened this morning down at Art Lam's place."

CHAPTER FIVE

"Detective Medeiros stopped by? Uh-oh." I dropped onto the couch.

"Molly." Donnie eyed me. "Why didn't you tell me?"

"Where are you going?"

"I'm going to get a glass of wine." Donnie turned away.

"It's a little early for you. Isn't it?"

"I sense I'm going to need it. Would you like one?"

"Yes, please."

Donnie brought a bottle and two glasses.

"I didn't want to spring it on you while you were at work," I said. "I figured a tree crashing through my window was enough bad news for one afternoon. What did Detective Medeiros tell you? Do they know who the victim was?"

"He didn't say. I had a bad feeling about you

driving all the way down there. At least you weren't alone." Donnie poured a glass of wine for me, and then one for himself. "This isn't the first time someone's biotech crop has been vandalized. Those activists can be unpredictable."

I took a sip. "You did say that. I remember."

"I'm just glad you're not hurt."

"On the bright side, I'm sure our other interviews will go a lot better than this one."

"Molly, you're not going to keep working on this grant after what happened this morning, are you? Aren't you worried?"

"I'm a nervous wreck. Of course I am. Donnie, you know me. I'm not a thrill seeker. I'm cautious, bordering on cowardly."

"Good," Donnie said.

"But this didn't have anything to do with Emma or me. We just happened to be in the wrong place at the wrong time."

"I know this grant is important to you. But it's not worth your life."

"Donnie, I realize you're worried about my safety, and I appreciate it. Really, I do. But I have to keep my research going. I can't just opt out. How about this? From here on out, Emma and I won't go anywhere remote. We'll talk to people right here in town, or we'll do our interviews by phone."

"Molly." Donnie took my hand. "You don't know who did this. How do you know they won't come after you next? You have to get as far away from this as you can."

"Well, what do you want me to do?" I pulled my hand away, picked up the wine bottle, and refilled my glass. "We can't just give the grant money back."

I wasn't sure it was true. But after all it had taken to get the grant, and how much work we'd already put into it, I had no intention of giving the money back.

"I thought you said there wasn't any money," Donnie said.

"Not in the form of a paycheck, but it helps us pay for recording equipment, conference travel, publication fees—"

"Publication *fees?*" Donnie set down his wine. "Are you telling me you have to pay to publish your articles? Aren't they supposed to pay you?"

"Not academic journals. You never get paid for an academic article. And more and more journals require pub fees."

"All this time I thought you were getting paid for publishing. Are you telling me it's been costing us money?"

"Donnie, it's not costing 'us' money. You and I still have separate bank accounts."

"I know. We still need to sit down and figure it all out."

Donnie and I had been having trouble working out the details of our shared finances. Specifically, there was the delicate matter of Donnie's awful son Davison, whom I wouldn't trust anywhere near my hard-earned money. Of course, I couldn't tell Donnie outright. Davison was my stepson now, and for Donnie's sake, I had to pretend to like him.

Before I met Donnie, young Davison had been enrolled in my Intro to Business Management class. There, he had distinguished himself as a remorseless cheater and a world-class suckup. While those qualities probably boded well for his future business career, they didn't make a great impression on me.

"I need to publish my research to get tenure," I said. "It's a requirement of my job. You've heard of publish or perish?"

I poured out the last of the wine, dividing it between us.

"Doesn't it seem like a racket to you?" Donnie said.

"It probably is. Donnie, listen. You don't need to worry about me. Emma and I are going to be very careful."

"I don't want some crazy person cutting your brake lines," Donnie said. "Or firebombing my restaurant."

"Emma and I are just asking questions. We're neutral. We're not the ones growing things, or telling people what to plant. No one's going to come after us."

"Okay," Donnie said, in a tone that signaled that he might have lost the battle, but we would see who'd win the war.

"Anyway," he said. "I do have some good news."

"Wonderful. I'd love to hear some good news right now."

"I talked to Davison this morning."

"Oh?"

"Looks like he'll be able to come out to visit us for his session break."

"Oh, great." I drained my wine glass and stood up.

"Where are you going?"

"To go open another bottle of wine."

"Molly, we've already finished a whole bottle between us. Do you really think you should—"

"Donnie, I've had a really, really bad day. No, you're right. I shouldn't be drinking this much on a weeknight. Maybe I should go up to the yoga studio. If I leave now, I can catch the last session of Restorative Yoga."

"Is the kid going to be there?" Donnie asked. "The one who used to be your student?"

"Oh, Primo? No. I told you. I'm not taking any more classes from him."

Far from being a "kid," Primo Nordmann was, in fact, pushing forty, despite his surfer-y blond good looks.

"One of the two sisters will probably be teaching, either Sharon or Sharla. When I went in the one time, I didn't realize I was taking a class from one of my former students until it was too late."

When Donnie had picked me up after the yoga session, the extroverted Primo had come over and introduced himself. The shirtless and well-built Primo had proceeded to say a number of complimentary things about my innate yoga talent, rattling on about how flexible I was and how I was one of the few women he knew who could throw her legs behind her head. It didn't sit well with my conservative husband.

"Good," Donnie said. "I don't trust him."

I stood up.

"Donnie, I already *said* I'm not going to take any more classes from him. What else do you want me to do? Is this how it's going to be? You're going to disapprove of *every single thing* I do?"

"No, Molly, I—"

"What I do for my job? What I do for exercise? What I do for fun? Oh, wait, I don't *do* anything for fun because I have no spare time because I don't have tenure yet, and despite my teaching load, I *still* have to publish my brains out, which apparently is something you don't approve of either. So what's the plan? You're just going to keep at it, drip, drip, drip, until I get fed up and leave, just like—"

I stopped myself before I said something irreparable. Donnie's first wife, Sherry, had walked out on him years earlier, leaving Donnie to raise Davison alone. Their history worried me a little, to be honest. At moments like this, I wondered if I would end up following suit.

"Molly, I don't want anything bad to happen to you. I—I'm very proud of you. You should know that."

I sank back down onto the couch.

"Sorry for getting snippy. This really hasn't been a good day."

"I know." Donnie put one arm around my

shoulder and gave me a squeeze. "Go to your yoga class. I'll get dinner started."

"I don't really have the energy now. I don't want to get back in the car and drive all the way back up to town. And I still have a pile of papers to grade. Oh, can I help with dinner?"

"No, no," Donnie said quickly. "Get your grading done. I'll take care of dinner."

CHAPTER SIX

The strains of Khachaturian's "Masquerade Waltz" broke through my sleep. I spent a few disoriented moments trying to figure out where I was. Once I had established I was in Donnie's bedroom, I quickly located my cell phone on the mango wood night table. Donnie had left for work already. I was alone on the vast platform bed.

"Molly," my phone said, in Pat Flanagan's voice. "Where are you?"

Pat used to be a crime reporter for the *County Courier*, before the layoffs. He now taught composition part-time at Mahina State, which was how I knew him. His adjunct position paid poorly, but it provided access to our library's news and market research databases. He made his real living from *Island Confidential*.

"I'm just waking up." I groaned.

"Emma and I are at the Pair-O-Dice. When can

you be here?"

"I'm still down at Donnie's."

"She's still at Donnie's." I heard Pat's voice.

"Tell her to catch a ride with Donnie," Emma said in the background. "Oh, maybe he starts work early."

"Earlier than you can imagine," I said. "I think he left hours ago."

"Doesn't it bother you that he's always at work?"

Pat, whose Irish Catholic parents stuck it out until death parted them, was not a fan of the institution of marriage. His wedding present to me had been an early edition chapbook of Charlotte Perkins Gilman's *The Yellow Wallpaper*.

I sat up.

"I really can't complain about the hours Donnie puts in. I think the only reason Donnie's Drive-Inn does so well is because Donnie's always down there supervising and helping out. If you want to make a restaurant work here, you have to be single-minded and detail-obsessed, the way he is. Those poor souls who get into the restaurant business because they love cooking and playing host? They're the ones who are out of business in two months. You're having breakfast at the Pair-O-Dice?"

"After a fashion," Pat said. "So what explains the fact that this place isn't out of business yet?"

"A very good question. Okay, I'll be there as soon as I can."

The Pair-O-Dice Bar and Grill in Downtown Mahina was the kind of place most sensible people would drive right by. Donnie didn't like it, of course. He thought it was a dump. The bar looked more impressive at night when its custom neon sign was illuminated. *Pair-O-Dice* was spelled out in curvy blue script, an animated pink pair of dice rolling from left to right, and green and yellow neon palm trees swaying jerkily on either side. During the daytime, the place had zero curb appeal and almost no customers. It was like having our own private club. As long as it stayed in business (and how it did was a mystery) Pat, Emma, and I were happy to spend time there.

Sitting together at one of the Pair-O-Dice's wobbly wooden tables, Pat Flanagan and Emma Nakamura looked like a living tableau meant to illustrate Human Diversity. While Emma was short, sturdy, and brown, Pat was well over six feet tall and gaunt. His Irish complexion fairly glowed in the penumbra.

"So what's for breakfast?" I took my seat, plucked a paper napkin from the chrome dispenser, and rubbed at a sticky stain on the table in front of me. It didn't help. The napkin stuck and then shredded, the pieces rolling into tiny white pills.

"I was telling Pat he's getting shaggy," Emma said.

"I don't know. To me it barely looks like a five o'clock shadow."

Pat rubbed his head. "Yeah, might be time to break out the razor again."

As part of his ongoing austerity project, Pat had

decided to stop paying for haircuts and simply shave his head instead. To his surprise (but no one else's), a rumor immediately sprang up among the students that Pat was a skinhead. In fact, Pat was a stalwart pacifist, and as progressive as they come.

"I was telling Pat what happened to us down at Art Lam's place yesterday," Emma said.

"Have you found out anything from your friends in Mahina PD? I was kind of hoping *you'd* tell *us* what was going on, Pat."

"They're not telling anyone anything," Emma said.

"No. Not until they've notified next of kin."

"Did Art Lam *have* any next of kin?" I asked. "I heard his wife died years ago, right?"

"Yeah," Emma said. "And no kids, either. Hey, I'm still hungry. I'm gonna get another Breakfast Bento. Molly, you want one?" A stack of black plastic bento boxes sat on the bar, each one fastened with a tan rubber band.

"They're just sitting out unrefrigerated," I said. "Are they safe to eat? Won't bacteria grow?"

"Yeah, it's probably like a microorganism zoo in there." Emma got up and helped herself to one.

"Can you get me one?" Pat asked. "Thanks, Emma."

"I'll just have some coffee," I said.

"I'd like to interview you two," Pat said when Emma returned with the bento boxes, "and get your story about what happened yesterday. I'll keep your names out of it if you want."

"I don't think we're supposed to talk," I said. "Couldn't it mess up the investigation? Sometimes they keep some details out of the paper on purpose."

"Yeah, Pat, try wait a couple days," Emma said. "What's the rush?"

Pat blew out a sigh. "I gotta put up some clickbait, stat. For the ad revenue."

"We know how it works," Emma said. "Molly's a business professor."

"Anyway, *Island Confidential* could really use a grisly murder. All I've had up lately is a bunch of stuff about the proposed waste incinerator. There wasn't even enough hurricane damage for more than one story."

"The waste incinerator articles are good journalism," I said. "People care about the issue. Or they should, anyway."

"I don't have the luxury of waiting for peoples' taste to improve," Pat said. "My landlord's selling my place, and I need a down payment to rent an apartment."

"Someone's buying that—I mean, your house?"

Pat lived off the grid twenty miles out of town, halfway up one of the five volcanic mounds comprising our island. The tiny cabin he called home sat at the end of a private dirt road that turned to muck whenever it rained. It wasn't my kind of place, but Pat liked the seclusion and the affordability.

"Who would wanna live all the way out *there*?" Emma chimed in. "Is it some nutcase with a truckload of canned food and guns?"

"Worse. Some overpaid idiot who wants to tear the whole thing down and build himself a swingin' bachelor pad."

"Isn't there anything else you can do for money, Pat?" Emma opened the bento box. "How about another section of comp?"

"Too late in the semester. My only option is the Faustian bargain."

"What Faustian bargain?" I asked.

"A job in Administration. Vice President Marshall Dixon's office."

"Really? Doing what?"

"Selling out," Emma offered.

"Is that the job description in its entirety?" I asked.

"She wants me to be the interim social media manager. I'd actually be working for her new marketing guy. Victor Santiago."

"Santiago's the guy with the little devil beard," Emma explained.

"He does have that Grand Inquisitor vibe, doesn't he?" Pat chuckled.

"Actually, Tomás de Torquemada was tonsured and clean shaven. You think of him as having a sinister goatee, but he didn't."

"You just happen to know that?" Emma challenged me. "About Torquemada's beard?"

"I said *no* beard. Pat, I think you should take the job. You'd be good at it. Look at the job you've done with *Island Confidential*."

"I think they're buying him off," Emma said. "If

he's on the university's payroll, he's gonna hafta stop reporting. He won't be able to do any more stories like the one he did about the library workers."

"Exactly," Pat said. "I can't do that."

"Good point. Just out of curiosity, what's the pay like?"

"If I took the job for just one year, I'd be able to *buy* a place in town, not just rent."

"Really?"

"What?" Pat asked, "Are you saying I should take it?"

"Of course. But I don't have any problem with selling out. I'm the one who went to work for the business school, don't forget."

"Smartest thing you ever did. You don't even want to know what's going on in the English department right now."

"What is it with Mahina State's English department, anyway?" Emma asked. "You guys always have some *mishegas* going on."

"It's not just Mahina State," I said. "My dissertation advisor used to say that hell has two English departments."

"There's something about studying the Greatest Expression of That Which is Human that brings out the worst in people," Pat said. "Speaking of which, I need to go teach my class."

"I have to get going too," I said.

"You didn't even have any breakfast." Emma proffered the remains of her bento box: gravy-stained rice, and a congealed fried chicken wing.

"Here, eat something."

"Thanks anyway, Emma, but I'm not really hungry."

CHAPTER SEVEN

It wasn't like me to sign up for yoga lessons, much less commit to six months' worth. But apparently some busybody government agency with too much time on its hands had come up with a set of completely unrealistic physical activity guidelines and sent them to every physician in the country. Including mine. At my last checkup, Dr. Cha urged me to start getting serious about exercise and stress reduction.

As soon as Emma caught wind of my doctor's diktat, she tried to recruit me into her paddling club. I knew better than to fall into her trap. Emma was the crew captain and extremely competitive. She was disappointed when I (once again) turned her down, but I wasn't keen on spending my afternoons getting yelled at by my best friend about my poor form and pitiful upper body strength. That would not have helped my stress level at all. To get Emma off my case, I bought a package deal from Laughing Lotus Yoga, which occupied the storefront left vacant when Tatsuya's Moderne Beauty closed.

Traffic had been smoother than I had expected, so I arrived a little early. I pulled in and parked in one of the strip mall's many vacant parking spots. The studio was flanked by an open-by-appointment dress shop, which never seemed to be open, and a new check-cashing store.

I signed in at the reception area and walked through to the main studio, planning to use the extra time to get myself "centered." This was real progress for me. A few months ago, I would have gone crazy thinking of all the ways I could have put that extra five minutes to better use. Unfortunately, I happened to walk in on a tense discussion between Sharon and Sharla, the studio's co-owners. The sisters were recent transplants to Mahina, and had brought along both their New England business savvy and their Boston bluntness. I tried to make myself invisible as I smoothed my yoga mat onto the sweat-pungent wooden floor.

"Molly, what do you think?" This was Sharon, whose deeply tanned, fat-free physique reminded me of those roasted chickens from Safeway. Her Southie accent flattened the vowels in my name to "Mah-ly."

"Shouldn't I be able to leave the money box out without worrying about someone stealing the cash?" Sharon demanded.

I looked around at the few other women in the space, rolling out their yoga mats, stretching, drinking water from stainless steel bottles. Why pick on me?

"I'm not sure I'm really the one who would—" I began.

"You're the business professor, right?" Sharon accused. "Don't you think you have to show your customers you trust them?"

"Someone *did* steal the money," Sharon's sister and business partner, Sharla, interrupted. Sharla had the same sun-worshipper's leathery complexion as her sister, but a plumper shape. While skinny Sharon sported form-fitting yoga pants, Sharla's modest batik skirt reached almost to the blurry dolphin tattoo on her deeply tanned ankle.

Fortunately, the sisters seemed to forget about me, and launched into a battle of truly impressive swearing. *If that's what it's really like to have a sister*, I thought, *maybe I should call my parents and tell them how grateful I am to be an only child.*

As more students filtered in, I carefully laid out my yoga mat, paying particular attention to keeping its edges parallel to the studio walls.

Sharla—who had been scolding her sister for leaving the cash box unattended—finally stormed out. She couldn't slam the door, because it was a beaded curtain, but she left a furious clacking in her wake.

The instructor came in through the swaying beads. She wore snug yoga pants, an abbreviated tank top, and an amethyst crystal suspended from a black leather choker. She was still young enough to sport a tan without looking weatherbeaten.

"Crystal." Sharla pointedly checked her watch. "Good. You made it. You got a full class, hon. Better get started."

Crystal led us through a number of moves that ranged from easy to impossible, gently encouraging us the whole time. I followed along to the best of my ability, even though to me the typical yoga class felt like this: Bend over and touch your fingertips to the ground. Now, put your right hand behind your back, leaving the fingertips of your left hand in contact with the earth. Now lift both your legs off the ground. The class was challenging, but when it was finally over I felt so calm I packed up my things in slow motion.

Crystal caught my eye. Suddenly I felt a little less relaxed. I had nothing against her personally, but conversation with strangers was always stressful. Unfortunately, it was too late to roll up my yoga mat and dash. We'd already established eye contact.

CHAPTER EIGHT

"Hi, Crystal. Great class."

I was usually bad at names, but "Crystal Phoenix" was pretty easy to remember. It evoked a striking mental image.

"I've never seen so many people in class before. When we did the half-moon, I kept worrying that I was going to kick the lady next to me."

"That wasn't a half-moon," she said. "I never called it a half-moon. It's a bending starfish. It's my own move."

"Sorry. I thought Primo called it a half moon when he—"

"Primo stole my move. It's okay, you wouldn't know. Watch. A half-moon looks like this." She bent to the side and lifted one leg in the air. "My bending starfish looks like this." She then did what, to me, looked like exactly the same move.

"See the difference?" she asked.

"Sure." I nodded.

"The earlier class was canceled." Crystal effortlessly straightened to a standing position. I wondered if I would ever be that graceful. "That's why it was so crowded. The extra students who couldn't go to the other class. You look a little tired, Molly."

"Oh, I've earned it. I've had a tiring couple of days."

"Are you drinking the supercharged water I told you about?"

As if to demonstrate the correct hydration protocol, Crystal unscrewed the bottle she was holding and drank from it. It was stainless steel, overlaid with a lacy black mandala pattern.

"Well, I—"

"I always bring some with me," she said. "You should get into the habit. Don't ever drink tap water. It's full of poisons."

Mahina's water tasted pretty good, actually. And according to Emma, who was trustworthy on matters of molecular biology, it was perfectly safe to drink.

"Most of the water I consume is in the form of coffee," I said. "*That* should count as supercharged, shouldn't it?"

"Molly, you're so funny." Crystal said it in the way people do when they know you're trying to be funny, but they don't really think you are.

The conversation went quiet. I supposed it was my turn to speak.

"So," I ventured, "what's new with you?"

"Oh, life is totally amazing right now. I'm going through a major change."

"Really?" I was genuinely surprised. I doubted Crystal was even thirty.

She rolled up her mat and slid it into its canvas carrier. "I've cleaned up some important issues, you know, and I think I'm ready for the Universe to send me a soulmate. Someone who can share my path."

"Ah." So she wasn't talking about menopause.

"So your stepson?"

"Stepson? I don't have a—oh, wait. Sorry. Yes, I do. Davison." I felt my serenity slipping away.

"I met him one time when your husband brought him into Natural High looking for calendula cream."

"That must have been when Davison was getting ready to go away to his new school. His father made him get his tattoos lasered off before he went. Apparently, it's not a painless process. So you have *two* jobs?"

"I have my own business, too."

We were in the reception area now and no one was behind the desk. "They don't like me to promote it here, but I do life coaching, including personal training and massage." She reached into her canvas bag and pulled out a small stack of rainbow-hued cards. "Here. Share them with your friends. Did the skin cream work out for him?"

"I guess so. I didn't examine him or anything. Listen, I really need to run."

"I want you to introduce us," she declared.

"Crystal, you're a lovely young lady. I'm sure you won't have any trouble meeting someone decent."

I did *not* want to get involved with playing matchmaker for Donnie's shiftless spawn. I pushed through the glass double doors in the front, into the warm and heavy air outside. Crystal followed me.

"I know I won't have any trouble." She smiled. "Because I'm putting my desire out there for the Universe to answer me."

"Okay." I gave her a noncommittal smile. Even if I hadn't been acquainted with the Biblical observations about the innocent suffering and the wicked prospering, not to mention the couple of millennia of martyrdoms, to me it was pretty self-evident that the Universe was neither just nor benevolent.

"The next time Davison comes home, you should bring him in with you for a free lesson."

"Sure." I scanned the parking lot. "*That* sounds like fun."

I had no trouble finding my turquoise and white convertible among the lifted pickup trucks (mostly black) and Japanese hatchbacks (mostly white) in the parking lot. I was the only person in Mahina who drove a 1959 Thunderbird. My competent but judgmental mechanic, Earl Miyashiro, made sure to remind me of this every time he had to special-order a replacement part for me.

I slid into the driver's seat, pressed the button down to lock the door, and started back to campus.

Serena, the dean's secretary, accosted me as I

reached my office door.

"Molly, do you ever check your voice mail?" She waved a handful of message slips at me.

"Sorry, Serena. I still haven't figured out the new system."

"You need another copy of the voice mail instructions?"

"No, I'm sure I can find it."

"Eh, terrible, that thing that happened down at Art Lam's place, yeah?"

"Yes. It was terrible."

"Chopped down his papaya trees too, then went broke his window. Can you imagine? So destructive."

"A broken window? Where did you hear about that?"

"Anyway," Serena said, "he's been trying to get a hold of you."

"Who has?"

"Art Lam."

"I'm sorry. Did you say *Art Lam*? The poor man who just—"

"That's what I said. He wants to talk to you."

"But I thought he was—"

Serena handed me the message slips.

"He just wanted to make sure you got his message."

I let myself into my office. Sure enough, the light on my phone was flashing. I dug through my email and found the instructions for retrieving voice mail messages. There were several from the Student

Retention Office, dating from the start of the semester. I deleted them.

The first message from Art Lam was timestamped October 28 at 5:12 a.m., the same morning Emma and I had gone down to his place.

"Hello professor, this is Art Lam. Sorry for the late notice, but something's come up and I have to go off-island today. I won't be able to make our interview this morning. Please give me a call to reschedule."

I pressed 9 to save the recording.

Then:

Yesterday. 6:22 pm.

"Hello again Professor, this is Art Lam. Just got back in. Heard you ran into some trouble at my place this morning. Give me a call when you get a chance. I still wanna do the interview, got a few things I wanna say." (Here a short, raspy laugh quickly devolved into a hacking cough.) "Anyways. You girls call me, we talk story."

Today. 9:14 am.

"Hello, Professor. Art Lam calling again. My attorney says I cannot talk to no one about da kine, even you university guys, so gotta cancel the interview. Eh, sorry, ah?"

CHAPTER NINE

The Chancellor's Welcome and Halloween party was scheduled for Friday night, at the lavish and taxpayer-funded Chancellor's Residence. I had been planning to skip it, but Dan Watanabe, the interim Dean of the College of Commerce, had waylaid me in the hallway to encourage me to attend. He made a very convincing case that, as I was going up for tenure this year, I needed to look like a "team player."

"You're a department chair now," Dan said. "It's going to be obvious if you aren't there."

"I'm only *interim* department chair," I countered.

"Still, you should attend. You don't want to snub the Chancellor when your tenure application might be sitting on his desk."

He'd convinced me. I trusted Dan. Dan Watanabe had always had my best interests at heart and had come through many times with support and good advice. (Unlike some other members of the management department. Not to name any names but Hanson Harrison, for all of his liberal posturing, clearly couldn't stomach the idea of a young-ish, female person serving as his department chair. If anything, I would have expected trouble from Rodge Cowper. Rodge, after all, had been the original inspiration for the Rodge Cowper Rule, the one that mandated faculty must keep their office doors open at an angle of at least forty-five degrees when a student was visiting. But Rodge hadn't been a problem at all. It was Hanson, the grandfatherly progressive, who had reflexively opposed me on everything from classroom assignments to final exam schedules to parking permits. At our last department meeting, he'd even publicly stated his opposition to a motion he'd introduced at our previous meeting, the only possible explanation being I had just spoken in favor of it.)

I had no idea where to find a costume on such short notice. Fortunately, Stephen Park, in the theater department, came through for me with a cockroach costume that had been constructed for a student production of Kafka's Metamorphosis. I had dated Stephen briefly, before I met Donnie. I'd heard rumors Stephen hadn't taken the news of my marriage well, so I was relieved that he seemed to harbor no ill will and was eager to help me out.

Donnie agreed to accompany me to the Chancellor's Welcome and Halloween party, but he refused to wear a costume. Instead, he dressed in his usual, conservative going-out clothes: crisply ironed navy blue and white aloha shirt tucked into black slacks.

Donnie's instincts, as it turns out, were correct. No one at the Chancellor's Welcome and Halloween Party was wearing a costume. Except for me. Even the wait staff made their champagne and canapé rounds in black trousers and white dress shirts.

I tried to blend in, although this was difficult when my ensemble included a solidly-constructed exoskeleton, a headpiece with long, waving antennae, and a third pair of limbs that sprouted from the waist and were wired to move in sync with my arms.

Of course, no one acknowledged my fashion faux pas. Everyone was far too polite. Even Donnie kept a straight face and said nothing. *At least none of my students is here to witness me trying to be inconspicuous while dressed as a giant arthropod,* I thought.

"Hey, Professor Barda."

I turned (cautiously, as my costume had many moving, waving parts) to see my student Lars Suzuki, dressed in too-long black trousers and an oversized white dress shirt. Donnie detached himself and went over to chat with our athletic director, who happened to be an old schoolmate of his.

"I'm supervising the caterers," Lars announced happily. "That's how come I get all dressed up." Lars had tucked his shirt in, which caused the excess fabric to balloon over the waistband. He was carrying a metal clipboard.

"Very nice. All you need now is a stopwatch."

He grinned.

"Frederick Taylor kine, ah? Eh, the costume's cool. Really realistic. I saw you and thought, ho, das one big cock-a-roach."

"Well, I thought it would be fun to get into the spirit of things. It is Halloween, after all, exactly the day when one might expect people to show up in costume."

"Eh, you get one extra pair of arms," Lars exclaimed. "You could probably hold four champagne glasses at one time. Hang on, I go get 'em, we try."

"No, no, it's not necessary." I imagined throttling Stephen Park with all six of my legs. "Listen, Lars, I see more guests coming in. I should probably let you get back to—"

"You know, I really like this job, professor. Keeping everything running, making sure everyone got their food and drinks and everything. I think I like work in hospitality when I graduate. You know, last summer I worked on a cruise ship?"

"I think you mentioned it. I've never been on a cruise ship. It sounds very glamorous."

"I wouldn't say glamorous. Lotta stomach flu going around. It gets kinda nasty."

"I can imagine."

"Worst thing, though, is you get people disappearing at sea. Either they jump overboard, or someone goes push 'em. And if no one sees it happen, cannot do nothing. Eh, if I was gonna murder someone, I'd do it on a cruise ship."

"Well, I'll certainly keep that in mind."

"Molly." Emma had just come in, looking elegant. She wore a simple black dress instead of her usual jeans-and-free-conference-t-shirt ensemble. Her black hair was brushed back from her face and fell in loose waves around her shoulders.

"Where's Yoshi?" I asked.

"At home. He didn't want to come. He just wanted to stay home and be a lump. How come you're dressed like a big cock-a-roach?"

"Because it's Halloween?"

"Did Stephen Park talk you into wearing it? He did, didn't he?"

"He didn't talk me into it. I asked him for ideas because I got summoned to this on such short notice. How did you know it was Stephen?"

"Because number one, who else would have a giant-size cock-a-roach costume sitting around, and number two, he's passive-aggressively getting back at you for getting married."

"Why would he care? We've been broken up for years."

"What kind of robot planet are you from, Molly? He's upset. You ended up in a serious relationship, and he didn't. Anyways, you gotta get out of that thing." She rapped my hard shell with her knuckles. "People are gonna think you're making fun."

"How was I supposed to know this wasn't a costume event?"

"This is the chancellor's house. Does this look like the kinda place you wear a giant bug outfit?" Emma gestured across the spacious, marble-tiled living room toward the floor-to-ceiling picture windows. Far below, the whitecaps of Mahina Bay glowed in the moonlight.

"I've never been to the chancellor's house before. I have no frame of reference."

"Let's go into the bathroom and get you out of that thing," she said. "What do you got on underneath?"

CHAPTER TEN

"All I'm wearing under this is a pair of brown tights and a bra," I said. Emma looked over my shoulder and waved her hand to shush me.

"It's Professor Barda," said a familiar (and disapproving) voice. "I should have known."

The voice belonged to Marshall Dixon, whose ensemble gave no hint of Halloween unless you counted the fact that her Italian knit taupe cardigan was trimmed with black bugle beads. As always, Marshall was an exemplar of subdued elegance, a living illustration of the advice that the wearer should be remembered, not the clothes. A wizened little woman in a purple shawl clung to Marshall's arm. The stranger wore her white hair pulled back in a loose bun, secured on one side by a giant purple rose.

"Miss Pfaff," Marshall Dixon said gently, "this is Molly Barda, from the College of Commerce, and

Emma Nakamura, from Biology. They're working on a grant together. Molly, Emma, this is Miss Dorothy Pfaff. She has arranged to donate several important works, and we're working on plans for a new library wing for preservation and display. Miss Pfaff has so many wonderful, innovative ideas. By this time next year, we may have in place a new scholarship fund for students in creative fields. And possibly an endowed chair in the Arts."

Translation: *This is an Important Donor. Don't embarrass me, you idiots.*

"I told Marshall I had to meet the giant Palmetto bug," Miss Dorothy Pfaff cackled. "*Love* your costume, Hon." She reached up to pluck at one of my antennae.

"Are you related to Mary Pfaff?" Emma asked.

"Mary Pfaff?" I exclaimed. "The Beatrix Potter of Hawaii?"

Dorothy beamed, obviously pleased that we knew about her famous grandmother. Only then did Marshall allow herself to smile, too.

"Sorry, Miss Pfaff, I didn't mean to gush. But I love Alice Mongoose."

"It's true," Emma said. "Molly's a huge fangirl. She wore her Alice the Mongoose t-shirt till it got all full of *pukas*, and now she sleeps in it."

"It's Alice Mongoose, Emma, not Alice *the* Mongoose. It's not Peter *the* Rabbit, right?"

Marshall murmured something and steered Miss Dorothy Pfaff away from us and toward a canapé-bearing waiter.

"I'm not sure everyone needed to know that about my t-shirt, Emma. Oh, good. Here's Donnie. Maybe he's ready to go home."

"Where's Pat?" Donnie asked us. "I thought he'd be here."

"Pat's a part-timer," Emma said. "They're never invited to these things."

"I forgot you know our athletic director. What were you two discussing over there?"

"Excuse me. I see champagne." Emma hurried off.

"Buck was bending my ear about the legislative budget cuts," Donnie said. "Having to do more with less. Same kinda thing you're always talking about. Are you ready?"

"Very. Let me grab my purse. Yeah, I love how they cut our appropriations, so *we* try to make up for the lost money by raising tuition, and then *they* get up and rack up political points by denouncing us for raising tuition and cut our budget even more."

My purse had fallen off the chair and ended up square underneath it. I tried to retrieve it by bending at the waist, then at the knees, but thanks to my stiff carapace, I was unable to reach the ground.

"I'll get it. Buck said something about steering a course between Scylla and Charybdis. What does that mean?" He retrieved my purse and handed it to me.

"It means trying to make your way between two evils without getting hurt by either one, like navigating a ship between a rocky shoal and a whirlpool. If you get far enough from one, you get too close to the other."

Donnie was quiet on the ride home. It wasn't until I had removed and bagged up the cockroach costume, showered, and climbed into Donnie's big bed that he finally spoke.

"Does it bother you that I don't have a college education?" Donnie asked.

"What? *No.* Seriously, no. Why should it bother me?"

"I'm not as educated as you are," Donnie said.

"No one's as educated as I am. Wait, that didn't sound right. I didn't mean it to sound like bragging. I'm just saying I rode the education train all the way to the last stop. Ph.D. And I have the student loan payments to show for it."

"Emma's husband has an MBA."

"Yoshi? Donnie, you are better than Yoshi in every possible way. I'm amazed at what you've accomplished, building your own business. I mean it. Especially since I got stuck teaching the business planning class. Ever since I was assigned the business planning class, I've realized how hard it is to do. How much goes into it. And how unlikely it is that a business will survive past five years. Anyone who can make it work has my admiration and respect. I couldn't do it."

"Scylla and Charybdis. What kind of class would you learn that in?"

"I'd say a literature class. Something that covers either Homer or James Joyce."

"It seems like everyone has a college degree now." I couldn't see Donnie's face in the dark, but from the tone of his voice, I could tell he was frowning.

"Actually, only about a third of American adults have a four-year degree."

"Really?"

"Yes, really. But look, if it's something you want to do, sign up for night classes at Mahina State. You could go part time and get your bachelor's in six years."

"No, I can't do that," Donnie said.

"Why not?"

"I can't afford the stigma of a Mahina State degree."

"What? The *stigma*? Of having a degree from the place where I've made my career?"

"Sorry, Molly, I didn't mean it that way." He stroked my hair. The gesture seemed condescending, like a pat on the head. "I'm really proud of what you do there. But you know what I mean. Image is important in my business. I can't have a degree from a college that advertises on television."

"Where did you hear that you're not supposed to get your degree from somewhere that advertises on TV?"

"From you, Molly. Don't you remember? When we were talking about where to send Davison?"

"There's nothing wrong with Mahina State," I insisted.

"Of course not." Donnie and I were close, our noses barely an inch apart. "How are you feeling,

Molly? Are you tired?"

"I'm not *tired*. But I *am* kind of *grumpy* now."

"Aw, that's a shame," he murmured. "Let's see if we can make you feel better."

CHAPTER ELEVEN

"So tell me again." I frowned at Donnie. "Why are we buying offal and bones now? Has your son joined a cult?"

Donnie and I were in Natural High Organic Foods, stocking up in anticipation of Davison Gonsalves' arrival in Mahina later in the day. I normally enjoyed shopping at Natural High, mostly for the gourmet snacks rather than for any particular health benefits. Tamari almonds, California rolls, blueberry smoothies, that sort of thing. Donnie claimed he could always tell when I'd been shopping there because my clothes would reek of dried ginseng.

"Not quite a cult." Donnie assessed the offerings. "He's on a big health kick. Some of the guys in his class got him into this whole foods thing. He says he's gotten good results so far at the gym."

"I always wondered who bought this expensive

almond flour." I watched Donnie place a small and astonishingly pricey bag of it into the hand basket. Natural High had green baskets, presumably because green plastic looked more environmentally responsible than other colors of plastic.

"I always had this image of college students living on instant noodles and bad coffee," Donnie said.

"They're *supposed* to."

Davison had emailed his shopping list to Donnie early in the morning, right before he got on the plane. I thought it was rude and entitled (also perfectly in character for Davison). When you're a guest at someone's house, it seemed to me, you eat what they put in front of you, and you say thank you.

And Davison's new diet plan was expensive. Organic vegetables, butter and beef from grass-fed cows, and cold-pressed olive oil were on the menu. Cheap staples like rice, canned meat, and instant noodles were out. You couldn't put together a more costly shopping list if you tried.

As luck would have it, Crystal Phoenix from the yoga studio was working at Natural High that day. She made a beeline for us—for Donnie, really.

"Well hi Molly," Crystal gushed, gazing into Donnie's eyes. Her golden hair was pulled back and pinned into a messy bun, exposing a graceful jawline. "And of course, I remember your husband. Donnie, it's so nice to see you again." She took Donnie's hand and held it, instead of letting go, as one would do with a normal handshake.

"It looks like Davison is coming back to Mahina

for a visit," I said.

"We're doing some grocery shopping for him," Donnie added.

"You should bring him by the studio for a free yoga lesson. Molly, did I give you my card?"

"Yes, you did." I spoke to Crystal's profile since she was still gazing at Donnie. "So it seems he's developed some very specific dietary requirements."

Donnie gently pulled his hand free from Crystal's grasp, set the basket down on the edge of the produce table, and read from the shopping list. "Coconut oil, olive oil, and butter are fine, he says. Yellow oils are off limits."

"Isn't butter yellow?" I asked.

"No, I know what he means. No industrial oils."

Donnie caught my expression. "It's only for a few days, Molly."

"I didn't say anything. I'm just looking at the avocados here."

I picked up an oversized green specimen from the bin and dropped it into our basket.

"No meat?" Crystal inquired hopefully.

"Meat is on the list," Donnie said, "but it has to be pastured or grass fed. Eggs need to be free range, preferably local, and supplemented with Omega-3. Cheese and other low-glycemic dairy products are acceptable as long as the milk comes from A2 cows."

"And it has to be served on a satin pillow stuffed with unicorn feathers," I added.

"Your son is taking good care of his body."

Crystal aimed her cool green eyes at Donnie. "What about you, Donnie? Are you taking care of yourself?"

"Uh," Donnie said.

"I can tell you have a *powerful* fitness practice." Her eyes wandered up and down his torso. "I'm a certified personal trainer, too. I'd love to—"

"He doesn't need a fitness practice," I said. "He gets *plenty* of physical activity already. From working all day at the restaurant, I mean. Donnie, I know you don't have time for any *extracurricular activities*."

Donnie patted my hand, which I realized I had placed on his bicep. Okay, maybe I was acting a *little* possessive. Who would blame me?

"You're probably tense with such an intense work schedule," Crystal murmured. "I do massage, too, First session is free."

"Wow, Crystal, you are really multitalented." It didn't escape my notice that she hadn't offered *me* a massage. "So Donnie, we should probably get this shopping done sometime before the sun cools."

Donnie smiled a little, as if something was funny about the situation, although if there was, I sure couldn't see it.

"So you think Davison's making a good choice here?" he asked.

"Your son is being very wise," Crystal said. "Let food be thy medicine."

Oh, come on, I thought. I was as pro-healthy-eating as the next person (actually no, I wasn't), but my mother was a medical doctor, and I'd heard enough stories about people who thought they could throw away their medication as soon as they were feeling a little better.

"What about letting *medicine* be your medicine?" I asked. "I mean, it's not like the secret cure for every disease on earth is hidden in, what?"

I peeked at the list in Donnie's hand.

"…fish oil and fermented soybeans?"

"Don't buy into the propaganda, Molly. You can't believe everything Monsanto tells you. Anything you get from the pharmaceutical industry has a better equivalent in nature."

"I'm not so sure about that." Why was I even engaging her?

"I'll show you an example." Crystal led us over to a computer terminal in the back of the store and pulled up a website with photographs of a plant that looked like spearmint with yellow flowers.

"It acts directly on the hormonal system," Crystal explained. "It can be used to treat bipolar disorder, and it's very energizing. Molly, this might even help you."

"I'm fine. Really. But thank you for the information. So, Donnie, we should get moving if we're going to meet the plane on time."

Davison's plane actually wasn't due for another four or five hours, but I wanted to wrap it up and get out of there.

"That's the girl who wanted to meet Davison?" Donnie asked once we were out on the sidewalk in front of Natural High. Each of us held a reusable shopping bag full of pastured, organic, free range, Omega-3-rich comestibles that pound for pound cost about as much as cocaine.

"She's the one. Although it seems pretty obvious to me she'll settle for *père* in the event that *fils* isn't available. Oh good, the rain's stopped."

"Who's available?" Donnie asked. "Did you say something about a pear?"

"Crystal was flirting with you."

"Do you really think she was—"

"Oh, come *on*. She was. At least she has good taste. Where did I park again?"

Across the street from the termite-eaten row of clapboard storefronts, the ocean sparkled. Small waves splashed playfully onto the black lava rock shore.

"Up there. Right around the corner. Remember?"

"Right."

Donnie took my grocery bag. I dug into my purse for my keys as we walked.

"She's a little out there," Donnie said.

"A little." I nodded.

I could tell Donnie was thinking something over. We walked quietly until we reached the Thunderbird.

"Ouch." I ran a finger over the gleaming paint. I need to go to the carwash. You can see every crumb of dirt in the sun."

"The situation with Sherry's been really hard on Davison," Donnie said. "I don't think it's healthy."

"I thought Sherry got back together with one of her ex-husbands."

"That's just it," Donnie said. "I don't think Davison's over her"

Donnie's ex-wife Sherry had walked out on Davison's eighth birthday. Davison and his former stepmother had reconnected many years later, neither one aware of the other's identity. By the time things were sorted out, it was too late. (As Sherry had put it, "Whaddaya want me to do? He's not a light bulb. I can't unscrew him.")

"Davison is an adult," I said. "We shouldn't mix in."

"I'm not saying we should mix in. But we can encourage him to meet some other people while he's here. Like this girl at the health food store. What was her name? Chrysalis?"

"Crystal." I slid the key into the lock. The trunk lid bounced up, revealing a spacious storage area, empty except for the spare tire propped up in the center. You really could fit a body or three into these old trunks. "Crystal Phoenix."

Donnie placed the grocery bags into the trunk, and I pushed the lid down, using most of my upper body strength to get it to latch.

"Phoenix?" Donnie gave me a skeptical look. "What kind of name is that?"

"A made-up one, I'm sure."

"Well, it's a little strange. But on the positive side, she's employed."

"That's the spirit. Aim high." I was already walking up to the driver's seat, and I don't think Donnie heard me.

CHAPTER TWELVE

I had a revise-and-resubmit due Monday, so after Natural High, I dropped Donnie off at his car, loaded the cockroach costume into my trunk, and drove up to campus. If Donnie wanted to chase around every grocery store in Mahina looking for all the things on Davison's magic list, he was welcome to it. I had to get my revision done and uploaded before the weekend was over. I'd learned the hard way a deadline of noon, East Coast time meant the crack of dawn in Hawaii.

Unfortunately, the air conditioning on campus was turned off on weekends, so I sweltered through my revisions, even with my desk fan rattling away on the highest setting. I had no one to blame but myself. I got the revise-and-resubmit back from the journal a month ago, and I'd kept putting it off. A major part of the revision (besides "add more tables" and "make it shorter") was the recommendation by one reviewer that I cite the relevant and outstanding work of a certain scholar. I was having a little trouble squeezing that work into my paper, as I didn't think it really pertained to the topic, but if it was important to someone who was going to decide whether my paper got published, it was important to me. (I also now had a pretty good idea who that anonymous reviewer was.)

I managed to finish, check my paper over, and get it uploaded while it was still light outside. One more errand, and then it was off to Donnie's for a joyous reunion with my stepson. Hooray.

Stephen looked up from his desk when I knocked on the open door of his office. Stephen had never been a terribly neat person, but his office was even messier than I remembered. Colorful gowns, headdresses, swords and plastic firearms hung from the coat rack. Costumes were heaped over the backs of his visitor chairs. Boots, curly-toed elf shoes, and stiletto heels were piled along the wall. A painted plywood palm tree, taller than the height of Stephen's office, was wedged against the wall.

Stephen himself looked gaunt and sickly under the fluorescent lights. His uniformly black hair (dyed, I'd bet money on it) was scraped back from his pale, angular face.

Stephen had spent some time in rehab a while back, and when he got out, he had started eating compulsively, substituting one addiction for another. After gaining seventy pounds or so, he had become an exercise fanatic, going up to the campus gym first thing in the morning and running on the treadmill for hours. He'd lost all the added weight (and then some), and now had the stringy, hollow-eyed look of a marathon runner.

"I just wanted to return this." I held up the bagged cockroach costume. "Thanks for letting me use it. I didn't see you at the Chancellor's Welcome and Halloween party."

"I had a lot to do."

Stephen didn't get up. He may not have been feeling well. Or perhaps he was just being rude.

"Well, it's too bad you missed the festivities, Stephen. You could've taken credit for my remarkable ensemble. By the way, I met Miss Dorothy Pfaff. Marshall Dixon has her on the hook for some major bucks."

"Ah. Did she sign your Alice Mongoose t-shirt?"

"No, but Emma told her all about it, much to my mortification."

Stephen had an issue of Variety spread out on his desk. He turned a page, and then another one, looking at nothing in particular.

"I'm sure you made a great impression on our benefactress, Molly. *That's* the most important thing."

Stephen was doing the thing he knew enraged me, positioning himself as the Morally Pure Artist, counterpoint to me, the Business School Sellout.

"Well, our funding from the state's been cut by forty percent. It's almost impossible to get grants with our crumbling infrastructure, and we're not allowed to raise tuition. So unless we all want to end up working for free, we'd better make nice with the local philanthropists. *You* know all this, Stephen. You go to the same budget meetings I do."

"Indeed, I do. Did your *Friend from the Business Community* accompany you?"

"Yes, Donnie came with me. He didn't have anyone *thoughtful* enough to provide him with a spectacular costume like this one, though, so *he* just wore his regular business clothes."

Stephen flipped open the carved wooden case on his desk, drew out a cigarette, clamped it into a wire cigarette holder and lit it. He closed his eyes and sucked in the smoke so hard his cheeks hollowed. One habit he'd never managed to kick was smoking his Indonesian clove cigarettes. Despite the campus-wide tobacco ban, Stephen's office still reeked of Gudang Garam smoke.

Stephen blew out a spicy cloud of exhaust.

"Of *course* he went with you. Can't let the little woman wander off by herself."

"Is there anything you need to talk about, Stephen?"

"How was the costume? Did it fit?"

"It was perfect," I said. "In fact, I'm going to miss the extra pair of limbs. They were quite useful. Should I just hang it over here?"

"Keep it."

"What?"

"Keep the costume. I don't have any place to store it. I don't have a prop room anymore."

"What do you mean you don't have a prop room? Isn't it just over—"

"That space houses the Office of Student Engagement now."

"Your *prop* room? They took it away?"

"The Student Retention Office concocted this space reallocation plan over the summer when most of the faculty were off campus. They didn't notify the theater department, of course."

Stephen rested the cigarette holder on the edge of his ashtray—a heavy vintage number from the sixties, molded out of golden glass—and looked directly at me for the first time.

"They piled all of my props and costumes in the hallway and moved in some new deanlet with his clutch of minions. So, keep the costume. Have fun. Re-enact *The Metamorphosis* for your accounting majors. I'm sure they'll enjoy it."

"Okay. Well, I guess I'll find some use for this. Thanks, Stephen."

I left Stephen in his dark office, sitting in a pool of sallow light from his desk lamp.

Donnie's house was still empty when I got back. The stew Donnie had started earlier was starting to smell delicious, although the savory meat aroma was mingled with a smell like suntan lotion. Maybe Donnie was trying out some new coconut-scented air freshener in anticipation of Davison's arrival.

I hung up the cockroach costume in the coat closet and found some simple white dishes in one of Donnie's cupboards. I put out three place settings on the dining room table, poured myself a glass of wine, and was just sitting down at the kitchen counter to read the day's paper when I heard the front door open.

"Guess who's here?" I heard Donnie sing out. "Molly? Are you home?"

After the draining experience of dealing with Stephen Park, I really didn't feel up to facing Davison. But I couldn't exactly hide and pretend not to be home. One, Donnie would be disappointed if I didn't show, and two, my distinctive Thunderbird was parked right in front of the house. I got up as Donnie came in through the living room, with Davison behind him. Donnie took Davison's duffel bag and gave him a little push to propel him toward me. I put down my wine and allowed Davison to squeeze me in a tight hug, enveloping me in the sour body odor that inevitably develops over twenty hours of uninterrupted travel.

"Long time, Molly." Davison pressed a stubbly kiss into my cheek. I wasn't crazy about the fact that my new stepson (and former student) was calling me by my first name. Unfortunately, I hadn't been able to come up with anything better. I certainly wasn't going to let him call me "Mommy."

"Go to your room and change." Donnie handed back Davison's bag. "Then we can have dinner."

Davison had his own room in Donnie's house, which was one reason I couldn't feel entirely at home there. A couple of years ago, Donnie had given him a furniture catalog and a blank check and told him he could pick out his own décor. The result was like *The Masque of the Red Death* as reimagined by a mob decorator, all red plush carpet, black and silver rococo furniture, and electric chandeliers with black leather candles. If the door happened to be ajar when I passed, I'd pull it shut.

"Oh, Molly, thanks for setting the table." Donnie went over to examine my work. He quietly gathered up the silverware, put it away, and brought out different flatware from another drawer. Then he rearranged everything on the table. When he was finished, he brought over a wine glass and sat next to me at the kitchen counter. I picked up the bottle of wine and poured for him.

"How was it?" I asked.

"Traffic wasn't too bad. I didn't recognize Davison right away. He was standing in front of me, and it still took me a second. Has he been gone that long?"

"It hasn't been that long. I think you didn't recognize him because you made him get all his tattoos lasered off before he left. What was wrong with the place settings?"

"Nothing," Donnie said. "I just like to do it a certain way."

"Could you explain your system to me? Maybe next time I can replicate it and save you the trouble of redoing it."

In fact, he could explain it, and he did. It had to do with which things could go in the dishwasher with which other things, and how many of each kind of place setting was on hand, and which pattern was still being manufactured, and which would be hard to replace, and some other parameters I didn't quite commit to memory. By the time he wrapped it up, it was nearly eight o'clock. I hadn't eaten since lunch, and my stomach was starting to make noises like a spoon caught in a garbage disposal.

We heard Davison's bedroom door open. Finally. A moist cloud of sweet shower gel fragrance wafted into the dining room ahead of him. He wore basketball shorts and a gray muscle shirt emblazoned with the name of his school in stencil font.

"Looking good," Donnie said. "Let's eat."

Davison looked more like Donnie than ever. He had his adoptive father's strong features and thick black hair. (Davison was Donnie's sister's baby, and for reasons still unclear to me, Donnie had taken him in and raised him. Donnie was always vague when I asked him about it, and as there was no reversing the decision at this point, I didn't feel I needed to know the details.)

Davison seemed to have lost some weight since I'd seen him last. His muscles looked functional, like Donnie's, rather than puffed-up and decorative. I'd always suspected Davison had been taking steroids to enhance his workouts. Maybe he'd given them up, or he didn't have the right connections at his new school.

"Wine?" Donnie asked Davison as we sat down.

"Nah. Dad, how many glasses you had today? You gotta practice moderation. Couple glasses a week, *maybe*, if you're highly active. But more than that, no can."

"*I'll* have some wine," I said.

"You gotta be careful too, Molly. Alcohol no good for *wahine*."

"*English*, Davison." Donnie ladled stew from the slow cooker into with my bowl.

"Donnie, this looks great. I'm so hungry."

"Dad, when you get ethanol in your system?" Davison persisted. "That's what the alcohol in drinks is called, ethanol. Your body burns ethanol first, so you don't burn fat. Lotta times when girls stop drinking, they lose weight, ah? That's how come. Eh, Molly, you quit drinking, you drop ten pounds right away I bet."

"You certainly are a font of advice today." I took the wine bottle and filled my own glass.

"I been learning a lot about nutrition. I been eating healthy, no alcohol, no trans fats, no rice or bread or nothing like that."

"Well. I did notice your acne's cleared up a little." I dug my spoon into the stew and stirred the chunks around.

"Davison, this is made entirely from ingredients on the list you sent me." Donnie ladled out Davison's portion. "I had to go to a few different places to find everything."

"Aw, thanks, ah?" Davison said. "Looks great."

"They didn't have everything at Natural High?" I asked. I brought the spoon halfway to my mouth. The suntan lotion smell intensified.

"They were out of coconut oil," Donnie said. "I had to buy that at Mizuno Mart."

I slowly lowered the spoon back into my bowl.

"The coconut oil was for us to *eat?* How *interesting.* What else is in here?"

"Grass fed beef," Donnie said, "and a few different kinds of greens. Onions and garlic. A little bit of fresh grated ginger."

"Well, that sounds nice."

"And some bone marrow and liver," Donnie added. "I've never cooked with this combination of ingredients before. I hope everyone likes it."

"Me too." I downed a fortifying gulp of wine. "Davison, you eat like this all the time?"

"Yeah. I'm gonna try eat clean the whole time I'm here."

"Terrific. Donnie, did I ever say thank you for calling Konishi Construction for me? It was so thoughtful of you. You think they'll finish the repairs on my house pretty soon?"

"Dad, you remember the fluoride-free toothpaste?"

"It's in your bathroom. Oh, Molly, I got the special shampoo and conditioner you like, the one for curly hair. It's already put away in the shower."

"Thanks.".

"You staying here now, Molly?" Davison asked.

"I am. An Albizia tree fell onto my house and crushed it."

"Good thing. Wife shouldn't be apart from her husband. You know what I'm saying? You two are man and wife now. You should act like it."

"Not really any of your business, buddy," Donnie said.

"Gosh, I'm so sleepy," I said. "I think I'll turn in."

"You've hardly eaten anything. Aren't you hungry?" Donnie reached over and squeezed my hand.

"Oh, I've had plenty. Really. I'll put the rest in the fridge and heat it up for lunch or something." I shuddered at the thought of warmed-over coconut-flavored liver. "You two probably want to catch up." I stood up, draped my arm around Donnie's shoulders, and got a peck on the cheek.

"We'll have a family breakfast tomorrow," Donnie said.

"Sounds great." I wrapped up my bowl and stuck it in the refrigerator, then quietly lifted a jar of peanuts out of the pantry and darted down the hallway to the master bedroom.

CHAPTER THIRTEEN

The sun hit me square in the face from Donnie's east-facing bedroom window. I'd invested in blackout shades for my own little house and had become accustomed to waking when my body told me to, rather than whenever the sun demanded. I'd have to remember to buy a sleep mask today. Donnie's window treatments were cream-colored muslin: light, elegant, and utterly ineffectual.

I didn't remember Donnie coming to bed. He was facing away from me now, his shoulder rising and falling in slow rhythm. I gave him a gentle kiss on the ear. He stirred and grunted.

"Want to go to St. Damien's with me this morning?"

"Huh?"

"Davison can come, too. We can all go to church together, as a family."

"I wanted to make us breakfast," Donnie said.

"Can't you stay and eat with us?"

"Of course. Want to go to the nine o'clock Mass afterward?"

"I don't think it'll work." Donnie sat up on the edge of the bed and pulled his hands through his unkempt hair. I lay there and stared at his beautifully formed back and shoulders. His white t-shirt glowed against his brown skin.

"Sunday's a busy day at the Drive-Inn," Donnie said.

"I know."

"It's already after seven. I'm going to get breakfast started. Come out whenever you're ready."

Donnie pushed himself into a standing position and stretched, which gave me the opportunity to admire him for a few moments longer. He went into the master bathroom and closed the door. I got up and rummaged in the closet until I found a bathrobe.

The heavy hem hit the tops of my feet, and the sleeves hung past my hands and had to be cuffed. I was uncomfortably warm. The bathrobe was my only option, though, other than getting completely dressed right away, or parading around in front of my stepson in sleep shorts and my laundered-to-translucence Alice Mongoose t-shirt.

I opened the bedroom door and peeked down the hallway. Davison's door was closed. *Good, he must still be asleep.* I went out through the front door and tiptoed down the wet asphalt driveway to retrieve the Sunday paper, enjoying the evaporating cool of the morning.

Like most homeowners in Mahina, Donnie had a box for delivery of the *County Courier* installed just below his mailbox. The Sunday paper wasn't in it. I checked the mailbox just in case, but it was empty, too. It wasn't like Donnie to let his subscription run out. I'd have to ask him about it. I picked up the hem of the robe and darted back inside.

I found the Sunday paper in the kitchen, along with Davison, who was already awake. Of course he was. His internal clock was still on Eastern Standard Time. He was reading the sports section. The rest of the paper was in pieces, strewn across the table.

"Eh, Molly." He didn't look up. He was shirtless, which created the off-putting illusion that he was sitting at the kitchen table naked. He reached up and scratched the back of his neck, displaying a wiry black armpit bush. How unfair was this? Here I was, trailing around in a big heavy bathrobe (which now had a wet hem), to spare my stepson the sight of my partially clothed body. He might have returned the favor.

Of course, I couldn't say anything to him. He'd make some inappropriate "joke" about it and then leer at me the way he did that time I accidentally walked into his hotel room, and I would immediately want to run out and put on five more bathrobes and a burqa.

"Good morning, Davison. I see you already got the paper."

"You gonna make coffee?" His eyes were still pinned on the sports section.

"Am *I* going to make coffee? Davison, didn't you grow up in this house?"

He set the paper down and looked at me with puppy dog eyes.

"The coffee machine's new." He tilted his bushy eyebrows into a sad a-frame. "Never used that kind before."

"Clever. Nice use of strategic incompetence."

"Huh?"

My students did it all the time. *Professor, the LMS won't let me upload my paper. Can I give it to you later? Professor, the syllabus is too long to read. Can't you just tell me what's on it? Professor, I can't figure out how to log into the library database.*

And students weren't the only ones guilty of this. My colleagues could be even worse. Hanson Harrison, for example, loved to play the part of the doddering technophobe who couldn't figure out how to submit his book orders online or upload his course grades. Serena, the dean's secretary, invariably would get fed up and do it for him. She even printed out Hanson's emails for him every day, as he insisted he was unable to read them on the computer.

"Making a cup of coffee is very simple. I'll demonstrate."

I took down a coffee mug from the cabinet, shaking my arm to let the bulky bathrobe sleeve fall out of the way. Then I retrieved a coffee pod from the drawer, inserted it into the coffeemaker, lowered the lid, and pressed a button. I watched the coffee stream into my cup, the flow slowing as the coffee maker gurgled its last.

"Just like that," I said. "Easy. One cup at a time. Pods are in this drawer. When the water gets low, just pour some into the reservoir here."

"It looks complicated."

"It's not complicated at all. It's simple. Now you try it."

I sat down at the kitchen table and rummaged through the mess of sections in search of the front page. I ignored Davison as he stood helplessly in front of the coffee machine. If anything, he should have made coffee for me. I was more of a guest in this house than he was.

The front section of the *County Courier* was filled with ads for the upcoming election. *Please vote for my friend Winston Agbayani. Kendrick Yamanaka, working hard for District 2. My name is Mercedes Yamashiro and I humbly ask for your vote.* I liked Mercedes Yamashiro. She was the owner of the Cloudforest Bed and Breakfast, and one of the first people I met when I moved to Hawaii. I wished I could vote for her, but unfortunately, I wasn't registered in her district. My choice was between the unprepossessing Winston Agbayani and the unremarkable Kendrick Yamanaka.

"Political campaigning is so polite here," I said. "On the mainland, it's all negative. No one humbly asks for anything. It's more like *Frank Smith eats live puppies and will raise your taxes. Frank Smith: Can you trust an alien shapeshifter who wears a suit of human skin?*"

Davison remained in front of the coffee machine,

inert.

"Get the pod from the drawer," I said, finally.

"What drawer?"

"The one right under the coffee machine."

He stood there for a while longer. When enough time had passed to convince him I really wasn't going to make his coffee for him, he managed to retrieve a coffee pod from the drawer and fit it into the holder.

"What I do now?"

"Press the brew button."

"There's three brew buttons," he countered.

"That's for six, eight, and ten-ounce cups. I usually choose the smallest cup, the six-ounce. Then I dilute it with water."

"That doesn't make sense. How come you don't just make a bigger cup?"

"When you run too much water over the coffee, you start to extract the bitter stuff at the end. When you select the small cup, you only get the best part of the brew, the nice aromatic extract."

"Too humbug. I'm gonna just make the big one. I like one big cup of coffee."

"Suit yourself."

He brewed his cup, sat back down, and drank. The only sounds were newspaper rustling and coffee slurping. I was reading the top story on the front page, about some ominous underground rumblings, which might presage a new lava flow, although it was uncertain where it was going to come out. According to the map that accompanied the story, my little house downtown was well out of danger. The lava would most likely miss Donnie's place as well, although it wasn't so certain.

"Eh Molly," Davison said.

"Yes?"

"Dad told me you wen' found one dead body."

"That's true."

"Aw, you get some bad luck, ah?"

"At least one person was having a worse day than I was. What did Donnie, I mean your dad, tell you about it?"

"Nothing. Just on the way from the airport, I asked him what was going on when I was outta town, and he said the usual, Molly tripped over another dead body."

"He said, 'The usual, I *tripped over another dead body?*'"

"Who was it?"

"I don't know who it was. They haven't announced the name. I think they're waiting to notify next of kin."

Donnie came into the kitchen, still wearing his t-shirt and pajama pants. He'd wet his hair down to smooth it, and looked less rumpled than he had earlier.

"Well, this is nice. The whole family's up." He grinned, came over and kissed me on the forehead, and then swung into action, producing bags of flour, cartons of eggs, and small jars of brown and white powders. From the aroma that wafted from the stainless steel gas range, I inferred that he was conjuring pancakes.

"Donnie, this is so sweet of you to cook for us. Especially since you'll be cooking for hundreds more people today at the Drive-Inn."

"I don't mind," Donnie said. "It's good to see people enjoying the food."

"Well, the pancakes smell delicious."

"Dad," Davison complained, "Pancakes? Cannot. Get white flour, ah?"

"I forgot," Donnie said. "I'll cook up some of your special bacon."

"You keep eating white flour an li' dat, you gonna get the kine, middle age dad gut."

"As long as my wife can put up with it."

"No problem. *I'll* eat your pancakes. There are worse things than being chubby and middle-aged."

Like being a know-it-all food Nazi, for example.

"Oh, Dad," Davison said. "You want to come to church with me today? You can come too, Molly."

"You want to go to St. Damien's?"

"Nah. We always go to St. Damien's. I wanna try go New Beginnings Chapel."

"The big box church?" I asked. "Why do you want to go there?"

"My strength and conditioning teacher said I should try it. When I told him I was gonna go visit back home, he looked it up online and told me try go New Beginnings Chapel when I'm here. When I get back, he's gonna ask me how it was."

"You have a faculty member telling students where they should go to church?"

"It's not a state school, Molly," Donnie said.

"Still. I can't imagine butting into my students' personal business."

"Sure, Davison," Donnie said. "We'll go with you. Is that okay, Molly?"

"Donnie, didn't you just tell me you couldn't go to church because you had to get to work this morning?"

"I think I can take a little time to go to church with my family."

I sighed. "Sure. Let's go. Maybe we'll hear the story of the Prodigal Son."

CHAPTER FOURTEEN

The parking lot of New Beginnings Chapel was crammed with supersized, lifted pickup trucks. New Beginnings, it seemed, did not draw an upmarket crowd. My initial impression was confirmed once we were inside. The pews were packed with neck and hand tattoos (the kind our university's career services office calls the "unemployables"), exposed bra straps, and everywhere, that heartbreaking obstacle to career opportunity: poor dental care.

The interior of New Beginnings Chapel was vast, about four times the size of the largest theater in the Mahina Mall's cinema multiplex. I estimated the ceiling to be three or four stories high. The seating was stadium-style, something I had never seen in a Catholic church. The expansive stage featured a podium in the center and potted palms on either side. Toward the rear, on the right, a band was setting up. High up on the wall behind the stage, where one might expect to see a crucifix (this being a church and all) was a gigantic television screen displaying a "New Beginnings Chapel" logo against a royal blue background.

New Beginnings Chapel should have a dental ministry, I thought. It sure looked like they had enough money to pull it off. As a child, I couldn't understand why my parents thought my teeth were so important.

"You're going to have your teeth for the rest of your life," they'd say as they dragged me to the dentist or denied me a second helping of dessert. Worst of all were the braces, constantly poking the inside of my cheeks and wearing away little sore spots. I dreaded going in to have my braces tightened; my entire skull would pulsate with pain for days afterward.

Now I felt grateful and a little bit guilty about all of the resistance I'd put up at the time.

"You okay, Molly?" Donnie asked. The front rows were already filled, and we had to climb up the aisle toward the back.

"Of course I am." I ran my tongue around the inside of my mouth as if to reassure myself everything was still intact. I told myself to get a grip and imagine what Iker Legazpi, my gentle and saintly colleague in the accounting department, might say in this situation. Iker had once told me church should be thought of as a hospital, not a country club, its purpose to heal the broken rather than to comfort the fortunate. He had gone on to quote the Book of

James and some things from the Old Testament. Iker was Catholic, like me, but for some reason, he seemed to know a lot of Bible verses.

Davison turned to enter a pew with enough space in the middle for all three of us (barely). Donnie and I followed him in, scooting past a young man in a long-sleeved fluorescent green t-shirt with *Konishi Construction* printed in black down one sleeve. A toddler lay half-asleep in the man's lap. The child stirred and opened his mouth to fuss, displaying silver stubs where his baby teeth should have been. The father produced a bottle full of red fruit punch and popped it into the kid's mouth.

If the church is a hospital, New Beginnings Chapel must be the free clinic.

"Is this good, Molly?" Donnie asked.

"Yes. Wonderful." I settled onto the cushioned pew, ending up wedged between my husband and my stepson. I picked up a paperback hymnal from the rack in front of me. All of the songs seemed to date from the 1970s through the early 1990s. Down on the distant stage, the praise band played a few chords by way of tuning up, confirming my worst suspicions about the kind of music we were in for. They launched into a repeating three-chord progression, the same one-four-five we'd beaten to death when I was in that punk band back in grad school. I preferred our version.

Davison nudged me.

"Eh Molly, you like go down there an' play?" He was grinning. Of course, Davison found it hilarious that I used to play bass for an all-female band called Phallus in Wonderland. (The name was Melanie Polewski's idea, by the way, not mine. She'd been into Lacan at the time.)

"I don't think so," I said.

"Not your kine music, ah?"

"This isn't about what kind of music we *prefer*. Being here is an act of worship and *sacrifice*."

In my opinion, sacred music had gone downhill right after the American Civil War, when it started to sound more suitable for a barbershop quartet than for a church choir.

"Time to stand up," Donnie whispered. I was the only one still sitting. I saw the lyrics projected on the big screen, so I tucked the hymnal back into the rack. Out of curiosity, I pulled out the pew Bible. It was a Protestant translation, what the church of my childhood would have called a "heretic" version. I opened it to a random page in the New Testament.

For if there should come into your assembly a man with gold rings, in fine apparel, and there should also come in a poor man in filthy clothes, and you pay attention to the one wearing the fine clothes and say to him, "You sit here in a good place," and say to the poor man, "You stand there," or, "Sit here at my footstool," have you not shown partiality among yourselves, and become judges with evil thoughts?

"What's that?" Donnie glanced over.

"Um, the Book of James." I closed the Bible, slid it back into the pew pocket, and started moving my lips along with the lyrics on screen.

People unfamiliar with the Catholic order of

worship have told me they found it hard to follow, but the New Beginnings service was downright baffling. The program indicated when we were to stand and sit, but there was also apparently some secret signal to tell the worshippers when to lift their hands and start swaying, or clap along to the music. Once in a while, someone would shout, "Amen," but such improvisation seemed to be optional, and restricted to the most advanced worshippers.

When the music ended, we sat down for the spoken part of the service. I realized the purpose of the giant monitor mounted behind the podium: it gave the faithful in the nosebleed seats a view of the events on stage. Without the close-up, I'd have had trouble picking the charismatic Pastor Skip Lewis out of a lineup. But on the high-definition Jumbotron, I could see tiny beads of sweat breaking out near Pastor Skip's hairline where the hot stage lights were hitting him, a ring of sweat forming on the collar of his aloha shirt, and orange-toned makeup collecting in the creases under his eyes.

As this was the first Sunday in November, the theme of the sermon was "Being Thankful." Pastor Skip offered as an example his own wife, whom he apparently counted as one of his life's foremost blessings because (a) she hadn't gained weight after they got married, and (b) she knew when to shut her yap and let him watch the game. The sermon was more standup routine than homily, with the humor of a "take my wife, please" variety.

Donnie leaned over and whispered, "You got mad

at me when I said happy wife, happy life. He just said the same thing."

"I did not get mad at you. And don't blame *me* for what that guy says. *I'm* not the one who picked this church." I glared at Davison, who had dragged us all up here in the first place, but he was busy with his cell phone.

"A boy comes home from school and tells his mother he has a part in the play." Pastor Skip was teeing up another one. "She asks, 'What part is it?' The boy says, 'I play the part of the husband.' The mother says, 'Go back and tell the teacher you want a speaking part'."

Of course, the Catholic Church wasn't much better in this respect, but at least you had hundreds of years of history and tradition to let you know what you were getting into. And the Catholic homily wasn't packed with groaners straight out of a vaudeville-era Catskills routine.

It was an hour and a half before the service let out. The fluorescent-shirted young man with the toddler stood up. Instead of standing back to let us out of the pew, he approached Donnie, still holding the kid's hand. The boy took the opportunity to suspend his full body weight and allow his toes to drag on the ground, swinging his bottle with his free hand.

"Mister Gonsalves?" The young man addressed Donnie. "Thought it was you guys. Eh Davison, long time, man."

"Eh, Curtis. Didn't recognize you. Howzit?"

The two younger men did a fist bump, Davison wandered off to talk to someone else he recognized, and Curtis got down to business.

"Mister Gonsalves, we found one wooden box in your house when we was doing the repair." The man was oblivious to the fact that his toddler had turned his juice bottle upside-down and was shaking it. Red droplets appeared briefly on the surface of the green carpet before soaking in. "Was in one cupboard that got painted over a long time ago. Probably you never even seen it. When the tree fell, it broke out the wall. Anyway, we cannot be responsible for the box. You gotta come pick it up."

"Are you talking about *my* house?" I interrupted. "What was inside the wall?"

Curtis looked to Donnie as if seeking his permission to address me directly.

"It's my wife's house," Donnie confirmed.

"Oh, sorry, missus. Was one old box. We didn't open it or nothing. Mister Konishi's in the office today. He got it there. He wants you to come get it when you can."

I felt a cold liquid spattering the top of my foot and looked down to see the little boy's silver-toothed grin.

"Da-da-da-da-*da*." He waved his bottle gleefully. Then released it. As it rolled downhill, the boy pulled the hymnals out of the pew one by one, dropping them onto the punch-soaked carpet.

"I can go get the box when we leave here." I stepped back out of the toddler's radius of destruction.

"Glad I seen you, Mister Gonsalves. You guys staying for the pancake breakfast?"

"Not today." Donnie shook his head. "I have to get to work."

"Yeah, Tessa got scheduled to work today. They don't let her know until the night before sometimes. Kinda humbug. Eh, no grumble you. Come on, we go get pancakes. Aw, *shoot*." Rage clouded the young father's face as he caught sight of the punch-spattered hymnbooks on the floor. "Stupid. What you did? Where you put your juice?"

"No worries, Curtis," Donnie said. "I got it. Say hello to Tessa for us." He bent down to retrieve the soggy hymnals, and I found a tissue pack in my purse. Donnie and I got the hymn books wiped off and put away in the pew rack as Curtis dragged the flailing toddler off in the direction of the Social Hall.

CHAPTER FIFTEEN

I had taken my own car up to New Beginnings Chapel that morning so that Donnie could leave for work directly from church. I said a quick goodbye to my husband at his car, and then Davison followed me to my Thunderbird.

"Eh, I like try drive this thing," Davison said.

"Sorry. You need a special license to drive a vintage car."

"Not," he protested, but I was already buckling myself into the driver's seat. I waited for him to get into the passenger side, pulled out, then waited some more until the orange-vested parking lot volunteer waved me into the line of trucks creeping out of New Beginnings Chapel's vast parking lot.

Davison opened my glove box and pulled out the case that contained our tablet.

"Ho, heavy, this thing," he exclaimed.

"Emma bought a top-of-the-line case for it.

Waterproof, fireproof, the whole thing. Please put it back. It's university property."

Davison unlatched the case. Too bad Emma hadn't gotten the stepson-proof model.

"Aw, sweet. This kine get the good camera on it."

"Yes, it's for our research. Please put it back"

"I like try the camera. I take one picture of you."

"Davison, would you *please*—"

"Molly, look out!"

I slammed the brakes just in time to avoid rear-ending the truck in front of us. The Thunderbird's nose plunged and the car skidded sideways. A driver behind us leaned on the horn.

Davison quickly stuffed the tablet back in the glove box and was quiet for the rest of the ride.

Konishi Construction was a few doors down from the Pair-O-Dice Bar and Grill, in the same shabby single-story building. I followed Davison in through the unlocked front door. Our arrival triggered a chime, which resonated from somewhere in the back. The reception area was dark, but down the hallway, a light shone from an open door.

"Eh Mister Konishi," Davison called out as he sauntered down the hallway. "It's Davison Gonsalves. Curtis said you gotta box for my dad, ah?"

"It's for *me*," I called after him. I didn't follow Davison. I didn't know Al Konishi and was happy to let Davison deal with him while I waited in the reception area.

I sat on an orange vinyl couch, which must have

been the height of style in the seventies. Now, even in the semi-darkness, I could see the vinyl was scuffed and the chrome legs were pitted.

I couldn't wait to see what was in the box. Historic documents? Priceless antiques? There was one person, at least, who would be as excited as I was to find out.

I called Pat Flanagan's number, but there was no answer at the headquarters of *Island Confidential*. The phone reception was patchy up on the mountainside where Pat's little cabin sat.

I called Emma next, but her number went straight to voicemail. I left a message for her and hung up just as Davison emerged holding what looked like a bundle of towels. I stood up.

"What is *that*? And why is it wrapped up?"

"Dusty is why," Davison said.

"Let's see."

He set the bundle down on the reception counter and pulled back the towel to reveal an ancient wooden crate, which looked to be exactly the size of a breadbox. The faded ink read Harper Twelvetrees Soap Powder. Grey wisps of spider webs dangled from the sides of the box. I tried to pick it up from the counter, but it was so heavy it felt like it had been nailed down.

"I got it." Davison lifted the box effortlessly. "Eh, good thing I came, ah?"

The twenty-minute drive down to Donnie's place took about an hour. No one (except me) seemed to be in any particular hurry. The motorists ahead took up both lanes in a leisurely blockade, apparently engaged in some kind of contest to see who could drive the slowest without coming to a complete stop.

Pat and Emma were waiting at Donnie's front door when we pulled up.

"Got your message," Emma said, as I unlocked the front door. Emma and Pat went in while Davison retrieved the box from the trunk. I hovered anxiously behind him to make sure he didn't drop it. By the time we were inside, Emma, who was really good at making herself feel at home, was already seated at the dining room table, drinking Donnie's good Sangiovese out of a coffee mug Donnie had picked up at the Cremona food expo a couple of years earlier. The decimated wine bottle was parked in front of her, within easy reach.

Pat sat at the dining room table next to Emma, checking his phone.

"Pat, make yourself some coffee," I called out as I hurried to the linen closet for a clean towel. "The pods are in the drawer under the machine."

I spread out the towel on the dining room table, and Davison set down the box.

"That thing looks old." Emma drew her mug of wine to her protectively. The box was made of pine, the label printed on the bare wood in orange and green inks.

Harper Twelvetrees Soap Powder. Bromley-by-bow, London.

"Are you going to open it right now?" Pat called from the kitchen.

"You better," Emma said. "That's how come you called us down here, right?"

"Don't we gotta wait until Dad gets home?" Davison asked.

"He said not to wait for him." I thought I remembered Donnie saying something like that. And I was dying to see what treasures lay inside the box.

For Washing Without Rubbing. A Penny Packet Equal to Ten Pennyworth of Soap.

I might find a long-buried secret. Or a time capsule. Or something so valuable I could retire and stop worrying about tenure.

"Hey, where were you this morning?" Emma asked.

"We went to New Beginnings Chapel," I said.

"With your hair uncovered like that?" Pat called from the kitchen. He emerged with a steaming mug of coffee. "Did the *mutaween* come and beat you with sticks for venturing out unveiled, you hussy?"

"Not this time. Fortunately, I was accompanied by male relatives. Okay, gather round everyone—"

The box appeared to have been nailed shut.

"Shoot," I said. "How are you supposed to open these things?"

"Gotta pry 'em," Emma said. "Davison, you get a crowbar or something?"

Davison disappeared into the kitchen and came out with a flat head screwdriver.

"Be careful," I said.

As Pat, Emma and I watched, Davison worked the flat blade of the screwdriver under the lid and rocked the screwdriver up and down. He did it next to each nail until an even gap separated the lid from the box. Eventually, he worked the lid free to reveal objects wrapped in yellowed newspaper.

Davison reached in and grabbed the paper-wrapped lump on top. The newspaper cracked like a shell in his grip, and crumbled onto the table, leaving him holding a sugar bowl. The silver had tarnished to a black finish with a rainbow shimmer.

"Wait," I cried.

"Sorry. I better go put away the screwdriver." He placed the sugar bowl back in the box and slunk away.

"Shoot," Emma said. "Now what?"

"From the typeface, it looks like this newspaper is from the mid to late nineteenth century." Pat leaned over the box and peered inside, but didn't touch anything.

"How do you know?" Emma asked.

"J-school. I can get Jeffrey to take a look at this."

"Who?" I asked.

"Jeffrey Voorhees. He's the manager of Bayfront Antiques and Collectibles. And he does some consulting for private collections."

"I know the guy you're talking about," Emma said. "He sold some old furniture for my dad. He seemed okay. Weird for a young guy to know so much about antiques."

"So he knows how to handle fragile things like this?" I asked. "Unlike you-know-who?"

"Jeffrey has this spray he uses for old paper," Pat

said. "It neutralizes the acid and keeps the paper from falling apart. You want him to see what he can do about unpacking your box?"

I heard Davison's bedroom door close.

"You were kinda hard on him, ah?" Emma said.

"Me? What did I do?"

"You gave him this look like he'd just run over your puppy," Pat said.

"He kind of *did*. What if the paper he crushed was valuable?"

"What?" Emma shoved my shoulder. "You think someone wrapped their tea set in the Declaration of Independence?"

"You don't like being stuck down here at Donnie's place," Pat said. *"That's* why you're so cranky."

"Ooh, Molly. You don't like living with your own *husband?*"

"Stop it. I *love* my husband. But maybe Pat has a point. I mean, for the past few days I've been living in not-my house, going to not-my church, eating not-my food. I thought whatever was in this little wooden box, at least, was mine. And even *that* has to get ruined. By you-know-who."

"I get it," Emma said. "Just, the boy was only trying to help."

"So is it going to be expensive? To have your antique dealer friend take a look at this?"

"I'll ask him not to do it if it looks like the contents aren't going to be worth it," Pat said.

"Sounds fair. How long will it take?"

"I'd give him a week, at least."

I placed the lid back on the soap powder box and pushed it over to Pat.

"I hate delaying gratification."

"Me too," Emma said.

"I know. I'll tell Jeffrey to get to it as soon as he can."

CHAPTER SIXTEEN

By Monday morning, I'd managed (with some effort) to stop obsessing over the contents of the box. I had more urgent matters to work out with Emma, anyway. We needed to decide what to do about continuing with our research, in light of the grisly murder on Art Lam's property, and Art Lam's subsequent vow of silence. I walked with Emma to her morning class, up the wide, covered concrete walkway that cut through the center of campus.

"I still don't think the murder has anything to do with us," Emma said. "If someone wanted to stop us, wouldn't they have sent us some kind of message? No one's even claimed responsibility."

"Seems like leaving a hacked-up body for us to see was supposed to send someone a message. But you're right. There's not really anything to connect it to us. On the other hand, should we just ignore that we found a hacked-up body?"

We were in the ten minutes between class periods, and Emma and I were pushing upstream through a tide of students. The air was heavy with cigarette smoke, cloying perfume, and the sour body odor born of warm, humid days and line-dried laundry.

"We don't even know who the guy was," Emma said. "Obviously wasn't Art Lam."

"Unless someone impersonated Art Lam on my phone messages."

"Who wouldn't want us to study attitudes toward biotech?" Emma asked. "How could anyone object? What kind of smoking gun do they think we'll dig up?"

"You don't dig up a smoking gun. It's not how the metaphor works."

"Fine. What kind of smoking gun do they think we'll *unearth*? Is that better?"

"You know, Donnie's right. This grant is great and everything, but it isn't worth my life. Or my career."

"Don't you dare think about quitting." Emma stopped walking and turned to me, tiny hands on her sturdy hips.

"Well, what are we supposed to do? We can't interview Art Lam. He said his lawyer won't let him talk to anyone, including us."

She sighed and resumed walking.

"So we write about what happened down at Art's place," Emma said. "It's qualitative data, right? You and me were eyewitnesses."

"There's not going to be much to our eyewitness

account. We didn't really see anything. Come to think of it, are we even sure it was a man? We assumed it was because we thought it was Art. The police aren't revealing the name of the victim pending notification of next of kin, whom they can't find. I was hoping Art Lam would be the start of our snowball sample. I thought he'd introduce us to other people we should talk to. But now we're at a dead end—"

Emma and I saw it at the same time. Among the posters taped to the concrete wall along the walkway was a flyer printed on fluorescent yellow paper. It was an announcement for an upcoming community forum on biotechnology.

"This Wednesday," Emma said. "Let's go."

"Do you think it's safe?"

"Look, it's sponsored by Students for a Better World and the Ag Club. How dangerous could it be? Molly, come *on*, don't be a wimp."

"It *would* be good for me to get out of the house for an evening. I'm sure Donnie would like to spend some quality time with his son. Without me there."

"That's the spirit. Okay, I gotta get to class. We're going to this event, yeah? Don't chicken out."

"I won't. In fact, I'll call Pat. He'll probably want to go."

"Good idea," Emma called back.

Donnie had made liver for dinner. It tasted pretty good, considering it was liver. He'd sliced it thin and fried it crisp, then topped it with browned onions and bacon slices. He served it with a side of some nutrient-dense leafy green thing that tasted like a chopped-up houseplant. It was certainly an improvement over that piña colada gizzard stew or whatever we had the first night Davison was back.

"Donnie, you've done a great job with these ingredients."

"It could be better," he said. "I'm working on it."

Davison was in a mood, making dinner glum for all three of us.

"So eating like this is going to make us healthier?" I asked, simply to make conversation. I was already healthy enough, and I wasn't particularly interested in adopting Davison's fun-free diet for the long term.

"It's not gonna work if you both keep drinking so much," Davison said.

"Davison." Donnie glared at him.

"No point in eating healthy if you're going to be grumpy and stressed-out all the time. Cheers." I raised my wine glass and took a big gulp.

"So you get in touch with your friends?" Donnie asked.

Davison shrugged. "Hardly anyone left. Everyone's gone to the mainland for work, or like Curtis, got kids already an' too busy to do anything. Only ones is Baron and Boyboy."

"Are the Balusteros brothers doing anything productive with their lives now?" Donnie asked.

"Both working at Strongman."

"What's Strongman?" I asked.

"Gym," Davison said. "The one downtown, used

to be called Iron Island."

"Oh Donnie, there's a meeting I was going to attend with Emma. Two of the student groups are sponsoring a debate on biotech. I thought it would be interesting."

"Is that the community forum with Randy Randolph?" Donnie asked.

"I don't know. Maybe? I don't know who Randy Randolph is."

"He's the new community liaison for Seed Solutions."

"Well if you're interested, it's on Wednesday night."

"I have something Wednesday," Donnie said. "Davison, maybe you'd like to go. You might learn something new."

"I dunno," Davison said.

"Oh, it's just going to be a long, boring debate about biotechnology. I don't think you'll want to sit through it, Davison. The only reason Emma and I are going is for work."

"Is Pat going to be there?" Donnie asked.

"Fifty/fifty. Pat told me he might not be able to make it."

"Davison, you should go with them," Donnie said.

"What? Don't force him. Davison, if you're bored, you can stay home and read a book."

Was that my mother's voice coming out of my mouth? It sure sounded like it.

"I have some good murder mysteries," I offered.

"They're in the drawer of the coffee table in the living room."

That was another reason Donnie's place didn't feel like home to me. If I was going to live here, we were going to need some bookshelves.

"Molly," Donnie interjected. "After what happened at Art Lam's place, you and Emma shouldn't be going out at night by yourself to this thing. Davison, you go with Molly and Emma. Make sure they don't get into trouble."

"Donnie, we don't need a *babysitter*."

"I'm sorry. I didn't mean for it to sound like that. But this is a night time event, and I want you to be safe."

"What if he doesn't want to go? I'm not going to force him."

"What if he *does* want to go?"

Both of us looked at Davison, who was pushing greens around on his plate.

"If he wants to go," I said, "of course he's welcome."

Donnie had a point, although I was loath to admit it. I didn't know who was going to show up at that meeting. The campus was dark at night, and security was thin on the ground. I was average-sized at best, and Emma was tiny, at least in the vertical dimension. Davison was a big kid and carried himself with the chest-out, chip-on-the-shoulder posture of someone who punches first and asks questions later. Maybe with Davison lurking around, people would think twice about messing with us.

"Sounds like a plan," Donnie said. "Davison, you good with it?"

"Yeah, I'll go. Nothing better to do."

CHAPTER SEVENTEEN

Emma, Davison, and I arrived on campus a few minutes before the scheduled start of the biotech debate and made our way to the Science Building. A desk was set up outside the door. My student, Lars Suzuki, was stationed behind it, making sure the attendees signed in.

"Oh, hey Professor," Lars chirped. "Glad you're here. Can you sign in right there? Your email too, if you don't mind. We need to document how many people showed up for when we do our report to the Student Events Board."

I filled in my information, then handed the pen to Emma.

"It's how we used to do it on the cruise ship," Lars went on. "You always have to count heads. You have thousands of people on one cruise. There's no way you can know who everyone is, and you don't wanna leave anyone behind."

Lars continued to expound on the operations management techniques used at his former cruise ship job as Emma, and then Davison, wrote in their contact information.

"Okay, we'd better let the next people sign in," I said, finally. "Nice to see you, Lars."

The event was being held in the big classroom, the newer one with stadium seating. Only a few empty seats remained, all of them in the middle of the rows, toward the front of the room. Four folding metal chairs had been arranged down in the front of the room, facing the audience. Davison sat on one side of Emma, I sat on the other.

Art Lam came down from the back of the room and sat in one of the four folding chairs facing the audience, elbows on his knees, hands folded, scowling.

"He's not dead." Emma elbowed me in the ribs.

"I know. facI can see him."

It was strange to see Art Lam sitting there alive and well. He briefly made eye contact, then looked away quickly without acknowledging me. I wondered what his lawyer had told him to make him afraid even to look at me.

A smirky fortyish dude in a pineapple-patterned aloha shirt and chinos swaggered out and sat down next to Art. After him came a hollow-eyed, grey-haired woman in flowing batik. The last folding chair remained empty.

I felt someone sit down beside me. It was Pat Flanagan.

Emma reached behind me and shoved Pat's shoulder by way of greeting. Davison looked over and gave Pat a cool-guy chin jut.

"Those are fab shoes," Pat whispered to me. "Love the buckles. How do you walk in them?"

"They're platforms." I turned my foot to show Pat the shoe's profile. "I'm high off the ground, but my foot's still at a comfortable angle. I don't have to do Barbie feet."

"I thought Coco Chanel said you weren't supposed to wear anything too memorable."

"Not exactly. She said, 'Dress shabbily and they remember the dress; dress impeccably and they remember the woman.' Anyway, Coco Chanel is not the boss of me. So this is weird to see Art Lam here."

"Is he still not talking to you?"

"He won't even make eye contact. What about those other two sitting down there? I assume Mister Business Casual is pro-biotech, and the lady in batik is anti."

"Right," Pat said. "The aging frat boy down there is Randy Randolph, the community liaison for Seed Solutions, formerly PlantGenex."

"Aging frat boy? What happened to your journalistic objectivity?"

"Randolph is the weaselly sack of unearned privilege who's buying my house out from under me."

"What about the other one? The woman who looks like she's on a hunger strike?"

"She's your councilwoman," Pat said.

"Looks like a mostly anti-biotech crowd," Emma remarked.

"How can you tell?" I asked.

"All the gray ponytails in the audience."

At around ten minutes after the hour, the crowd hushed as Crystal Phoenix from the yoga studio walked to the podium. She wore a close-fitting clay-dyed tank dress, which was just a shade darker than her sun-warmed skin. Davison leaned forward and stared.

Crystal welcomed the crowd, thanked the student organizations for arranging the debate, and introduced the three panelists and the moderator. Then she walked over to the vacant folding chair and rested her hand on the back.

"Primo Nordmann was planning to be here tonight," she announced. "Unfortunately, he wasn't able to make it. I know Primo is with us in spirit. Please give a warm welcome to our guests."

Davison watched Crystal walk offstage, swiveling his head to follow her up to the back of the room. I pulled the tablet out and started up the note-taking app. I was still getting used to the interface, which allowed me to take notes as sound and video were recorded. I got the recording started and braced the tablet on the little flip-down arm desk at the correct angle to record the three panelists, farmer Art Lam, biotech executive Randy Randolph, and county councilwoman Alohalani Zabek, as they made their opening statements. From there the debate meandered along in a free-form style, with minimal intervention from the moderator.

I took notes, but by this time, I was so familiar with the arguments, I could have written them out in advance:

We're helping farmers to feed the world / You're poisoning the ecosystem and making farmers dependent. / If biotech food is so great, why won't you label it so we know what we're buying? / Biotech food is just as safe as any other food, so why should we have to label it? Genetic modifications have been going on for millennia / But not across species. It can't happen in nature / What's so great about nature? Nature will kill you the minute she gets a chance.

When it was time for the presenters to make their closing statements, Art Lam did not speak. Instead, we were shown a clip of Art Lam's October 28 testimony to the legislature.

"Looks like Art Lam really was out of town that morning," Pat whispered.

"He coulda done the murder the night before," Emma suggested. "And then flown over to the capitol that morning."

"And left the mess there for us to find?" I whispered.

"Maybe he didn't think it through."

When the closing statements were finished, the questions from the audience began, more or less recapitulating the same arguments but occasionally hijacking the discussion over to the questioner's pet issue. Emma was right; it was an overwhelmingly anti-biotech crowd, and the discussion didn't seem to change anyone's opinion.

More interesting to me than the arguments themselves were the rhetorical styles of the panelists. The wispy-haired councilwoman may not have looked like a professional politician, but she struck exactly the right note: earnest, gentle, and above all, *concerned*. As a local farmer, the cantankerous Art Lam should have been a sympathetic figure, but he seemed like he was itching to wave us all off with a shotgun. Being under his lawyer's gag order didn't help; he made an oblique reference to vandalism on his property, and complained about his broken window. Then he changed the subject and refused to say anything more about the incident, which made him seem evasive and paranoid.

Randy Randolph's performance on behalf of Seed Solutions was slick and flawless. Of the three panelists, I found him the least sympathetic. Maybe it was because of what Pat had told me, although how can you fault someone for wanting to buy a house? It wasn't like he was displacing Pat on purpose.

When the audience questions had finally petered out, Pat, Emma, Davison, and I repaired to the back of the room for gluten-free cookies, courtesy of Students for a Better World, and locally grown coffee provided by the Ag club. Davison grabbed a handful of cookies and wandered off into the crowd.

Emma waved a cookie at me.

"It says GMO-free on the box, but that's a lie. Do they know that the wheat used in cookies has been genetically modified over millennia? This is biotech right here. Hey everyone, you're eating biotech food right now."

"It's not the same," Pat said. "You could use conventional breeding techniques forever, but you'll never be able to import a gene from one species into another. *That's* what people are freaked out about."

"I notice there's an anti-vaccine faction here. Is that usual?"

"Every friggin' time," Emma said. "And don't forget about those people who think they can fly and communicate with dolphins."

"The alliances are interesting," Pat said. "The antivaxxers and the anti-biotech people are usually on the same side. Which I guess makes sense, because both positions are pro-nature. But then, you have your libertarians. They tend to be anti-vax but pro-GMO."

"Make a note, Molly."

I patted my bag. "Still recording audio," I said.

"Hey, what about my civil rights?" Pat protested.

"Put in a section on alliance-building," I said to my bag. "And look into the flying dolphins."

"Make sure you talk to that chiropractor who claimed she was a mermaid," Emma said.

"I don't see her. It looks like she's already left."

"Guess she swam back home. And it's flying AND dolphins," Emma pointedly told my laptop bag, "not flying dolphins. Hey, what happened to

Davison? Isn't he supposed to be hanging around looking menacing?"

"He's over there, talking to Crystal," Pat said.

Crystal and Davison were down by the whiteboard, standing much closer than they needed to.

"Well, look at that," Emma said. "The hippie chick and the military academy boy. You know what? If I was that girl, not knowing Davison's personality or anything, he'd probably look pretty good to me. Look, he got a nice aloha shirt on and everything."

"Donnie made him dress up for this. I guess he does look less loutish than usual."

"And that scar tissue on the side of his face and neck looks like some kind of heroic battlefield injury," Pat said.

"Instead of what it really is. The residue of his lasered-off neck tattoo. Fine. Crystal can keep Davison occupied while we collect some data. Okay, how should we do the interviews now? Art already said he wasn't going to talk to us. Maybe one of us should take Randy Randolph, and one of us should take Councilwoman Zabek. There's a long line for her, though."

"I'll wait for Zabek," Emma said. "You go talk to Randolph."

"There's only the one tablet to record the interviews. Maybe we should have requisitioned one for each of us."

"I'll go with Emma," Pat said. "You take the

tablet. I'll remember the conversation."

Pat wasn't bragging. I knew he could do it. I'd seen him interview people for his *Island Confidential* pieces, committing the conversation to memory in real time. That way there was no notepad to lose, no tape recorder to get stolen or stomped on.

"I'll go talk to Randolph then," I said.

"Good," Emma said. "Better you than me. I can't trust myself not to punch his smug face."

"What are you talking about? He's pro-biotech. He's on your side."

"That smarmy little schmuck is kicking Pat out of his house. I hate him."

"As long as we keep our Scientific Objectivity," I said.

I walked over to introduce myself to Randy Randolph.

CHAPTER EIGHTEEN

Randy Randolph of Seed Solutions sat alone in his metal folding chair at the front of the lecture hall.

"Hi, I'm Molly Barda." I extended my hand. "I teach in the College of Commerce here. I just wanted to say hello, and thanks for coming out to talk to us."

He took my hand and squeezed it briefly. I thought I caught a whiff of booze breath. Maybe he'd gone out to dinner before the forum.

"You're a teacher here? Should I call you Professor?" He snickered, as if there were something humorous about my being a professor.

"Just call me Molly." I settled into the folding chair next to him. "So you mentioned in your intro you're new to Hawaii. I just moved here a few years ago myself. Are you adjusting?"

When I had been watching Randolph from the audience, the pineapple pattern of his aloha shirt had masked the stains spreading under his arms. Sitting beside him now, I could see he was drenched with sweat.

"Trying to buy a house. Takes forever to get things done around here. Some ridiculous holdup with a tenant."

"I'm doing some research about attitudes toward biotech," I said. "I wonder if you wouldn't mind if I recorded—"

"One down, a thousand to go," he said.

"I'm sorry? What was that?"

"I've been at *way* too many of these things already, and it's just the beginning."

He seemed willing to speak candidly. This was better than I'd expected. I'd already asked his permission to record our conversation, right? I was set.

"Why do you say too many?" I asked.

"'Cause everyone's got their minds made up already. These things are all the same. When my boss told me I was going to Hawaii, I was expecting sandy beaches and beautiful hula girls. Instead I get a bunch of old hippies from California spouting off about the *keiki* and the `aina and all that crap."

He looked around, as if he were about to impart a great secret to me.

"And then—I probably shouldn't say this. But every single time, some chunky Hawaiian chick stands up at the end and says, 'Oh, I don't know about DNA or anything, but my grandmother taught me about fish ponds.' Then she goes off about her ancestors and Pele and blah blah blah."

So much for my scientific objectivity. I did not like this guy at all. *Chunky?* That woman wasn't any bigger than I was.

"Hey, you're not writing any of this down, are you?" he said.

I held up my hands to show him I wasn't holding any writing instruments. Over on the other side of the lecture hall, Emma and Pat finished their conversation with Councilwoman Zabek and made their way toward the upper exit. (We were in one of the newer classrooms, which had been built with two doors. In the event a mad gunman came in through one, people had a chance of escaping through the other.)

Emma paused when she reached the door, turned around, and made a rude gesture meant for my eyes only. Maybe it was a good thing I'd come to talk to Randy Randolph by myself. He might not have been so forthcoming with his opinions about the natives had Emma been standing right there. Also, Emma probably *would* have punched him by now, which would have been hard to explain to our Human Subjects Board.

"So what do you think of Art Lam?" I asked.

"Art's a good man," Randy said. "He's rational. Orientals are very practical people. Alls he wants to do is grow food to feed people, and he has to sit there and listen to these loonies accuse him of poisoning the land."

"Councilwoman Zabek?" I asked.

"Typical politician. Just does whatever the crazies in her district tell her to."

"What about Primo Nordmann, who was scheduled to be your fourth panel member? What do you think of him?"

Randy Randolph's expression went opaque, like a shutter being pulled down over a storefront.

"You probably need to talk to one of the organizers about him. I gotta get going. Hey, nice to meet you, Melody. Give me a call if you want to talk some more."

"It's Molly."

He pressed a Seed Solutions card into my hand—green ink on cardstock the color of a grocery bag—and left, trailing a tang of alcohol and flop sweat. I tucked the card into my bag and made my way over to where Davison and Crystal were still chatting.

"I hope you didn't believe everything Randy Randolph told you," Crystal said.

"Do you know him?" I asked.

"He's a client."

Davison's face clouded. "You're massaging this guy?"

"We just started Randy on a strength training program. I'm doing personal training and life coaching for him."

"So what happened to Primo Nordmann?" I asked. "The fourth panelist? Why wasn't he here tonight?"

"Who?" Davison asked.

"Primo Nordmann. He was a student here. Maybe

you knew him when you were here?"

"Nah," Davison said. "Doesn't sound familiar."

"Come to think of it," I said, "I haven't seen Primo around the yoga studio lately. Is he okay?"

Crystal flicked a glance at Davison, and then at me.

"You don't know," she said.

"Know what?"

"Neither of you can say anything about this."

"I won't," I assured her.

"Primo attracted some bad energy." Crystal paused to make sure we understood how significant that was.

"How did he do that?" I asked. "What happened?"

Crystal motioned us to come closer.

"Didn't you hear about that body found in Art Lam's papaya field? It was Primo."

"That was *Primo*? Primo is *dead*?"

"Oh, the papaya field guy," Davison exclaimed. "Molly, he's the one you—"

Davison caught my panicked look. Fortunately, he was smart enough to catch on and change the subject.

"Yeah, I heard about it," he mumbled.

It wasn't common knowledge that Emma and I had discovered the body. Detective Medeiros had asked (ordered) Emma and me to keep it quiet, and we were more than happy to comply. We didn't need the celebrity, and we didn't want to mess up the police investigation.

"Crystal, how did you find this out? About Primo?"

How did Crystal Phoenix the yoga instructor/ personal trainer/ life coach/ masseuse/ supplement saleswoman know who the murder victim was, when Emma and I had no idea? When we were the ones who discovered the body? Some kind of researchers *we* were.

"The police came and talked to all of us at the studio. But they told us not to tell anyone. Molly, you can't say anything, okay?"

"Who would do something like that? I mean, I know Art Lam is kind of a grumpy guy, but if he caught someone cutting down his trees, I think he'd just yell at them and call the police. He doesn't seem like a—" I was going to say he doesn't seem like a dismembering kind of guy, but I remembered just in time no one had said anything about Primo's manner of death.

Davison was looking from Crystal to me and back to Crystal, as if he were watching a tennis match.

"Sometimes it isn't ours to know," Crystal said. "Some secrets belong to the Universe."

"How horrible," I said. "Poor guy."

Having Primo Nordmann as a student hadn't exactly been the highlight of my teaching career. In class, he often showed up without having done the reading, and then "made up" for it by pursuing class participation points with extra vigor. He derailed and dominated the conversation with his anti-corporate rants, which was not particularly helpful to the other students in the business planning class. Outside of class, Primo was an office-hours pest, lobbying me to convert to his all-fruit diet and trying to get my approval for a number of insane business ideas. (My favorite: smashing global capitalism by setting up an alternate worldwide supply chain for all manufactured goods.)

But even at his worst (which I'd have to say was when he filed a grievance against me for insensitively eating cheese in front of him during my office hours) I just hoped he would chill out a little and stop hectoring me. I couldn't imagine anyone wanting to kill him, much less going about it so viciously.

"It's getting late. And cold. I'm ready to go home. I have class tomorrow, and I have to finish prepping my lecture."

I rubbed my upper arms to generate some warmth. "Davison, do you need a ride back, or...?"

"I'll take him home," Crystal purred.

"Great. Thanks, Crystal. Davison, I'll let your dad know you'll be home whenever. No rush."

CHAPTER NINETEEN

I drove back down to Donnie's place, slipped my shoes off at the front door, and let myself in to the empty house. I figured something must have come up at Donnie's Drive-Inn to keep him working so late. I showered and changed into a comfortable t-shirt and sweatpants, got myself a glass of wine and a murder mystery, and went back to the master bedroom. I slid into the ultra-high-thread-count sheets of Donnie's platform bed and got comfortable.

I must have fallen asleep, because I woke to the bumping sensation of someone trying to crawl into bed without disturbing me.

"Hey," came a voice from somewhere in the dark. The rain was making a low roar on the metal roof and blocking out the moonlight. I felt Donnie lean over to give me a minty kiss.

"You were out late," I groped around for my

book, and found it on my chest. I placed it onto the night table, almost knocking over my glass of wine.

"Sorry about waking you up," Donnie said. "Maybe we should look into getting one of those memory foam mattresses."

"Your hair's wet. Did you already shower? I must've been fast asleep."

"It's nice to come home and find you here." I sensed Donnie settling in to his side of the bed.

"Well that's sweet," I said. "I was kind of hoping *you'd* be home when *I* got back."

"I didn't see Davison. Did he come back with you?"

"You'll be glad to hear he's with Crystal Phoenix. She said she'd give him a ride home."

"Who?"

"Crystal. The one you wanted me to set him up with. You met her at Natural High organic foods when we were buying Davison's weird food for him. Blonde hippie girl? The one who was flirting with you?"

"Oh, her. Sorry, I didn't make the connection. She was at your biotech meeting?"

"She actually introduced the speakers. She definitely caught Davison's eye."

I heard Donnie sigh.

"You know, we flew him all the way back here from the East Coast so he could spend some time with his *parents*."

"Donnie, Davison didn't want to come back with me. What was I supposed to do? Throw him over my shoulder and carry him back to the car? I think it's fine. He doesn't need to spend every waking second with us."

"I hoped he'd be able to spend a little more time with *you*."

"Donnie, is this you lecturing me on how I'm doing everything wrong? Again? *You* were the one who wanted Davison to find nice girl his own age, remember? Now you're mad at *me* because things worked out exactly the way you wanted?"

"No, Molly, it's not what I—"

"Anyway, when he was talking with her, it was maybe the first time I've really seen him look happy this whole trip. If *that* means anything to you."

"I was just trying to—did you get some good research done tonight?"

"Oh, speaking of research. Guess what I found out? The body in Art Lam's papaya grove? It was Primo Nordmann."

"Who?"

"My former student? The one who was working at the yoga studio?"

"Oh. The yoga teacher. The one who was so impressed with the way you could put your legs—"

"That's the one."

"He's dead?"

"According to Crystal. He was actually scheduled as one of the panelists tonight, and he didn't show up. Poor guy. What a horrible way to go."

"That's why Ka`imi Medeiros has been asking me so many questions about you," Donnie said.

"Detective Medeiros? What kind of questions?"

"It's probably because of your history with the murder victim."

"My *history*? Donnie, I do not have a *history* with Primo Nordmann."

"Wasn't he the one with the cheese? He filed a complaint about you, right?"

"Oh. *That* history. So what, Medeiros thinks I hacked up my former student and a bunch of Art Lam's papaya trees and then left all the parts strewn around because what? Because I was holding a grudge about that stupid cheese thing?"

"Ka`imi has to be suspicious. It's part of his job."

"He doesn't have to be *that* suspicious. It's pathological, if you ask me."

"Molly, neither one of us has worked in law enforcement. We don't know what it's like. Ka`imi sees the worst of human nature every day."

"That's what *he* thinks. He's never served on a General Education committee. Hey, I met your friend Randy Randolph, from Seed Solutions."

"What did you think of him?"

"He did *not* make a good impression on me. He's like if you took the spoiled rich-boy bully character from every teen '80s movie, and added a couple of decades and a drinking problem. He told me he was disappointed when Mahina wasn't full of beautiful hula girls. Reducing a centuries-old art form to some trivial erotic diversion."

"That's surprising. My impression of him was he plays his cards close. He doesn't seem to say what he's really thinking."

"Yeah, maybe not to you. Lucky me. I got the white person all-access pass to his inner thoughts. So, speaking of meetings, where did *you* go tonight?"

"Oh, just something I had to go to," Donnie said.

"No, really. Where were you? I know the Drive-Inn closes at—"

"Molly."

Donnie moved closer. I smelled toothpaste and shampoo, and his warm, wet skin.

"Seriously, Donnie? You think I won't notice you're changing the subject to avoid answering my question?"

"Is it working?"

"Are you going to tell me where you were?"

"I will," he murmured into my hair. "I promise."

On the one hand, I was annoyed at Donnie's evasiveness. On the other hand, we had some privacy with Davison out of the house, and Donnie was rather effectively pressing his suit, as it were.

"You know I'll find out." But I had already lost interest in whatever it was we'd been arguing about.

CHAPTER TWENTY

The next morning, Emma and Pat came by my office, as they often do. I'd like to say it was because they enjoyed my company, but I think it had more to do with my fancy coffee machine than with my engaging personality. And of course, I had enough chairs for everyone to sit down.

Budget cuts had eliminated funding for faculty office furniture, so we all had to pay for our own desks and chairs. When Tatsuya's Moderne Beauty went out of business, Pat bought a set of attached hot pink vinyl hairdryer chairs for twenty-five dollars. They took up half his office, and would have been reasonably comfortable had the chrome hairdryer bonnets not still been attached.

Emma's office was even less welcoming than Pat's. Emma refused to spend her own money to buy work furniture, so her office had no place for visitors to sit. The rare student who got up the nerve to visit her in her office had to stand and stare at the brain in a jar she had sitting on her file cabinet.

Emma pushed in to my office first. She claimed my more comfortable chair (which I'd scrounged from one of the Student Retention Office's remodels) and handed me her coffee mug. It bore the logo of a well-known and widely vilified chemical company.

"You carrying this around just to annoy the anti-biotech people?" I brewed a dose of coffee into the mug.

"What? I got it at a conference. I'm supposed to turn down free stuff now?"

Pat unfolded the metal chair I had leaning against my wall.

"So what's the latest?" he asked as I took his mug, the big one with the C-Span logo.

"Oh, this is *huge*. Right after you two left the biotech forum, I found out the body in the papaya field was Primo Nordmann."

"Oh yeah," Emma said. "I knew that.

"What? How did you know?"

"Pat told me,"

"Pat, you knew?"

"Not a hundred percent. But I knew the police had been asking around at the yoga studio. Primo Nordmann was the only instructor there who hadn't shown up for his classes."

"Why didn't you tell me, Pat?"

"They actually warned me not to say anything to you."

"Who is *they*? And why not?"

"Medeiros guys," Emma said.

"*Et tu*, Emma? What, the stupid cheese incident again?"

Pat shrugged. So it *was* the stupid cheese incident.

"What do they think happened? What exactly is their working hypothesis here?"

"They're just being cautious," Pat said.

"It's not like you're a *suspect*, exactly," Emma added.

"Exactly? I shouldn't be a suspect at *all*. What is wrong with people? I can't believe Medeiros doesn't trust me. I've been nothing but helpful and law-abiding. When have I ever caused him any trouble?"

"What about when you had to be rescued this summer?" Emma asked.

"Oh, yeah." Pat chuckled. "He was telling me they had to divert most of the island's emergency vehicles—"

"That could've happened to anyone."

I handed Pat's mug back to him and finally set my own onto the platform, impatiently watching the stream thin and peter out as my cup filled.

"So what are the facts so far? You two go out to Art Lam's farm to do research on attitudes toward biotech. You show up, not knowing Art has conveniently been called away to testify at the Ledge, of which he has video proof."

"I bet one of those enviro-nuts killed Primo Nordmann," Emma said.

"But Primo was one of those 'enviro-nuts',

Emma. He was scheduled to speak on the anti-biotech side at the forum, remember? Now, if the victim had been Randy Randolph from Seed Solutions, you'd have a point. But who would want to get rid of Primo Nordmann?"

"So in other words, we have *bupkis*," Emma said.

"What scares me is whoever did it is still out there," I said. "And there's no logic to it. No one's claimed responsibility."

"I'm not worried," Emma said. "The police are on it, and better yet, so is Pat. If the Mahina PD don't catch the guy right away, *Island Confidential* is gonna get to the bottom of it."

"Please be careful, Pat," I said.

"Sure." Pat didn't look at either of us.

"Pat?" Emma asked. "You're going to follow this story, aren't you? You're not gonna let the murderers get away, are you?"

"You're not doing the story?" I stared. "Did Detective Medeiros tell you to back off?"

"It doesn't have anything to do with Medeiros." Pat folded his arms and leaned back in the metal chair. "I've decided to take the job."

"What do you mean take the job?" Emma demanded.

"With the Mahina State University marketing department."

"Oy," Emma exclaimed. "The marketing department yet. What a sellout."

"What did they tempt you with?" I asked. "Immortality? Unimaginable wealth?"

"I'd be completely in charge of our social media strategy."

"Listen to Mister Big Shot," Emma scoffed. "*Our* social media strategy, he says."

"Do they know about *Island Confidential*, with all of those scathing exposes about our university administration?" I asked. "Do they know it's you?"

"Oh yeah. Your article about the library workers? If they ever find out you're behind the story, you're gonna be out on your *tochas* so fast."

"They know about *Island Confidential*. They're okay with it."

"Who's *they* exactly?" I asked. "To whom are you reporting?"

"Victor Santiago from Dixon's office."

"You're working for Torquemada?" Emma crossed her arms. "You're dead to me."

"He said I'd done a great job of building *Island Confidential's* brand. They wanted to infuse that edgy spirit into their social media outreach."

"I thought you hated words like branding and edgy and infuse," I said. "Anyway, are you sure you'll have enough time for *Island Confidential* if you take this on?"

"Molly, I'm getting full health, vision, and dental. And five times what I'm making now teaching intro comp."

"Well, when you put it that way," Emma said. "I see your point. Pat, you should totally take the marketing job."

"What about *Island Confidential?*" I persisted.

"Well, that's the catch. I'll have to suspend publication."

"You have to stop publishing *Island Confidential?*" I exclaimed. "Pat, this is classic co-optation. *That's* what this is about. The administration doesn't want a social media manager. They want to shut down *Island Confidential.* They've decided that your investigative reporting is a threat. They're neutralizing you."

"That's a great insight, Molly, coming from a well-compensated, tenure-track professor with a cushy benefits package and a nice pension."

"I'm not saying you don't deserve a living wage, Pat, but are you sure you want to—"

"Maybe they want to hire me because they think I'll do a good job. Did that ever occur to you?"

"Of course you'd do a good job. You'd be great at it. But Pat, think about it. When has actual competence ever mattered to these people?"

"I have to go. I'm going to be late to class." Pat stood and left.

"I didn't mean to insult him," I said to Emma.

"And yet, you managed to."

"Emma, I think someone in the administration doesn't want Pat looking into this murder."

"You think it's because of the murder?" She emptied her cup. "It's not all he was working on, you know. What about his column on how our Student Retention Office is spending its Foundation grant? Or the series about the chancellor's research trips to Cancun? Or that new campus network that redirects our private emails onto the scrolling LED display in the Compliance Office?"

"He wasn't able to verify the thing about the scrolling display. But you just confirmed my point. The administration has a *lot* of reasons to shut him down."

"I know you've seen all those emails from the chancellor," Emma said, "About how we need to attract and retain more students to keep those tuition dollars coming in. Maybe the administration thinks this social media thing will help. And they know Pat will do a good job."

"Of course he will. You're right. Maybe I'm being too suspicious. It's just sometimes I get the feeling that the administration is watching our every—"

My office phone rang.

"What is it?" Emma asked when I'd hung up.

"That was Marshall Dixon's secretary. Vice President Marshall Dixon wants us to report to her office."

"When?"

"Now."

CHAPTER TWENTY-ONE

Vice President Marshall Dixon was located in the new Student Retention Office Complex, a gleaming edifice of glass and steel, as out of place on our shabby little campus as a spaceship. Emma and I made our way through the vast, chilly lobby, our footsteps ringing on the hard floor, to where the receptionist sat hunched against the cold.

She stood and pulled her puffy white sweater tight around her as we approached, and rubbed her arms for warmth.

"Right through here, Professors." Her voice echoed off the glass walls and metal girders. She led us down a series of hallways to Marshall Dixon's office, quickly announced us, and scurried away.

Vice President Marshall Dixon presided over a sleek, clutter-free koa desk. A separate conversation area featured a couch and two upholstered chairs arranged around a low coffee table. The decor was like Marshall Dixon's outfits—expensive, beige, and understated to the point of being utterly forgettable. Coco Chanel would approve.

Already seated in one of the chairs was a compact, wiry man, whom I recognized as Victor Santiago, the new marketing director. (His actual title was something else, much longer than "marketing director" and impossible for me to remember.).

Emma and I hovered uncertainly in front of the couch until Marshall nodded an invitation to seat ourselves. We sat down right next to each other, like two naughty little girls who were about to get a scolding.

"First of all, congratulations again to both of you on bringing in that grant," Marshall said. "With our reduced appropriations from the legislature, returned overhead is crucial to our operations."

Emma and I mumbled thanks. I was certain Marshall didn't call an urgent meeting just to say nice things about our grant. There was a "but" on the way.

"But a sensitive issue has come up," she continued. "Do you know Victor Santiago, our new Associate Vice President in Charge of Student Outreach and Community Relations?"

Santiago's red aloha shirt with yellow hibiscus shapes looked similar to one Donnie had. It must have been from the same local designer. If the vivid pattern was intended to make the glowering Victor look any less menacing, it failed. The too-cheery colors made his island version of business casual look like an unconvincing disguise.

Emma and I exchanged handshakes and murmured nice-to-meet-yous with the Associate Vice President in Charge of Student Outreach and Community Relations. Victor Santiago's stiff attempt at a smile only made him look more villainous.

"Are you the one who did the cash register ad?" Emma asked.

"Oh, I've seen that one," I added. It was the nicest thing I could think of to say and still be truthful.

I had been watching the evening news with Donnie when the ad came on. MAHINA STATE: A GREAT VALUE. A crudely drawn cash register wearing a mortarboard cap danced on a white background as dollar signs popped out in sync with tacky music. A local radio announcer provided a voiceover trumpeting our bargain-basement tuition rates and Mahina's low cost of living.

Donnie had thought the cheesy commercial was funny. I was mortified.

"We've discontinued the campaign." Victor said it with such finality it sounded like the person responsible for it had been "discontinued" as well.

"Our research shows our target customer sees college as a luxury good. Like a designer handbag. Anyway, Marshall, should I go ahead with..?"

She nodded.

"So, as Marshall said, we appreciate you professors who bring in outside funding. We are very aware of the role your research plays in raising the profile of the university. Unfortunately, high visibility is a two-edged sword. The incident at Art Lam's farm has become a concern."

Emma winced at the phrase "two-edged sword." I didn't think it was the best choice of words either, under the circumstances.

"The victim was a student here," Marshall said. "Harold Nordmann."

"Harold?" Emma said.

"He sometimes went by Primo," Marshall added.

"I thought they hadn't released the name of the victim," I said.

"Not publicly," Victor said. "Molly, Harold Nordmann was enrolled in your business planning class. In the seventh week of the semester he filed, and later withdrew, a harassment complaint against you. Now you happen to be first on the scene when his body is discovered."

"That wasn't public knowledge either," I protested.

"No one is accusing you of anything," Marshall interjected. "But we do need to know any relevant information so we're not blindsided. What can you tell us about the cheese incident?"

I stared at my folded hands. I hadn't done anything wrong. Marshall Dixon and Victor Santiago were making me feel like a criminal.

"I'd missed lunch that day." I heard a scratching sound and looked up to see Victor taking notes on a yellow pad. "It wasn't even during my posted office hours. I usually leave my office door propped open for airflow, because the air conditioning doesn't work well. So, Primo saw my open door, came in, saw me eating a piece of string cheese, and—"

"Freaked out," Emma interrupted.

"He took it personally," I interrupted back. "As if I were eating my cheese *at* him, when really I was just hungry."

"How did you get him to withdraw the complaint?" Victor asked.

"I think someone in administration told him it wouldn't go anywhere. It was when the owner of Malama Dairy was on our board of trustees."

"He remained enrolled in your class," Victor said. "And you gave him a passing grade in the end."

"He *earned* a passing grade."

"Did you have any other contact with him?" Victor asked.

"After he left Mahina State, I didn't see him for a long time until I happened to run into him at the yoga studio in town."

"Did he remember you?" Victor asked.

"Yes. And he was perfectly friendly. No hard feelings, apparently."

"He was *very* friendly," Emma said. "You should ask Molly's husband about it."

I glared at Emma, but fortunately, Marshall was already moving on.

"There's another issue here," Marshall said. "Harold, or Primo if you prefer, had become very active in the anti-biotech movement."

"And you have a biotech grant," Victor added.

"It's a grant to investigate *attitudes* toward biotech," Emma said. "We're not taking a position on it."

"But you understand this creates a perception issue," Marshall said. "Especially with Mr. Nordmann's high profile."

"High profile?" I said.

"His blog," Victor said.

"Now, no one is trying to tell either of you how to do your research," Marshall said. "At Mahina State, academic freedom is sacrosanct."

I nodded, thinking how much "academic freedom is sacrosanct" sounded like "people are our most important asset," "we respect your privacy," and similar corporate eyewash.

"However," she continued, "what's at stake is not just the reputation of the university. Your personal safety and the security of our physical plant are our immediate concerns."

"Our *personal* safety?" I said.

"You think someone's gonna try bomb my lab or what?" Emma said.

"We can't rule it out," Victor said. "There have been incidents at other institutions."

Emma and I looked at each other.

"What should we do?" I asked.

"You don't want us to give the grant back, do you?" Emma said.

Giving the money back didn't seem like such a bad idea now. Not after all this talk of physical safety and lab bombings.

"Returning the grant won't be necessary," Marshall Dixon said.

"But we think both of you should keep a low profile for the time being," Victor said. "With your permission, we're going to announce you've suspended work on the grant for the time being out of respect for the deceased. Hopefully it'll make you less of a target. We've just hired a new social media director, so he'll start spreading the word right away."

"I believe you know him," Marshall said. "Patrick Flanagan. We're excited about what he can bring to the table."

"Now, in the meantime," Victor said, "we don't want you to go into hiding."

"I don't mind hiding," I said.

"Our development office will be having a dinner for a few of our most important prospects," Marshall said. "Some of them are very interested in getting to know our faculty. When we were working on our seating plans, both of your names came up. We trust you'll make time in your busy schedules for this important event."

"You are both assets to Mahina State at this point in time," Victor said. "The fact that your research program has been halted by tragedy makes you both seem very relatable and sympathetic."

"*Seem?*" Emma said.

"We'll be there. At the donor dinner. No problem. Right Emma?"

As we left Marshall's office, I caught a glimpse of

Victor leaning over to Marshall and whispering into her ear. Emma saw it too. We waited until we were outside, in the hazy afternoon sunshine, before we dared to speak.

"Isn't she married?" Emma asked. "Marshall Dixon?"

"I know she was married," I said. "But I heard she's divorced now. I think."

"*In*teresting."

CHAPTER TWENTY-TWO

My sunglasses fogged up the minute we stepped outside, so great was the difference between the refrigerated air of the Student Retention Office and the humid outdoors. I removed my temporarily opaque eyewear and shielded my eyes with my hand.

"So Marshall Dixon works for the Student Retention Office now?" Emma squinted at me. "I thought she was higher ranking."

"It's an administrative thing," I said. "They keep moving positions into the SRO, so the SRO's grant can cover the salaries. That's one of the reasons they keep growing."

"Have you ever noticed how the Student Retention Office Complex is *mauka* of the campus, above everyone else?" Emma said.

I turned and squinted back at the soaring glass and metal edifice looming over the squat, tin-roofed buildings below it.

"The symbolism is purely accidental, I'm sure."

"They think they run the place," Emma said.

"They *do* run the place. They decided the psych department's required stats sequence was 'discouraging' students. Next thing you know, statistics is optional. Students complain history is boring. Boom. History's no longer a graduation requirement. Oh, and remember what happened to our computer engineering major?"

"I keep forgetting we used to have a computer engineering major," Emma said. "Hey, you have to be anywhere right now? I wanna go back to your office and check out Primo Nordmann's blog."

"I thought they didn't want us doing any more research for the grant right now."

"Nah, nah. They don't want us doing it *publicly*, that's all. We can go online an' look stuff up. Who's gonna know?"

We were coming up on the double glass doors of the library.

"Okay. But let's do it here. Not in my office."

"The library?" Emma asked.

"The library computers are open to everyone, so they can't trace who's using them. The computers in the library lab don't require a login. Not to sound paranoid or anything, but they told us to back off, and I'm pretty sure they can see what we do on our office computers."

"You mean you don't wanna end up broken on the rack, which is probably what happened to that poor *schlemiel* who did that cash register commercial."

"Exactly."

The library's glass door wheezed open to admit Emma and me to an architectural time capsule. The terrazzo floor, teak shelves, and avocado vinyl chairs with the chrome legs had been installed somewhere around the middle of the last century. The original plans had been drawn up before such a thing as a student computer lab existed, so the lab was an add-on afterthought, tucked behind the government documents collection. The lab looked sparsely populated, but it wasn't for lack of student demand. It was because most of the available monitors were connected to nothing. Most of the computers had died and never been replaced.

Once Emma and I finally claimed a functioning computer, a quick search turned up Primo Nordmann online.

"Bananawrangler-dot-com," Emma exclaimed. "His website is called *Banana Wrangler?*"

Emma's voice echoed in the suddenly quiet computer lab. Two girls at the next station turned from their spreadsheet to stare at us.

"I think it's supposed to be a reference to his diet," I whispered. "Look. Tantric Zenmaster. Fruititarian Warrior."

"Are you sure?" Emma said. "Cause he likes to eat fruit? Cause to me, banana wrangler sounds like a double entenuendo."

"Emma, there's no such word as—"

"Oh, this guy. I remember him. He was the older

student who would come by your office all the time, right? And give you those flyers about how to take care of your colon and stuff?"

"That's Primo," I agreed.

"I loved how you'd always get rid of him by saying you had to go to a meeting right then, like, 'Oh, I'm late to my two-seventeen meeting,' like anyone would schedule a meeting at two-seventeen."

Bananawrangler-dot-com wasn't a great example of state-of-the-art website design. It had five columns of small print in various typefaces interspersed with pictures of Primo. The photos showed him variously chinning up on a tree branch, stuffing jaboticaba berries into his mouth, and performing a one-armed balancing plank on the low rock wall fronting Mahina Harbor.

"How come he has his shirt off in all his pictures?" Emma asked.

"I guess he's proud of his physique."

"He looks like a scarecrow. Let's see what else there is." She moved the mouse and clicked, and we waited for the superannuated graphics processor to refresh the screen. "Well this is interesting."

Primo's last blog entry featured a photograph of Randy Randolph, Community Liaison for Seed Solutions. The picture looked like it might have been lifted from the company website. Randy Randolph wore a suit and tie, and looked at least ten years younger than he had last night.

The post was titled *Five Things You Need to Know about Seed Solutions.*

"Number one," I read. "Randy Randolph is a gigantic—oh dear. Primo really went for the ad hominem here."

"Whoa, three drunk driving arrests. And a link to Randolph's divorce papers. Hey, you think Randy Randolph is the one who hacked Primo into stew meat?"

The spreadsheet girls glared at us.

"Let me print this to an image file and mail it to myself," I said.

"Just send yourself the link," Emma said.

"What if the page gets taken down?"

"Everything gets cached," Emma said.

"I'm not going to count on it. Oh wait, if I mail this to my address that then there'll be a record of it. I'll just send it to Detective Medeiros. No wait, I don't think Mahina PD has email."

"Send it to me then," Emma said. "I wanna show Yoshi."

"Is your husband involved in this biotech thing?"

"Nah. Just, he was feeling kind of down the other day about how everyone else from his MBA class was *Somebody* now, and he was just a freelance artist. He was even saying he shoulda had that Seed Solutions job instead of Randy Randolph. He'll feel better when he finds out what a schmuck Randolph is."

"Okay, sending it now. Happy to help spread a little sunshine. Ready to go?"

As Emma and I reached the turnstile to exit the library, Emma said, "Hey, isn't that Donnie? What's he doing here?"

CHAPTER TWENTY-THREE

"That *is* my husband. What the heck? Why isn't he at work?"

Donnie was seated at one of the reference workstations, the ones hooked right into our special subscription-only databases. He was facing away from the front entrance, his back to Emma and me, so he wasn't aware of us until we were practically on top of him.

"Eh, Donnie."

At the sound of Emma's voice, Donnie leaped to his feet and logged out in a single, fluid motion.

"Donnie, what a nice surprise to see you. What are you doing in the library?"

"I was on my lunch break and I thought I'd come over and look some things up."

"Kinda late for lunch," Emma pointed out.

"I take my lunch after the lunch rush at the restaurant."

"Lucky they let you use this terminal, brah. It's supposed to be just for faculty and students. One time, ah? Yoshi tried to use my login to look up places where he could sell his artwork, and the reference librarian wen' kick 'em out."

Donnie turned to look at the terminal he'd just logged out of as if he had just been made aware of its presence ("What? A computer terminal? What's that doing back there?")

"Did you find everything you needed?" I asked. "You didn't have to stop what you were doing."

"No, I'm done. I should get back to the Drive-Inn."

"Anything I can help with?" I asked. "I know my way around the databases pretty well."

"No. See you at home."

Donnie bent down to give me a quick kiss on the forehead and left. Emma and I exchanged a look, then watched him push through the turnstile and exit through the glass doors.

As soon as he was out of sight, I plunked down in the still-warm chair.

"What are you doing?" Emma asked.

"Browser history."

She dragged another chair over from the adjacent workstation.

"Can you see anything?" she asked.

"No. He logged out. Darn."

"He's probably just looking up some population data or something," Emma said. "Maybe he's thinking about building another Donnie's Drive-Inn location."

"If he was looking for a new location, why wouldn't he tell me? I mean, I teach a *class* in business planning."

"Maybe it's cause he thinks that those who can't do, teach," Emma said.

"Maybe he's communicating with someone, and he doesn't want me to know. He doesn't want an incriminating electron trail. So he's emailing whoever-she-is from an anonymous computer."

"This is the reference workstation, Molly. Does it even have internet access?"

"It does. See, here's the browser. With no history, of course, because he logged out, which wiped everything. What if it's Jennifer Yamazaki?"

"Who's Jennifer Yamazaki?"

"Sole proprietor of Yamazaki Sports Massage. She's in Business Boosters. She's an entrepreneur, like Donnie. And she's young, skinny, and *cute*."

"Oh, stop it, Molly. Donnie doesn't want someone young, skinny, and cute. He wants *you*."

"Thanks for the reassurance. Okay, I have to get to class." I got up and for the second time, headed for the library exit.

Emma followed me. "Hey, are you going to yoga tonight?"

"I don't know. I'm going to be knackered after teaching for three hours straight."

Emma pushed in front of me and went through the turnstile. I followed her, lifting my hands out of the way, and turning to move the metal bar with my hip. I could only imagine how many hundreds of germy hands had been on the thing just today, and I doubted anyone disinfected it at night.

"I'll come with you," Emma said. "To yoga."

"You're going to do yoga?"

"I wanna find out more about Primo. Our murder victim. Maybe we can figure out what happened to him."

"Emma, I don't mind doing some research online, but I don't think we should go around interrogating people. We don't know who did it. If we go poking around asking questions, who knows what the murderer might do?"

"I can keep it low key."

"You? Stop right there. Emma. Just leave it alone."

"Molly, don't you see? We're stuck. We can't really get our research going again, and we sure can't *publish* anything from this until this murder is solved. The sooner the murderer's caught, the sooner we're back in business."

The student worker behind the checkout counter, a boy with a spiky black anime hairdo and smudgy black eyeliner, wasn't even trying to pretend he wasn't staring at us. I hustled Emma outside.

"Solving murders was not in the RFP, Emma. We can work on the literature review for now, maybe do some online research from home. But we shouldn't go around like, 'Excuse me sir, did you happen to murder Primo Nordmann?'"

"Maybe I just want to do some yoga. You're not

gonna try stop me from taking one little yoga lesson, are you?"

I sighed.

"Fine. I'll swing by your house and pick you up on the way over."

CHAPTER TWENTY-FOUR

Sharon, the skinny sister, was leading the yoga class. Attendance was sparse. Perhaps the rain, heavy even by Mahina standards, encouraged people to stay home. Maybe Sharon's paint-peeling Boston accent didn't engender feelings of serenity. Or possibly word of Primo Nordmann's demise was getting around, and people didn't want to catch his bad karma.

I wondered how Emma was going to manage to strike up a conversation with Sharon when we were through, but it turned out not to be a problem. As soon as the class was over, Sharon zoomed right over to Emma, asked if she was new, and complimented her upper body development.

"Are you a canoe paddler?" Sharon asked. "I'm thinking about joining one of the clubs."

And they were off. Emma's crew was perpetually one or two women short, so as the rest of the students packed up and left the room, Emma laid on a sales pitch about the many benefits of canoe paddling. When we were the only three people remaining in the room, Emma wrapped it up by inviting Sharon to come out and paddle with her crew.

Rapport thus established, Emma abruptly stopped talking and looked at me expectantly. This was where we were supposed to circle around to the real reason we had come tonight.

"I was so sorry to hear about Primo," I said.

"Did they make it public already? The police came in and grilled us about it, but they told us not to say anything."

"Do you think he had bad karma?" Emma asked. "I heard a rumor about it, that's why. Cause he must've done something bad to someone."

"No," Sharon protested. "Primo? Ridiculous. He was a little lamb. I don't know anyone who would wanna hurt him."

"Then why would someone say he had bad karma?" I asked.

"Aw, that's not hard to figure out." Sharla, Sharon's sister, entered the studio, carrying a broom and dustpan. "You all finished in here, Shar? It's okay. You guys don't have to leave."

Sharla started sweeping the edges where the wooden floors met the molding.

"People can't get their heads around the fact that some maniac can come along outta nowhere and chop you into little pieces. Sorry, I know people don't like hearing it, but sometimes, bad stuff just happens for no reason. And you couldn't have done anything to prevent it. Nothing to do with karma, or the balance of the universe, or anything like that."

"Primo was so dedicated." Sharon slid her rolled-up yoga mat into a hemp shopping bag and slung it over her shoulder. "He'd go to yoga conferences with us, pay his own way. He'd attend the other instructors' classes, just to learn from them."

"And steal their poses, supposedly." Sharla continued to sweep. "I can't believe some of the dumb stuff people can bicker about."

"Did Primo steal anyone's poses?" Emma asked.

"No," Sharla said, looking directly at Sharon. "Because there's *no such thing in yoga*. It's about *sharing*. And supporting one another. Right, *Sharon?*"

"Oh, whatever. I gotta go get cleaned up."

Sharon turned and pushed through the clacking beaded curtain. Her sister seemed to have managed to push her buttons in the special way only family members can. I grew up without siblings, but I do have two parents, so I have some idea what it's like.

"I did the same thing when I first came to Mahina State," I said, to keep the conversation going with Sharla. "Visited the classes of the other professors in the management department."

"It helps, right?" Sharla said.

"It might've," Emma said, "if her department wasn't such a freak show. Hey, you ever see Primo Nordmann's website?"

"Oh, the banana wrangler?" Sharla laughed. "We

gave him a lotta grief about the name."

"Do you think he had a stalker or something?" Emma asked.

"The police asked us the exact same question. But as far as any of us could remember, nah, he never said anything about a stalker. It didn't seem like there was anyone he was scared of. I mean, people were always arguing with each other in the comments. And Primo loved to take potshots at the big companies, like Monsanto and Seed Solutions. But those big guys aren't gonna go after some little guy like Primo. Listen, girls, don't wanna run you off, but I'm gonna have to sweep that side now."

Emma and I made sure to talk about nothing important as we left, just in case we were overheard.

"That was a great workout." I announced a little too loudly.

"I will definitely come to Laughing Lotus yoga studio again," Emma agreed.

Only when we were safely inside my car did we feel comfortable speaking normally.

"You're a terrible actor," Emma said.

"I don't think either of us should quit our day jobs."

"Monsanto's not even doing anything on this island." Emma buckled in. "How come everyone keeps bringing them up? Hey, you finally got new seatbelts."

"The ones I had were rotting. I had to mail order these. Finally got them in. The shipping and installation cost even more than the actual seatbelts."

"How come you didn't just go down to Lanakila Auto Parts? They got seatbelts. And they'd probably put 'em in for cheap. What's so special about these?"

"They're perfect reproductions of the originals."

The seatbelts in question were simple turquoise webbing with a rounded buckle.

"Oh, and that's so important 'cause why? 'Cause the Ghost of 1959 is gonna come audit you or something?"

"So did we find out anything useful about Primo? Other than the fact that he was really into yoga?"

"Nah. Waste of time."

I backed out of the parking spot with great care, glancing from my side mirror to my rear view mirror and back. The parking lot was dark. The closest light was burned out, and the moonlight was obscured by clouds.

"What about the papayas?" I suggested. "Do you think Primo meant to kill the papaya trees? Or steal the papayas? Or both?"

"Kill, maybe. Steal, no. Those genetically modified papayas were 'contaminated' as far as he was concerned. He wouldn't want to 'poison' himself by eating them."

"It seems like Primo was pretty well-liked at the yoga studio. No stalkers from his website as far as we can tell. Who would want to do him in?"

"Randy Randolph from Seed Solutions, of course," Emma said. "Primo *humiliated* him, posting his arrest records and divorce papers and everything."

"Maybe. I'd *like* the murderer to be Randolph, because he's such a jerk."

"Hey, I never knew about you going into the other professors' classes. For real, did it help?"

"Dan Watanabe's class was good." I stopped at the spot where the parking lot opened onto the dark road, looking both ways several times just to make sure I'd be safe pulling out into traffic. Mahina did have streetlights, but they were the dimmest possible kind, designed so light pollution wouldn't interfere with the telescopes on the mountain.

"Dan has this nice way of explaining to the students why things in his class are set up the way they are," I continued. "He tells them about how all this research on attention and learning goes into how he designs his assignments. I think the students appreciated it, knowing they weren't being asked to do things for no reason."

"Dan seems like he would be a good teacher," Emma said.

"The other classroom visits weren't quite as helpful. Hanson Harrison just walked in and started pontificating about something he'd heard on NPR that morning. His students were all texting each other or dozing off. Hanson either didn't notice, or didn't care."

"He's like that in meetings, too," Emma agreed. "He just goes on and on, and doesn't realize half the table's falling asleep."

"And Larry Schneider—he talks fast. You know he has a New York accent, and when the class started to fall behind, he'd say something like, 'My next comment is addressed to the two individuals in this classroom who actually *belong* in college.' It seemed a little harsh to me."

"Is that your phone?" Emma asked.

"In my purse. Can you get it?"

"It's Pat. I guess he's decided he's speaking to you again."

"Put it on speaker."

"Molly." Pat sounded excited, which was unusual for him. "I got your box back from Jeffrey, the antique dealer. Do you have some time tomorrow?"

CHAPTER TWENTY-FIVE

Friday was a big news day in Mahina. A front-page, below-the-fold item in the *County Courier* carried the official announcement that the remains on Art Lam's farm were those of local anti-biotech gadfly Primo Nordmann. The article also mentioned that two "university employees" made the discovery, but fortunately for Emma and me, it didn't get more specific.

Al Konishi of Konishi Construction called with glorious news. The work on my house was completed, the damage done by the falling tree was fixed, and I could move back in any time I wanted.

Most thrilling of all, Pat's antique-dealer friend, Jeffrey, had unpacked the contents of the box discovered during my house repair, and I was about to find out more about my buried treasure.

Emma, Pat, and I met for lunch at the Pair-O-Dice Bar and Grill, just a few doors down from the offices of Konishi Construction. Even at noon, the Pair-O-Dice was nearly empty. A lone fan wobbled bravely against the humid air. One couple (an office romance, maybe?) huddled in the farthest, darkest corner, sharing a pitcher of beer and a basket of fries.

"So where's my box?" I asked Pat, as we got seated. We chose a table for four, close to the window, behind the distinctive neon sign.

"I wanted to make sure we had a place to sit first," Pat said.

Emma and I watched through the not-so-clean glass storefront as Pat went to his car (he was still driving that cooking-oil-burning Mercedes) and retrieved a cardboard box from the trunk. He came back inside and placed it on the table.

"Where's my wooden soap box?" I asked. "The Twelve Trees, whatever it was?"

"I have it. It's in my trunk. Jeffrey cleaned off the dust. He also rewrapped the silver items in this special tissue paper he has, and preserved the original newspapers the items were wrapped in."

"How much did it cost?" I realized how ungrateful I sounded, so I added, "Thank you, Pat."

"Here's your bill, and an estimate of the values." Pat handed me a printout.

"Seems like a lot just to unpack a box."

"It's a lot of work."

Emma snatched the invoice from me.

"Is this how much Molly's silver is worth? It seems like it should be more."

"It's free money out of nowhere," Pat said. "I wouldn't complain. The pieces are silver-plate, not solid, but they're in good condition. Jeffrey says you should keep the collection together if you want to sell any of it. It's worth more that way. And you don't have to count on the Mahina market. He'll auction them online and get you a better price. Or you can try to sell them yourself."

I held out my hand, and Emma returned the paper to me. I scanned down the valuation list and made a quick mental calculation. Jeffrey had thoughtfully taken a photograph of each piece, and placed a thumbnail image next to each line item. I saw a coffee pot, a teapot, an ice bucket, a creamer and sugar bowl, several teaspoons, a small cup, and a tray. The silver was so tarnished the pieces were nearly black.

"Well, this isn't bad. If I manage to sell this, I'll get something like a third of what Earl Miyashiro wants me to pay him to fix my front end."

"Pat's right," Emma said. "It is money you didn't think you had. So you shouldn't look so disappointed."

"I know. It's kind of a letdown. Here was this mysterious long-hidden box, unearthed through a quirk of fate and bad weather."

"So what did you want, a genie to pop out?" Emma asked.

I pulled the box toward me and lifted out one of the wrapped pieces. It was about the size of a baseball, probably a sugar bowl or creamer.

"Those'll look nice once you polish them," Pat said.

"Yeah. That'll be a fun project for a rainy day. Maybe I will keep them. I don't have any nice dishes or glassware or anything like that."

"There's something else. Jeffrey said he doesn't want to carry this in his shop, or sell it online under his store name. But he says *someone* out there might be willing to pay a lot for it."

Pat produced a large manila envelope and pulled out a plastic bag containing a folded piece of newspaper. Jeffrey Voorhees had painstakingly unfolded, smoothed, preserved, refolded, and sealed it.

"Here." Pat placed it in front of me. Even after the treatment, the paper inside the plastic was as brittle as piecrust. I picked up the bag by the edges and tipped my head until I could read it without interference from the reflected light from the window. It was an editorial cartoon.

"Ugh." Emma reached out to grab it. "Burn it."

"Wait." I pulled the cartoon out of her reach.

It was ugly, no question: a caricature of Queen Liliuokalani, the last queen of Hawaii, dressed in a getup that looked like a showgirl costume for an African-themed Vegas show. The half-naked queen was offering the "crown" of Hawaii to a fish-lipped, hook-nosed pawnbroker.

"When was the overthrow of Liliuokalani?" I asked Emma.

"The coup was January 17, 1893." Emma

reluctantly withdrew her hand.

"The date on the newspaper is February 3," Pat said.

"That's why the pawnbroker in the cartoon tells her the crown isn't worth a wisp of hay," I said.

"The kingdom was lost by then." Emma frowned.

"These caricatures are horrible." I set down the bag. "Did anyone think they were clever?"

Pat nodded. "What, no drunken Irishman? I'm feeling kind of left out here."

"So this is actually worth something?" I asked. "Who would want to pay for this thing?"

"It's rare. Jeffrey told me there are no microfilms of this paper before 1901. There was a big fire. The building burned down, and the newspaper's archives were destroyed."

"So this might be the only copy of the cartoon?" Emma stared at it again.

"That's right. Molly, you were lucky it was stored in your house, away from sunlight. Because of the post and pier construction, you had circulation under the house, so it must not have been too damp."

"Please don't tell anyone about this cartoon," I said. "Either of you. I mean, it has historic value, so I don't want to throw it away, but I really don't want to be associated with it, either."

"I don't blame you," Pat said. "Jeffrey felt exactly the same way. Oh, one more thing. The signature's visible, and the artist might be someone of interest to collectors, so he offered to do some research on it if you want."

"How much would he charge? Never mind, I'm sure it's reasonable. Sure. Why not?"

"How much would he charge? Never mind, I'm sure it's reasonable. Sure. Why not?"

CHAPTER TWENTY-SIX

"It seems like we just had one of these university things last week." I was trying on various outfits in Donnie's big master bedroom in front of the mirrored closets.

"We did," Donnie said. "The Halloween party."

"Was it just last week? I guess I repressed the memory. Well, I'm not going to wear a cockroach costume this time. My fashion philosophy for tonight will be: try not to frighten small children or big donors."

Donnie sat on the edge of the bed and watched me twist my hair into different configurations. His eyes met mine in the mirror, and he sucked in his breath as if preparing to say something.

"What?"

"I'm really sorry, Molly. I can't go with you tonight."

"The donor dinner? You told me you were

coming. What do you mean you can't go?"

"I have a deadline coming up. I need to work on it tonight."

"I have to go by myself? Donnie, I RSVP'd for both of us. You said you'd be able to go. Victor Santiago's going to have me in thumbscrews when he sees an empty chair at the donor dinner."

"Already taken care of. Davison's going with you. No, it's okay. He *wants* to go. I'm not forcing him."

"Davison? Seriously? Donnie, this is the *donor dinner*. The whole point is to make a favorable impr—look. These things aren't fun. You have to be on your best behavior the whole time. *You* know how to handle yourself, but are you sure Davison wants to be under this kind of pressure? I mean, he came back home to relax, not to *work*, right?"

"Molly, he'll be fine, and it's good practice for him. He needs to learn how to network. You have to admit, he's been well behaved this trip. Hasn't he?"

"Depends what you mean by *well behaved*. Ever since he stepped off the plane with his buckle hat and his blunderbuss, he's been lobbying to have me burned at the stake."

"What are you talking about?"

"He's all Mister Scoldy-Preachy now. He keeps telling me I need to cut down on my drinking."

"It's because he cares about you. He wants you to be healthy. At least he didn't warn you about getting middle-aged dad gut."

"And he's acting all judgmental about me living in my own house. Did you tell him I was going back up there tonight? Because he just brought it up. *Again*."

"Well, he wants his family to be together. I don't like it that we're living apart. Do you?"

"Of *course* I'd prefer it if you and I lived together, Donnie. We just need to work out the details."

I loved my husband, but I also loved having my own place. Sure, Donnie's house was gorgeous with its gleaming wood floors and its perfectly placed quarter-sawn oak side tables and its professional kitchen. And its museum-quality pieces like that celadon vase I'd been afraid to go near ever since I found out it was worth more than a year's worth of student loan payments. But I liked coming home to someplace of my own, even if the decor was nothing more than chili-pepper Christmas lights and a Felix the Cat wall clock and an affordable living room set from Balusteros World of Furniture, and where my little electric oven had no higher purpose other than storing my extra shoes.

"Seriously, Donnie, you're not coming with me? Is there any way I can change your mind?"

"I thought I'd be able to get everything done in time, but I miscalculated. I'm sorry. I'll make it up to you."

I tried on the fanciest thing I had handy at Donnie's, a pair of loose-fitting silver silk trousers I hadn't worn for a year. At least I remembered them as loose fitting. To my dismay, I could barely get them up over my hips.

"Something wrong?" Donnie asked.

"I think the dry cleaner did something to these

pants."

I had imagined somehow when I got married, I'd shed the last ten or fifteen pounds. My new husband was a gourmet chef, and I loved to eat, so I'm not sure where that idea came from. Wishful thinking, probably. I found a flowing ivory silk top to pair nicely with the pants. With my hair twisted up into a sort of victory roll, and a bold pair of earrings, I decided I was presentable.

I was never going to look like Donnie's ex-wife Sherry, who, as far as I could tell, maintained her spare figure with a diet of 7-and-7s and Virginia Slims. Donnie came up behind me and ran his hands over my hips, their embarrassing heft highlighted by the shimmering grey silk of my too-tight trousers.

"Come back and stay with me tonight," he murmured into my ear.

"Sounds tempting, except we won't have any privacy." Unlike the other night, Davison was going to be a few feet down the hallway. "Anyway, it's time to get going. You're sure you can't come?"

"I'll drive you both up to campus. I can get my work done at the university library."

Davison was waiting for us in the living room. He wore a decent looking aloha shirt, a print of *laule'a* leaves in pale blue on a black background. He stood up wordlessly and followed us out to the garage.

Donnie opened the passenger door for me, but I urged Davison to sit shotgun. I opened the back door and slid all the way in until I was sitting behind Donnie.

"It's fine. You two hang out. I'll be happy back here." My mother, who started her medical career in the emergency department, refers to the passenger seat as the "death seat." The phrase has always stuck with me.

Our drive to campus was uneventful until we were almost at the parking lot. A tree-trimming rig had blocked the right lane, abruptly narrowing the two-lane road to one. A dark blue BMW jumped in front of us from the blocked-off lane, forcing Donnie to slam on the brakes. Donnie simply shook his head.

Davison, on the other hand, couldn't let it go. He reached over between Donnie's arms and leaned hard on the horn.

The BMW slammed on its brakes, and the driver stuck his arm out and made an obscene gesture.

Davison muttered something. I only caught the last word: *haole*.

"Davison." Donnie briefly took his eyes of the road to glare at his son.

"Oh. Forgot. Sorry, Molly."

"Well," I said from the back seat. "I sure hope that wasn't one of our big donors. Oh look, he's making a left into the university parking lot."

"Is there another way in? I don't want a confrontation right before your event." Donnie spoke these words emphatically in Davison's direction.

"Needs to learn some respect," Davison grumbled.

"Take it easy, Davison," Donnie warned.

"Keep going straight, and then make a left at the next intersection. We'll park up near the Student Retention Office and walk down. That way, we won't have to meet this guy in the parking lot."

I watched the blue BMW pull in and park across two spots. Donnie was focused on driving, but I saw Davison staring at the parking lot, too. Randy Randolph from Seed Solutions climbed out of the car.

"Eh, I know that guy," Davison said.

"Who is that?" Donnie asked. "I can't look. I'm driving."

"It's Randy Randolph," I said. "He was one of the speakers at the community forum."

"The Seed Solutions community liaison?"

"The very same. Every bit as charming as I remember him."

Donnie pulled into one of the visitor spaces at the Student Retention Office, right next to Vice President Marshall Dixon's platinum Lexus.

"Where will we meet?" I asked.

"You two come get me in the library when you're done. Your dinner's not going past ten, I assume."

Donnie departed for the library, and Davison and I headed down to the Campus Dining Center. During the day, it was our main cafeteria. But for special events, it was dressed up with white tablecloths and real metal utensils instead of the flimsy low-bidder sporks we got at lunchtime. Inside, Serena Castro, the dean's secretary, manned the reception table.

"Eh, Serena." Davison brightened when he recognized her. "Howzit? Long time, ah?"

Serena stood and clasped him in a hug.

"Aw, all grown up, you. I heard you're at West Point now."

"Nah. Not West Point." Davison seemed pleased Serena might think so. "Military academy, but."

"You miss Mahina." This sounded more like a statement than a question.

"Feels good to be home. East Coast school. I'm the only one in my class from Hawaii. Even when I was in Cali, was plenty Hawaii kids."

Serena examined the guest list. "So, where's your father?" Then to me: "Donnie couldn't make it tonight?"

"He's at the library. He said he had some things to take care of for work."

"Here, Davison, I print you one name tag." She typed something into her laptop, and a few seconds later, pulled a printed paper name tag from the miniature printer next to it.

"Nice setup," I said.

"Yeah, there's always some unexpected changes to the guest list, or someone's name spelled wrong. And these high maka maka kine, you don't wanna hand 'em a Sharpie and tell 'em do 'em yourself. Well, lucky Davison could fill in tonight."

"Yes. I feel very fortunate. Serena, are you going to get a chance to eat?"

"I'll make a plate after. You two are sitting at the

table over there. You're with Victor Santiago and Randy Randolph."

"Randy Randolph?" I repeated, helplessly.

I heard Davison suck his breath in, as if he were puffing himself up for a fight. Great.

"We want to make sure Mister Randolph has a nice time tonight," Serena said. "He's from Seed Solutions, that big agricultural company. I hear they're considering making a major donation to our university."

"Serena, we don't have to take the *best* seats. I'm sure there are plenty of people who are *dying* to sit with someone as important as Randy Randolph. You can put us somewhere else. We won't mind."

I was already dreading an evening of socializing with strangers. Now I had to keep my hotheaded stepson from getting into a brawl with a major donor.

"No, they were very particular about the seating chart. And you have a good table, not too far from the podium. Go. Have a good time."

Of the six seats at the table, only one was occupied. Victor Santiago had taken the least desirable place, the one facing directly away from the podium. He was examining a printout. Probably the results of his office's latest marketing survey, or a list of tonight's guests and their net worth. When we approached, Victor stood up to greet us and shook Davison's hand cordially. He probably would have preferred to have had Donnie there, but fortunately, he didn't seem upset at the bait-and-switch.

"Donnie's Drive-Inn has been a great friend and supporter of our university." Victor gave Davison a pointy-bearded grin, which showed lots of lower teeth. We got seated, and I noticed to my immense relief that two of the places were reserved for Pat Flanagan and Emma Nakamura.

Pat walked up, carrying a tiny ceramic coffee cup and wearing his usual getup: Gleaming shaved head, beat-up plaid shirt with a white Danzig t-shirt underneath, ratty jeans, and big black boots. Victor glanced up and greeted him, then handed him a page from his stack of reports. I was amazed Victor made no attempt to whisk Pat out of sight before his appearance offended some donor. Maybe the marketing office really was serious about wanting to project an "edgy" image.

"Eh, Mister Flanagan." Davison offered Pat a fist-bump.

It didn't seem fair. To Davison, Pat and Emma were still Mister Flanagan and Professor Nakamura, while I had been demoted to "Molly." On the other hand, it would be weird to have Davison calling his stepmother "Professor."

"So are you officially the social media person now?" I asked.

"That's me." Pat placed his coffee cup next to his name card and then seated himself. "I'm in charge of curating Mahina State University's brand on those newfangled social media platforms the kids like these days."

"That doesn't even make sense. What do you

mean, you're curating our brand? You're just sticking random trendy buzzwords together."

Victor Santiago looked to be on high alert. He was scanning the room, probably checking to make sure the donors seemed happy and the tables were filling as planned.

"Aw, Mister Flanagan," Davison said. "You get a new job, that's how come no more *Island Confidential?*"

"Davison, you read *Island Confidential?*" I asked.

"Nah. But Crystal does. She says it's the only place to get real news. Cause the *County Courier* is just paid advertising for big companies or something."

Emma joined us next, bringing our table's count to five: Me, Pat, Emma, Victor Santiago, and Davison. The charmless Randy Randolph of Seed Solutions had parked himself at the open bar.

Victor quietly cleared his throat.

"Molly, Emma, uh Davidson, Seed Solutions is shaping up to be a very important partner for the university. We're looking at significant development potential."

"We have to be extra nice to Randy Randolph, is what you're saying?" Emma asked.

"Yes."

Vice President Marshall Dixon strode to the podium, causing the conversation in the room to quiet. She made some welcoming remarks, namechecked the big shots in the room, and then introduced our chancellor.

"Is *that* our chancellor?" Emma whispered.

"I don't know," I whispered back. "I guess that guy sort of looks like the picture on our website."

Emma leaned over and whispered something to Pat. He looked up at the podium and whispered something back to Emma. She socked him in the shoulder, so I inferred whatever information he'd given her wasn't very helpful.

Randy Randolph remained at the bar until the chancellor's comments were finished, then staggered over and plopped into the remaining vacant seat, which was right next to me.

"Hey, it's Professor Mindy," Randy slurred, blasting me with alcohol breath. He leaned close and squinted at my paper nametag.

"What's an ass professor?"

"That's *Assistant* Professor," I corrected him.

"Randy," Victor jumped in. "Let me introduce you."

Victor did a good job of acting like we were all his close friends. He'd never even met Davison before this evening, although you wouldn't know it from his easy introduction. The only problem was Victor kept pronouncing it Davidson, with an extra "d." Pat, Emma, and I did nice-to-see-you-agains. Davison gave Randy a clenched-jaw nod paired with a white-knuckle handshake that made Randy's hand bones crack.

Even in his impaired state, Randy recognized the challenge.

"Hey there, Chief." He pulled his hand back to safety. "You like older women, huh?"

Emma's eyes widened. Pat stared down at the white tablecloth. Davison glowered so fiercely he was practically incandescent.

"Davison is my *stepson*," I said. "I think you've met my husband. Donnie Gonsalves. Donnie's Drive-Inn."

"Oh yeah?" Randy's gaze remained locked on Davison. "I wouldn't let *my* wife step out with some young *buck*." The last word was drawn out with a long belch.

"Randy," Victor interrupted. "I think all of us would like to hear about Seed Solutions' plans for an exciting new scholarship program."

"Sure. Seed Solutions knows students are our future. Hey." He addressed Davison again. "*You* ever think about college, sport?"

"Davison is attending a private university back east," I said. "I'd love to hear more about your scholarship program. It sounds fascinating."

The arrival of our salads broke the tension. As white-jacketed culinary students set out our plates, Randy recited the particulars of Seed Solutions' proposal, which included paid summer internships at Seed Solutions, textbook subsidies, and a housing allowance. It sounded like a good deal for our students. Even Emma thought so.

The student servers brought us our main course (seared ahi heaped with shredded carrots and something purple—beets, maybe?) and kept our glasses full. Randy kept talking, moving from the topic of the scholarship program to farming and the debate over biotech and then his own career and the marriage that didn't survive his move to Mahina. The rest of us ate quietly as he rambled on. I tuned him out. Until he said,

"I've never been in a place with so little amount of white people. Look at this table, for example. Just you and me, Pat. And maybe you, Misty. What are you, Italian?"

"Albanian," I muttered, not wanting to be part of this conversation.

"Looks like us Caucasians are a rare and endangered species. You better hang on to this one, son," he belched in Davison's direction, grasping my upper arm. "Fast as *you* people are breeding, gal like *her's* gonna be a collector's item pretty soon."

Davison was fairly vibrating with rage. His black eyes beamed pure hate at Randy Randolph. I fully expected a brawl to erupt if someone didn't do something soon.

Pat went for the nuclear option.

"Randy. Did you see this morning's paper? About the murder at Art Lam's farm? The victim was Primo Nordmann. You must've known him."

A server came by to refill water glasses. The ice clanked loudly in the silence. Victor Santiago said nothing. His eyes darted from person to person. I held my breath.

Finally, Randy spoke.

"It's a darned shame, what happened." I wondered whether Randy had seen Primo's last blog post trumpeting Randy Randolph's DUI arrests, the details of his divorce, and other humiliating private information. Of course he had. As had Primo Nordmann's ten thousand followers.

"Very tragic." Victor assumed a mournful expression.

"Look," Randy sputtered. "Seed Solutions does not condone violence. We embrace and encourage civil discourse."

A student server quietly placed another tall glass of Kona Longboard in front of Randy. Victor used the interruption to jump in and change the subject to the culinary program, and to praise the food and the service. Davison glowered quietly for the rest of the dinner and left his dessert untouched. I hoped it was because of his weird diet, and not because he was too furious to eat.

When it was finally time to leave, Randy handed me his card, oblivious to the fact that he'd already given me one at the public forum two days earlier.

"I didn't forget about our interview, Masie. We need to talk some more, you and me."

"Oh, we've put our research on hold for now. Um, haven't we?" I looked to Victor for guidance.

"Officially, yes. The study is on hold for the moment." Victor nodded.

"Seems kinda unfair." Randy was slurring his words, and drenched with sweat. I hoped he wasn't planning to drive himself home. "We're always the bad guy. We never get to tell our side of the story. ThassallIwant, tell our side of the story."

"Well, I'm sure Emma and Molly are both willing

to dialogue with you," Victor said. "As are Pat and I. Mahina State's door is always open."

"Good man." Randy turned to Davison. "Hey buddy, you gotta good set a guns." He aimed a manly punch at Davison's upper arm, but missed and nearly toppled over. "You work out? I got a private gym. You gotta come up and check it out."

I thought I heard Randy telling Davison he could bench press four hundred pounds, but I must have misunderstood.

"Well, goodness," I exclaimed, "look at the time."

I had to get out of there before Randy and Davison started bashing antlers. I said hasty goodbyes to everyone at the table and exited the Campus Dining Center quickly, hoping Davison would follow. (He did, but grudgingly and at a distance, as if I were dragging him on a leash.)

I had hoped to catch Donnie in the act (of what, I wasn't sure), but he was waiting just outside the library's glass doors for us.

"How was dinner?" Donnie asked as the three of us started for the parking lot. "See anyone you know?"

"Emma was at our table. That was nice to have her there. And Serena, the dean's secretary? She was glad to see Davison. The food was all done by the culinary students, and I think they did a nice job."

I was lightly editing the evening's events for Donnie's benefit. Or *curating* them, as Pat might say. Not that I had anything to hide, but Donnie had never been crazy about Pat Flanagan.

Donnie's antipathy to Pat wasn't conventional jealousy. Even Donnie had to admit it was unlikely Pat would switch teams just for me. Pat was like a brother (or so I'd imagine, never having had actual siblings), but it meant I was close to Pat in a way I'd never be with Donnie. Donnie didn't like that.

"Pat Flanagan was at our table," Davison volunteered. "Molly, forgetful you, ah? Cannot even remember your best friend."

Tattletale.

"Yes. Thank you for reminding me, Davison."

"Maybe you drinking is why," Davison persisted. "Gonna rot your brain, you drink all that wine."

"And speaking of that, Randy Randolph was sitting with us too. Fortunately he didn't seem to recognize us from our little road rage incident."

Davison muttered something not worth repeating.

"I don't like him either, Davison. But unfortunately, we have to be nice to our donors."

"You don't *gotta* be nice to him," Davison snorted. "Everyone kissing up just 'cause he got money. Made me wanna puke."

"Language," Donnie warned.

"So you think you'll never to have to ingratiate yourself to anyone, Davison?"

"That's how come I'm getting my degree. Don't wanna end up like Curtis, all tied down, gotta clock in and li'dat."

"I have news for you. A degree's not some kind of magical armor. I have as much education as a person can possibly have. And did you not see me in there just now, forcing myself to be polite to that awful man? Unless and until you're independently wealthy, you have to kowtow to someone. That's just how the world works."

"Nah, Molly. I'm gonna work for myself. I'm gonna be a entrepreneur. Like my dad. I don't wanna answer to a boss."

"Being in business for yourself doesn't mean you don't have a boss," Donnie said. "It means you have a lot of bosses. The health department. The zoning commission. Every one of your customers. So did you two manage to make a good impression?"

"I think so." I hoped Randy wouldn't pursue his idea of my interviewing him. Maybe the notion would evaporate along with his booze buzz.

The ride back down to Donnie's house was quiet. I dozed in the back seat, Davison sulked in the front, and Donnie concentrated on the dark road. He stopped the car when we reached his driveway, and Davison jumped out to get the mail.

"Letter for you, Molly." Davison climbed back into the passenger seat and handed back a thin envelope. The printed return address was the Mahina State University administrative office.

"What's that?" Donnie asked.

"I don't know."

I stared at the envelope, afraid to open it. No news was good news. That's what everyone told me about the tenure application process. And this looked like news.

CHAPTER TWENTY-SEVEN

Donnie let us in to the house, and Davison lumbered off to his room. I sat down at the kitchen counter and tore open the envelope, not even bothering to find a pair of scissors to slit it neatly.

It was exactly what I was afraid it would be: notice of a not-completely-favorable vote from my departmental tenure committee. The vote had been three for and only one against, so it could have been worse, but my application was going forward without unanimous support from my own department.

Which one of my colleagues, the ones I saw every day, had voted against me? Dan Watanabe, the interim dean, who had always been a mentor? Rodge Cowper, who was pretty much phoning it in by this point, and scarcely seemed to care enough to hold a grudge against anyone? Who would have cast a no vote, knowing the tenure decision was up or out? If I didn't make it, my academic career was over.

I felt Donnie's arm around me. "Bad news?"

"Not great. Someone in my department voted against my tenure bid."

"You said it was risky being department chair without tenure."

"I didn't *ask* to be department chair. I was forced into it. This negative vote could kill my chances, Donnie. What am I going to do?"

Donnie pulled me close.

"You'll be fine. We're in good financial shape. You don't need to work. You can stay home."

"So I should just end my career? After making it through a top ten Ph.D. program, and switching fields, and publishing my brains out, and twisting myself into pretzel knots to provide the right level of 'customer service' so I can get decent student evals?"

"I didn't say you should end your career."

"No? How does that not end my career if I stop working and stay home? What kind of cold-blooded thing is that to suggest? How would *you* like it if you couldn't work? How would you feel if someone took away your livelihood? Your only outlet for achievement?"

"Molly, I was just—"

"Does it sound like fun to you to be under *house arrest* for the rest of your life? How would *you* like to have to beg for money for every little thing you wanted to buy, as if you were a *child?* Because that's how it would be, Donnie. 'Molly, don't you already have a dress just like it? Molly, are you sure you need another pair of shoes?' You *already* say stuff like that to me, and I'm buying those things with *my* money."

"I'm trying to be supportive. You're worried about what happens if you don't get tenure, and I'm just telling you we'll be okay no matter what happens. I'm on your side. What do you want me to say?"

"I know. You were trying to make me feel better. I'm just—this past few days, I've had to be so careful not to take up too much space or get in anyone's way. *Davison* has his own entire room in this house. *I* don't even rate a foot of closet space. I can't imagine how much more of a nightmare it would be if I were financially dependent on you."

Davison emerged from his room, avoiding eye contact with us. He beelined to the fridge and got himself a sports drink.

"I'm not here." He zoomed back to his room.

"I thought you didn't allow food or drink in the bedrooms," I said.

"You feel like being married to me is a *nightmare?*"

"It's not what I said, exactly. But it's interesting how you let *Davison* take his drink back to his room. Remember what happened the one time I took my coffee—"

"Is that what you want, your own room? I thought a married couple was supposed to share a bedroom."

"We're not *sharing* a bedroom, Donnie. *I'm* staying in *your* bedroom. Believe me, I can tell the difference."

"I know I need to clear out the closet to make room for your things. But there's no point in getting all ready for you to move in if you have no intention of doing it."

"Chicken and egg, Donnie. I'm not going to move in when in your entire huge house, there's somehow no room for me."

"Molly, this whole house is yours, too. I'll give you as much closet space as you want. Just say the word. Oh, that reminds me. That cockroach costume was taking up too much room in the closet. I moved it."

"Of course you did. Where'd you put it?"

"Davison's closet."

"Listen, I think I'm going to drive back home tonight."

"Really? I was looking forward to you staying here with me." He moved closer, and buried his face in my hair.

"I should spend the night in town. I need to be close to campus."

"Tomorrow's Saturday. Why do you need to be close to campus?"

"Fine. You caught me. I just want to spend the night at home. It's been a few days, and I want to make sure everything's okay there. And thank you for calling Konishi Construction to come fix it. It was very thoughtful of you. We're still on for tomorrow night though, right?"

"As long as you're not mad at me. Molly, please remember, *I'm* not the one who voted against you. I want you to get tenure. I really do."

"Really?"

"Really. Because imagine how cranky you'd be—hey, whoa, I'm *kidding*."

I went out to where my car was parked, half on the narrow road and half on Donnie's lawn. I buckled in, started the engine, pulled out my cell phone and called Pat, hoping he hadn't gone back up the hill yet.

"Pat. I'm glad I got hold of you. You and Emma want to come over? To my house?"

"Aren't you spending the night with your husband?"

"No. We both agreed it would be a good idea for me to spend the night in town, make sure everything's okay there."

"I figured you would've had enough of your happy little family by now."

"Are you coming over or not?"

"Want to go over to Molly's?" Pat asked.

"Sure," I heard Emma reply.

Pat and Emma were sitting on the couch in my living room when I got home. I smelled coffee.

"You guys are drinking coffee now? Isn't it kind of late? And did Konishi leave my door unlocked?"

Pat and Emma exchanged a look.

"You need to replace the box of cabernet," Emma said. "I drank the last of it. So what's going on?"

"I didn't get a chance to tell you guys what happened when we were driving to the donor dinner." I related the story of Randy Randolph's cutting us off and his subsequent bad behavior on the road.

"Yeah, Randolph's a schmuck," Emma said. "No news there."

"But think about it. Don't you think he could've been the one who killed Primo Nordmann?"

"I don't know." Pat looked thoughtful. "Whoever committed the murder was somewhat competent. Randy Randolph is a drunken buffoon."

"Maybe it's a cover," Emma suggested.

"He obviously has a temper," I said. "And you both saw at dinner how he is. He's clearly a narcissist and a sociopath. And totally lacking in empathy. Did you see how he was winding Davison up?"

"You think just 'cause someone likes to quote Ayn Rand, they're automatically a narcissist and a sociopath?" Pat said. "Oh wait. *I'm* the one who thinks that."

"I thought Davison was gonna snap his neck." Emma sounded disappointed that he hadn't "I wouldn't blame him, either. So what then? What should we do?"

"Let's tell Detective Medeiros." I poured myself a cup of coffee and joined them on the couch.

"We can do better than that," Emma socked my shoulder. "Randy Randolph gave you his card. He's willing to talk to you."

"It was actually the second time he gave me his card."

"He gave you his card twice?" Pat smirked. "Randolph is clearly willing to do *something* with you. Not sure it has much to do with talking."

"Molly, you should call him and set up another interview. Pat, you—"

"Not me." Pat held up a hand. "I have a good-paying gig now. I'm not gonna go around spying on our donors."

"Fine, Captain Sellout. We don't need you. Molly and I will do it."

"What? No way, Emma. I don't want to be alone with him. I think we should tell Detective Medeiros."

Emma looked like she was going to object.

"I'm going to call Medeiros first thing tomorrow morning," I said.

"Tomorrow's Saturday."

"If he's not in, I'll leave a message."

"Good luck with that, ladies." Pat set his cup on the coffee table. "I hope you nail him. Now, since we're all here, let's talk about something more important. I want your opinion on a new campaign I'm planning."

CHAPTER TWENTY-EIGHT

It was glorious to greet the morning in my own bedroom. I woke up rested, having slept like a rock. I pulled open my light-blocking curtains, setting my bedroom ablaze with sunshine. My backyard still looked a little ragged. My Albizia trees hadn't been the only casualties of the storm. The birds of paradise drooped, muddy puddles dotted the lawn, and one banana tree lay where it had toppled.

Waking in Donnie's bed the past few days had been a treat, and I did miss it. But there was no grumpy stepson right down the hallway, and no off-limits, too-nice-to-use silverware in the kitchen. For the first time in over a week, I was finally home. And I had some things to cross off my to-do list.

Donnie wouldn't approve of my calling Detective Ka`imi Medeiros, but he wasn't there to stop me, and what business was it of his, anyway? I placed the call to the Mahina Police Department. Detective

Medeiros wasn't there. I debated leaving a message, and finally decided in the affirmative. If someone had an insight that would help me do my job better, I'd want them to share it with me. It was only fair to extend that courtesy to Detective Medeiros.

"This is about the incident at Art Lam's farm," I told the receptionist. "October twenty-eighth."

"Oh, the papaya grove murder. Terrible, that thing."

"Please tell Detective Medeiros to look at the blog of Bananawrangler-dot-com."

"Banana what?"

"How about this. Just tell him to look into Randy Randolph of Seed Solutions. Randy Randolph."

"Randy Randolph," she repeated. "This is for who now?"

"Detective Medeiros."

"Which one?"

"Ka`imi Medeiros. There's more than one Detective Medeiros?"

"Ka`imi. Anything else?"

"That's it. Thank you for your help."

Better to keep it simple. Too bad Detective Medeiros didn't have an email address.

"No worries, professor. You have a good day, ah?"

Professor? Had I told her who I was?

An enthusiastic hammering on my door signaled Emma's arrival. I let her in and told her what I'd just done.

"You think the police haven't already thought of

Randolph as a suspect? They're not stupid, Molly. Eh, you got some coffee?"

"I was so excited about calling Detective Medeiros that I forgot to make any. No wonder I'm getting a headache"

I heard muffled music playing in my laptop bag as I brought out our cups.

"What's the scary song?" Emma stared at my bag. "It sounds like a haunted house."

"It's Khachaturian's 'Masquerade Waltz.' It's not scary. It's dramatic."

"Oh, right." Emma nodded. "Your *revenge* song."

The caller was patient enough to stay on the line until I dug my phone out. The caller ID was blocked.

"Maybe it's Detective Medeiros calling back." I set Emma's coffee down in front of her and switched on the speakerphone. "He realizes I might have something to contribute to this case."

"Good morning, *professor.*" Randy Randolph's voice squawked on the speaker. "Guess who?"

"Oh, gosh, I couldn't possibly—"

"This is Randy Randolph. Aw, don't tell me you forgot about me already. We had such a good time last night."

"Mister Randolph. What a delightful surprise."

"Call me Randy. So like I was saying, I think your research sounds really interesting. I'd like to get a chance to sit down and talk story. Hopefully without your *bodyguard* there."

"Did he say talk *story*?" Emma said.

"Shh."

"Who was that?" Randy asked.

"That's Dr. Nakamura. She was at our table last night. She's a biologist, and has done some research on transgenic organisms—"

"Ah, the little Hawaiian girl with the big—eyes?"

Emma vigorously pantomimed sticking her finger down her throat.

"Mister Randolph, were you thinking the three of us could chat sometime, over coffee?"

"I'm off island for the weekend," he said.

"Probably on some quickie third world sex tour," Emma muttered.

"What was that?" Randy asked.

"Static."

"How about Monday?"

"*This* Monday? Day after tomorrow?"

"Come by my apartment around nine. I'll be done with my workout by then."

Emma wrinkled her nose.

"His *apartment?*" she whispered.

"It'll be easier for you girls. I'm right in town. The Seed Solutions office is all the way out in Pohaku."

"Sounds fine." I ignored Emma, who was pantomiming retching on the floor. "We'll see you then. What's the address?"

"Why did you agree to that?" Emma asked when I had gotten the address and hung up.

"Because we've been ordered to be nice to our donors. What do you think would happen if I told Randolph to get stuffed, and then he went and complained to Marshall and Victor?"

"Wow, you're a jumpy little rabbit this morning."

"Emma, I got a negative vote from my department. I just got the registered letter last night. I didn't want to bring it up in front of Pat, because I'm not sure where his loyalties lie now."

"They all voted against you?"

"No, there was just one no-vote. But it wasn't a unanimous yes."

"I see. You have to stay on the administration's good side now. Fine. But if Randolph answers the door in a velvet bathrobe, I'm outta there. Hey, I'm ready for a second cup."

Emma drained her mug and handed it to me. I stood up to get refills.

"I'm calling Detective Medeiros again. I'm just going to let him know about our appointment with Randolph on Monday. I think it's better if we keep him informed."

"Good idea, Molly. You don't want him to think you're a loose cannon or anything."

CHAPTER TWENTY-NINE

One benefit of living apart from my husband was that date nights felt special. Tonight, Donnie was planning to cook a gourmet Italian meal for the two of us, and I was looking forward to it.

I wore a retro-styled red dress with three-quarter sleeves, a deep V-neck, and a flattering A-line skirt cut to guide the eye past my burgeoning hips. While the silhouette was mid-twentieth century, the dress was made of a decidedly twenty-first century stretch fabric, which was the reason I could still squeeze myself into it. On the way out of my house, I caught a glimpse of myself in the mirror and sighed. The dress was so tight I was ready to pop out of it, and it was too late to go back and change. I *really* had to lose some weight. Maybe Donnie would be so busy cooking that he wouldn't notice my dress was two sizes too small.

Unfortunately, he did notice. When I walked into

the kitchen, he looked up from the stove and stared. His eyes traveled slowly down to my fishnet-stocking-clad feet and back up again. Only a sudden, frantic sizzling drew his attention back to the pan he was holding.

"You look *great*." He focused on pouring liquid into the pan and unsticking something from the bottom. "Sorry, I'm kind of chained to the stove right now."

"Well, thanks for the compliment. Can I help?"

"No, no. Sit. Keep me company. I just opened a bottle."

I sat at the kitchen counter, where I could watch Donnie's deltoids and latissimus dorsi working through his silk shirt as he cooked. He'd set a wine glass out for me on the counter, next to the uncorked bottle. I poured a glass.

"So where's Davison tonight?"

"He went out earlier with that girl, Crystal. Seems like they're really getting along."

"That's great."

"Yeah, I hope it doesn't cause a problem when he has to go back to school."

I took a sip of wine, and sighed with contentment. Funny what a treat it was being down here at Donnie's house, as long as I could think of myself as a visitor and not a permanent resident. *Nice place to visit, but I wouldn't want to live here.* What was wrong with me, that I felt this way about spending time with my own husband? I adored Donnie, so what was my problem? My mother often accused me of having commitment issues. Well, maybe I did, but come on, no one *chooses* to have commitment issues, so really, whose fault was it, *Mom*? She also liked to say I blamed everyone but myself for my problems.

"So, you and Davison have a nice time at dinner last night? I never got to hear what happened."

Donnie was doing his best to ignore the previous night's unpleasantness between us. Maybe that wasn't such a bad idea.

"Donnie, I'm sorry I was so cranky. Dinner was stressful. We all had to be polite to that awful Randy Randolph, all because there's a chance he might cough up some Seed Solutions money for the university. And then getting that letter about the negative vote on my tenure application was the last straw. And you know what? I think Randy Randolph killed Primo Nordmann."

"You think so?" Donnie spoke over his shoulder in a sort of sideways direction. It was hard to hear him over the sizzling sounds, which filled the kitchen, along with heavenly aromas of tomato, garlic, wine, and mushrooms.

"I don't know about means and opportunity, but he sure had motive," I continued. "You didn't see the last post Primo put up on his website, documenting all of Randolph's shortcomings and failures."

"I know Randolph didn't make a very good impression on Davison. I heard him complaining to his girlfriend on the phone. The guy really got under his skin. Funny, both of you had a negative reaction to him. I never saw it. He's always seemed fine to me. Until that incident when he cut in front of us yesterday."

"He knows exactly what he can get away with." I took another sip.

"Well, the donor dinner's over now. Neither of you needs to spend any more time with him."

Now probably wouldn't be the best time to tell Donnie that I was planning to visit Randy Randolph's apartment on Monday.

"I think the guy's a sociopath," I said.

"I guess I should be glad you and Davison agree on something."

"When does Davison go back? Doesn't his school term start Monday?"

"It does. But he couldn't get a flight. He's on a waiting list for something later next week. He might even be able to stay here for his birthday. He says he's worked it all out with his professors."

"A couple of years ago, I remember you talking about Vegas for Davison's twenty-first birthday. Have your plans changed?"

"He's not interested in Vegas anymore." Donnie splashed some liquid into the pan so it sizzled and spattered. "Good thing, too. You ask me, gambling's a waste of money."

I started to feel warm and relaxed from the wine. And brave.

"Donnie, why did you really have to go to the library last night?"

"I told you. I had to look up some information."

He turned off the stove, arranged the pasta on two oversized white plates, and carried them out to the dining room table.

I got up and picked up my glass and the bottle of Sangiovese.

"You went to the library to look up some information is like saying you went shopping to procure some merchandise."

Donnie laughed, and deftly changed the subject. "Normally, I wouldn't use shiitake mushrooms in an Italian dish. I thought I'd take a chance and try it. Tell me what you think."

CHAPTER THIRTY

It took me a while to get oriented when I woke up at Donnie's the next morning. The duvet lay in a heap on the floor. I leaned over and pulled it aside. Underneath, I found my dress, knotted up like a big red piece of chewed gum.

I looked through Donnie's closet for something church-appropriate and found a modest navy blue suit I had brought at some point and forgotten. I dressed quietly and made myself a cup of coffee, which I enjoyed in pleasant solitude at the kitchen table. Donnie had already left for the Drive-Inn, and Davison was probably still asleep in his room, assuming he had come home at all. I left (red dress stuffed in my purse) for the early service at St. Damien's. After church, I went back to my house to change into Sunday loafing clothes, and occupied myself with chores until it was time to meet Pat and Emma for brunch at the Pair-O-Dice Bar and Grill.

Pat and Emma were the only people inside when I arrived. Pat was enjoying a cup of the Pair-O-Dice's bar coffee, which no matter when you ordered it, always seemed to have spent hours sitting in its glass carafe on the hot plate. Emma was already drinking beer, even though it was still well before noon. I went to the bar and ordered a bourbon straight up from the (apparently) teenaged bartender, then went to sit with Emma and Pat.

"So, you two have a date with Randy Randolph tomorrow morning," Pat said.

"Ucch." Emma gagged.

"I'll be glad to get it over with," I agreed.

"I told Pat about your letter," Emma said.

"It's not the end of the world, Molly. Marshall Dixon has a lot of power. If she likes you, she can make tenure happen. Just make sure you stay on her good side."

"The thing is, these are my colleagues. The guys in my own department. Which one of them would vote against my getting tenure? Which means, voting for the end of my career."

"Chill, Molly, it's just one vote. It's not gonna spike your tenure—oh, hey, Davison."

There was my stepson, making his way toward our table.

"Davison," I exclaimed. "No New Beginnings Chapel this morning?"

"I already went."

"Well, what a surprise. I certainly didn't expect to see you here."

"Crystal had to go to work. She's over at Natural High, so I walked up. Thought I'd probably find you at the Pair-O-Dice."

"You already eat?" Emma said. "Come sit."

Emma's invitation was superfluous since Davison had already pulled up a chair.

"How did you know we'd be here?" I asked.

"Dad said you guys like slumming here." Davison gave a side-eye to Emma's pre-noon beer.

"So what do you do at New Beginnings?" Pat asked. "Burn a witch, stone an adulteress, sing a few hymns?"

"Nah. What?" Davison looked confused. He'd wedged himself into the chair and somehow managed to take up way more room than anyone else at the table, even long-limbed Pat.

I scooted sideways to relieve the pressure of Davison's leg against mine.

"Did you see your friend from Konishi Construction?" I asked. (Scoot.) "The one who told us about the box?" (Scoot.)

"Nah. Seeing Curtis again was kinda, I dunno. Kinda depressing."

"Classmate?" Emma asked.

Davison nodded. "We used to be pretty close back in the day. But when Tessa came *hapai*, couldn't hang out, 'cause the baby. All the family responsibility and stuff. I dunno how he can deal with it."

"Yes, having a baby and all that responsibility must be very difficult for *him*," I said.

The bartender arrived with my bourbon.

"You want some coffee or something?" Emma asked.

"Yeah, get me a coffee." Davison addressed the young man.

"Thank you," I added, because no one else had said it. The bartender nodded in my direction and left to get Davison a cup of the Pair-O-Dice's stale, burned coffee.

"Not twenty-one yet?"

"I don't drink, Professor Nakamura. I'm keeping my metabolism well-tuned and my body fat down. You know, your digestive system treats ethanol like a—"

"Eh, Davison." Emma peered under the table. "There's no room for the rest of us under there. You really gotta sit with your knees in two different time zones?"

"What? Oh. Sorry." He moved his chair back and rearranged his legs.

I said nothing. With Davison there, I didn't feel comfortable discussing either my own tenure woes or Primo Nordmann's murder. And I certainly wasn't going to bring up the topic of Randy Randolph.

"Hey Molly," Emma said, "you going to yoga today?"

"No. I think I'm going to rest—"

"Good," she interrupted. "You can come with me to the gym today, get your exercise there."

"Too crowded and noisy." I shook my head.

"We can make sure to get in before one," Emma insisted.

"Not today. Thanks, anyway."

"You need to work on your upper arms, Molly. You gotta do something." She reached over and jiggled my upper arm. I smacked her hand away.

"Mahina State gym's pretty good," Davison said. "We useta laugh about it. How the library's old and it's closed half the time, and the gym's all new and full of the latest and greatest stuffs, and open twenty-four seven."

"Priorities," Pat agreed.

"Hey, you can come work out with us," Emma offered.

"I'm *sure* Davison has better things to do on his break, Emma."

"Cannot. Not a Mahina State student anymore. Anyway, I been going to Strongman. Couple of my classmates work there now. Nothing fancy, but they get the basics. Barbells, dumbbells, li'dat. Crystal comes with me to Strongman an' helps spot." He grinned. "Makes the workout go faster."

"I remember she mentioned she worked as a personal trainer. At least that's what she claimed when she offered her services to your father."

"Hey," Emma said, "so what's our plan for Randy Randolph tomorrow?"

I felt Davison stiffen next to me at the mention of Randolph's name. I tried a subtle head shake to warn Emma off, but she plowed ahead.

"Make sure you shine up that wedding ring nice

and bright before we go, Molly. I think we'll have to keep reminding him you're married."

"Whatever you do," Pat said, "make sure he ends up feeling warm and fuzzy about Mahina State. It's all my management cares about."

"Remember when he was going on and on about Molly's 'exotic' looks, and her 'kinky' hair?" Emma laughed.

"I shoulda punched that faka's face in." Davison stalked out without paying for his coffee.

"Emma, Donnie's not supposed to know about our meeting with Randy Randolph."

"Whoops," Emma said.

CHAPTER THIRTY-ONE

Pat watched the front door of the Pair-O-Dice close behind Davison, the sliver of outdoor light slowly narrowing to nothing.

"This job is killing me," Pat said.

"What do you mean?" I asked.

"You just started," Emma added.

"I had my first meeting with the athletics boosters this morning."

"They make you work on Sunday?" I asked.

"We have *boosters*?" Emma echoed.

"Yup. I had to attend their monthly breakfast meeting to assure them that our athletic program is our number one priority. And then on Friday, I'm going to go stand in front of the faculty senate and tell them *academics* is our number one priority. Our chancellor refuses to say no to anyone, and it's my job to somehow keep everyone happy."

"Well, that's why you're getting the big bucks," I

said.

"Tough gig," Emma sympathized. "Chancellor makes all these promises, then goes and hides till Pat and Victor can figure out how to make it all work."

"That's pretty much it," Pat sighed. "And something else I didn't expect about this job. Suddenly I'm privy to all this sensitive internal information. In a way, it's the worst part."

"That sounds like the *best* part," Emma said.

"Seriously," I agreed. "So what's the dish?"

Pat shook his head despairingly. "Sometimes ignorance really is bliss. Molly, I already knew about your tenure vote. In fact, I know exactly what happened."

"You do? Those committees are supposed to be confidential."

"Nothing's confidential. Seriously. Nothing. Not what goes on in closed meetings, not what you buy from your office computer, nothing that goes over the campus network, even if it's from your private email account. Victor and I see *everything*. I'm gonna get more coffee." Pat stood up and went up to the bar.

Emma and I looked at each other. Emma's eyes were wide.

"They see everything we do on our computers?"

"That's what he just said."

"You think Pat and Victor know about that back massager I ordered?"

"I wouldn't worry, Emma. They're both guys. They probably think it's actually for back pain."

Pat returned, his Styrofoam cup brimming with watery tan brew.

"So what happened with Molly's tenure vote?" Emma demanded.

"It was Hanson Harrison." Pat set the cup down and took his seat. "He said he found your methodology 'reductive,' whatever that's supposed to mean."

"Yeah, well it was good enough to get a federal grant," Emma snorted.

"Harrison?" I exclaimed. "I knew we had our differences, but he actually tried to destroy my career?"

"That's the kicker. He didn't realize this was your up-or-out tenure vote. He doesn't read his email. Everyone else voted in your favor. And Larry Schneider went out of his way to stick up for you."

"That's just because Larry Schneider and Hanson Harrison hate each other."

"So Pat," Emma said, "why don't you just walk away from this job, if it's so bad?"

"I'll tell you why. Because with my big fat salary, I now qualify for a home loan."

"Wonderful," I said. "Congratulations."

"Yeah, I've just put in a backup offer for my cabin, in case Randy Randolph's deal falls out of escrow."

"Do you have any reason to think he'll fall out of escrow?"

"No." Pat sighed. "Not unless someone drops an anvil on his head, or something."

"Well, we can dream," Emma said.

"Emma, you know what? I do feel like working out now."

"Really?" Emma said.

"Yes. All of a sudden, I feel like hitting something. Pat, do you want to go with us?"

"Me, work out?" Pat said. "Have we met? Anyway, I'm supposed to finish the position paper on our Golf Course Management major."

"What *is* our position on the Golf Course Management major?" I asked.

"Our position is, yes, Mister Yamada, your wonderful idea for a Golf Course Management major is going through, and before you know it, we'll be putting out graduates who are ready and willing to work at your resort. And also, no, Senator Kamoku, of *course* we're not considering offering a major in golf as a taxpayer-subsidized sop to our most powerful trustee. The very *idea*."

"That'll take some wordsmithing," I said.

"You girls have fun at the gym." Pat stood up. "Oh, and Emma, be careful lifting those weights. Back pain is no laughing matter."

Unlike the Mahina State library, the Mahina State student gym was open on Sunday. Also unlike our library, it was packed with students.

"I'm losing my motivation now, Emma. I don't want to wait in line for some sweaty machine. Maybe I can go home and punch a pillow or something."

"They have classes in the back." Emma led me through the clanging and grunting of the cavernous main workout space. "Let's go see what's there."

Room "A" had a crowded high-impact dance class. Neither of us felt coordinated enough to jump in to what looked like a complicated routine. Room "B" had a spin class. All the stationary bikes were occupied. Room "C" had a Tai Chi class with only a few students. It was a maybe. Room "D" had a Katana class starting at half past the hour.

"What's Katana?" I asked.

"I think it's sword fighting."

"That sounds kind of fun."

The door to the room was closed. We peeked through the narrow glass window. A lone man, dressed in wide-legged black trousers and a snug white t-shirt, expertly maneuvered a large sword. He whipped it around over his head, brought it around sideways, brandished and retracted it with such expertise it looked like a dance.

"No way could I do that. I'd walk out with an arm missing."

"Wanna go back to the Tai Chi class?" Emma asked.

"I think I'll just do the treadmill. Wait a minute. Is that…"

It was.

"Victor Santiago is the *katana* instructor?"

"Looks like it," Emma said.

"He sure can handle that sword."

"I *know*."

We looked at each other.

"You think?" Emma said. "*Victor*? What's he have

against Primo Nordmann?”

“Are you kidding? That’s the easy part. His whole reason for being is to keep our donors happy. Like our *favorite* biotech guy, Randy Randolph.”

“Nah. Seriously?” Emma stared at him.

Victor caught sight of us lurking at the window. He rested the sword, point down, on the mat and looked straight at us, as if daring us to come in. I waved idiotically and ducked out of sight.

“He saw us,” Emma gasped.

“It’s the campus gym. We have every right to be here.”

“So you want to go take his class?”

“What? *No.* I’m just going to go walk on the treadmill.”

Emma took one last peek through the window. “He’s kinda sexy and dangerous.”

“Stop it, Emma. You’re married. Remember?”

“Well, he sure knows how to move.” Emma pulled away reluctantly from the window. “They never did find the weapon, did they? I’ll come do the treadmill with you.”

“No. I don’t think they ever did find the weapon.”

CHAPTER THIRTY-TWO

On Monday morning, Emma picked me up at my house, and we drove the few short blocks to Randy Randolph's Bayfront apartment.

"He better not come to the door with a towel around his neck, slapping on aftershave," Emma said, as we approached the building.

"Maybe Randy isn't my prime suspect anymore," I said.

"I hear you. After seeing Victor Santiago's katana routine? *Man.*"

"And Victor's the one who engineered our suspending our work on this grant. It sure seems like he wants to keep *something* secret."

"So, what are we going to do about it?"

"As long as I still don't have tenure? Nothing. *That's* what we're going to do. We're going to keep our heads down, stick with the phony story about voluntarily suspending work on the grant, and then quietly interview Randy Randolph because he's a potential donor who wants to be interviewed, and our administration wants us to appease him."

Randolph's salmon-pink apartment complex stood out as one of the very few new structures in Mahina's dilapidated downtown. After one too many tsunamis had deluged the business district, the building codes had been revised to require expensive safety measures like concrete pilings and ground-floor parking. As a result, building owners had refused to remodel, preferring to wring as much rental income as possible out of the termite-infested structures before they collapsed completely.

As we approached Randolph's complex we saw an armada of emergency vehicles parked up and down the block, lights flashing. I recognized Detective Medeiros' police cruiser.

"Detective Medeiros must have gotten my message," I said. "I don't think they needed all these police cars, though. One would've been enough."

"Maybe this doesn't have anything to do with Randy Randolph. Maybe something's going on somewhere else in his building."

"Good point."

We finally found a legal parking spot two blocks up the hill from Randy Randolph's building. Emma and I walked back down. The front gate was propped open, so we didn't bother to ring. I double-checked the unit number and we mounted the steps to Randy's second floor apartment.

The door to Randy's unit was open. We

approached, looked in, and saw workers in dark blue (police) and white (medical) uniforms swarming inside.

"Make way," a male voice ordered.

We stepped aside to allow a large man in a white uniform to roll a gurney past us. Lying on it was a white plastic bag, which appeared to contain a human-shaped object. The zipper was completely closed.

Detective Medeiros stepped out behind the gurney.

"I'd like a word with you two." It sounded as if he was talking to me from very far away.

"Molly." Emma was in my face, shouting at me. "Get a grip. Come on. Don't get sick like you did last time."

"I did not get sick."

"Did. Soon as you saw the foot lying there, you turned green, and your legs went out from under you."

"The ground was uneven," I protested. "I tripped."

"Professor Barda," Detective Medeiros said (now speaking at a normal distance). "We received your message. Unfortunately, we arrived too late. Please. We need to talk."

Detective Medeiros led us downstairs to a picnic bench in the prettily planted courtyard. *I never have to deal with the odious Randy Randolph again*, I thought, with a shameful and short-lived sense of relief. Short-lived because I realized whoever did this to

Randolph was still out there. Randolph certainly wasn't the most charming fellow I'd ever met, but who hated him enough to go to his apartment and kill him? I couldn't imagine who would do something so—

Uh-oh. Yes I could.

We sat on the concrete lip of a planter, and Medeiros took out a small notebook.

"So what happened?" I asked.

"After we got your tip, we sent Officer Freitas over this morning to check it out. He went to the unit and knocked, but no answer. He looked in through the windows and saw the deceased in his workout room."

"How did he die?" Emma asked.

"His neck was crushed under the bar. We still have to wait for the pathology report, but that's how they found him. Still with the bar lying across his neck. What do you know about this?"

"Molly." Emma reached over and rubbed my back. "Put your head between your knees."

"I'm fine. And I don't know anything about this. I called you because I thought Randy Randolph had killed Primo Nordmann. Did you see his website?"

"It's called bananawrangler.com," Emma added.

"The post exposing details of Randolph's personal life? Yes, we're aware of it."

"Randolph could still be the murderer," Emma said. "Maybe this thing was an accident."

"Maybe." Medeiros nodded. "Maybe it's *pure coincidence* that you left an urgent message for me to check on Randy Randolph, and we show up at his apartment and find him dead."

When Medeiros put it that way, it did seem unlikely.

"Professor Barda, Professor Nakamura, if there's anything you know about this, please tell me now. You hold something back, all you're doing is helping someone get away with murder. Did the deceased have any kind of disagreement or fight with anyone recently?"

"Randy Randolph was at the donor dinner Friday night, on campus," I said. "Emma and I were at his table. He was drunk and obnoxious."

"Did he have a conflict with anyone in particular?"

"He was really provoking my stepson. Davison Gonsalves." *Sorry, Donnie, but I'm not going to lie to the police.*

"Provoking him how?"

"Male competition stuff," Emma said. "Like the kind of thing you'd see in a documentary about baboons."

"He invited Davison to come work out with him. Although it was more like a challenge, like *I* can bench press four hundred pounds, what can *you* do? Kind of like that."

"Did he say four hundred pounds?" Medeiros asked. "Were those his exact words?"

"I think so. I remember thinking, that's impossible. It seems like Olympic weightlifter level. I assumed Randolph was exaggerating for effect.

Why?"

"He had exactly four hundred pounds loaded on the bar," Medeiros said. "Two hundred each side."

Emma and I looked at each other.

"There were no signs of forced entry," Medeiros said. "Whoever it was, it appears Randolph let him in voluntarily. Anyone else have a grudge against Randolph?"

"He was going to buy Pat Flanagan's house," Emma said. "Don't give me that look, Molly. They would've found out about it anyway. Pat's saving money to buy the house he's living in now and renting, but Randolph was already in escrow and was trying to kick Pat out."

The apartment building had apparently been modeled on a sunny Southwestern template. The builders hadn't counted on Mahina's three hundred inches of annual rainfall. As the drizzle turned to a downpour, the three of us got up and moved under the overhang next to the laundry room. The clean starchy scent mingled with the smell of rain.

"So this is what's troubling me," Medeiros said. "You two go down to interview Art Lam on his farm. You happen to find Primo Nordmann's body. You're still our only eyewitnesses. You two haven't remembered anything else about that, have you?"

"No," Emma and I said in unison.

"Now you leave me a message about Randy Randolph," Medeiros continued. "We come to check it out and find Randolph dead. And here you two are, on the scene. Again, about to conduct an interview. Correct?"

"Sounds right," I said.

"So both times you've tried to interview someone, you show up, and there's a dead body."

"He has a point," Emma said.

"Professor Barda. I saw in the newspaper you and Professor Nakamura put your research on hold. Is that correct?"

"Yes. At the request of our administration, following the Primo Nordmann incident. They wanted us to keep a low profile. Stay out of harm's way."

"But this morning, you and Professor Nakamura came to Randy Randolph's apartment for the purpose of interviewing him."

"Our fundraising people were cultivating Randy Randolph as a donor. When he saw the announcement about our suspending work on the grant, I guess he wasn't happy about it. At the dinner, he was complaining, saying he wanted to tell his side of the story. So, our fundraising people made it very clear to Emma and me we should interview Randy Randolph if it was what he wanted. After the dinner, Randolph called me to set up the interview."

"It's true, Detective. *Randy* was the one who wanted to talk to *us*. Although I really think he just wanted to see Molly again."

"Do you agree with your administration's decision?" Medeiros asked. "You think you might be in danger?"

"No," Emma said.

"Yes," I said.

"Don't be paranoid, Molly. Why would anyone want to come after us?"

"Why would anyone want to come after Primo Nordmann?" Medeiros asked. "Or Randy Randolph?"

"Primo was anti-biotech," I said, "and Randy Randolph was the face of the biotech industry. They were on opposite sides. It doesn't seem like the same person would want to do away with both of them."

"You two need to be careful," Medeiros warned. "And let me know if you find out anything relevant. We want to catch this guy before anyone else gets hurt."

CHAPTER THIRTY-THREE

I had a quiet dinner with Donnie that night. We ate linguine *alle vongole* at the dining room table, with the correct silverware, the cloth napkins, and the proper wineglasses. Unlike at my house, where I don't even own real wineglasses and use repurposed *furikake* jars for my box wine.

"I can't believe it," Donnie said. "It must've been an accident. What else could it be?"

"Donnie, you need to talk to Davison. Maybe you can convince him to go in and see Medeiros voluntarily."

"You don't think Davison had anything to do with this, do you?"

"These forensics people, it's amazing what they can find. If Davison was in Randy Randolph's apartment, they'll know. Even if he was wearing gloves, people shed hair and skin cells."

"How would Davison have gotten into Randy

Randolph's apartment in the first place?"

"Oh, that's easy. At the dinner, Randolph invited Davison, challenged him actually, to work out with him. So, he could've gone over that morning, and Randolph would've let him in. Or even if he didn't go there by himself, his girlfriend, Crystal, said she was Randolph's personal trainer. Maybe Davison got in through her, got the access code from her or something."

Donnie put his fork down on his barely touched mound of linguine. Maybe he hadn't really wanted a detailed and plausible case for Davison's guilt.

"As a single father, you always feel guilty about something. If you're at work, you feel bad because you should be spending time with your kid. And when you're with your kid, you feel bad because you should be out working to bring in money."

"Donnie, I think you did a—you've done the best you could." I reached over and rested my hand on his. "I think you're amazing. Where is Davison, by the way? Is he out with Crystal again?"

"I think so."

Excellent. Donnie and I would have the evening to ourselves.

"It's hard for a boy to grow up without a mother." Donnie looked at his plate, but I didn't think he noticed the food. "Sherry is the closest he's had. And she didn't stick around very long. Well, he has you now."

Great. A romantic evening where I get to hear my husband reminisce about his ex-wife. Nothing personal against

Sherry, but I hated when Donnie brought her up. It was bad enough when people told me I looked so much like Sherry I must be her long lost twin. Her *fatter* long lost twin. What galled me was Donnie married Sherry first. Years after she ran off with someone else, he'd decided to throw his lot in with me. It made me feel like the consolation prize. Especially when he would slip and call me "Sherry."

"Is there anything you haven't told me?" Donnie looked up at me. "About what went on between Randolph and Davison?"

"I think you have the basics. Randolph was drinking. A lot. And he's an ugly drunk. *Was* an ugly drunk. I don't know how a guy like that ends up with a job as a community liaison."

"The Mahina assignment might not have been one of Seed Solutions' most desirable postings. *You* seem to like it here so far, but for a lot of people from the mainland, it's a backwater. It's why they usually end up leaving after a couple of years."

"It's no excuse for Randolph's behavior." I shook my head. "He was awful. If I had the upper body strength, I might've been tempted to drop a barbell onto his neck myself."

"Molly."

"Sorry."

I took a gulp of wine, an earthy Albanian merlot. It tasted like it had been fermented in a stable. I wasn't going to complain. Donnie had gone out of his way to special order it from Hagiwara's, thinking I'd appreciate the nod to my Balkan heritage.

I had assumed when Donnie, an inveterate Italophile, found out I wasn't really Italian, he'd lose interest. In fact, not only did he not break our engagement, he took the news quite well. He'd even tried cooking Albanian cuisine (which was as unfamiliar to me as it was to him). It was sweet of him. Donnie really was a catch. Too bad about the rotten stepson.

"We all had to sit around with pleasant smiles pasted on our faces while he was being as boorish as could be, just because Seed Solutions has money. The whole thing was revolting."

The front door burst open, and we heard two adult voices, giggling like children.

"Davison," Donnie called out. The voices shushed, and Davison peered around the corner to see Donnie and me at the dinner table.

"Oh, hey, Dad. Hey Molly. Crystal's here."

"Have you eaten?"

"Yeah. We're just gonna hang out."

"You take in the propane tanks like I asked you?"

"Aw, forgot. Too dark now. I get to it tomorrow."

"You get your closet sorted out?"

"Yeah, we go do that right now."

"We need to talk to you about something," Donnie called after Davison. "Later, when you don't have company. And remember to lock the front door."

CHAPTER THIRTY-FOUR

Donnie and I had a comfortable after-dinner routine. While Donnie looked over the Drive-Inn's daily sales reports, or perused *Pacific Business News* or *Hospitality Hawaii*, I settled on Donnie's genuine Sottsass sofa and graded papers or caught up on my journal reading. We had been engaged in this agreeable activity for about twenty minutes when a muffled giggle broke the quiet.

"Sounds like Crystal's still here." I stopped reading and looked at Donnie.

"As long as he keeps it in his room."

"Don't you have a 'not under my roof' rule for Davison?"

"He'll be fine."

"Let me ask you this, Donnie. What if we had a *daughter*? Would you let *her* have a *guest* in her room?"

"What? Of course I—I'm not answering that question. Anyway, Davison's a grown man. What am

I supposed to say to him?"

"Look, we both know the horse is out of the barn. Maybe I could've phrased that better. But I think we should at least officially disapprove of overnight guests, shouldn't we? I don't think it's good for parents to condone premarital sleepovers."

"It would be a little hypocritical, wouldn't it? What about the time you and I—"

"We don't need to discuss this anymore. Davison's *your* son, I'll defer to *your* judgment. I need to get my lecture ready for tomorrow. They came out with a new edition of the Intro textbook, *again*, and scrambled all of the chapters around, so I can't use last semester's notes."

"Intro's the one Davison took from you, right? He told me he liked your class."

"Marvelous." What my stepson undoubtedly *liked* about it was the fact I wasn't allowed to do anything about his flagrant cheating, thanks to my "student centered" former dean.

Intro to Business Management reminded me of one of those ten-cities-in-seven-days European bus tours, where you went careening from one business field to the next, covering everything in a single semester. The current topic was financial ratios, which for me—to stick with the European bus tour analogy—was the equivalent of visiting Oslo in February.

The giggling from Davison's room abruptly escalated to a shriek. A door slammed. Crystal burst out of the hallway, stormed through the living room, and pushed out the front door, letting it bang shut behind her.

"Aw, c'mon baby." Davison's voice followed her exit. "Don't be mad. It's funny."

Davison emerged into the living room wearing the cockroach costume. The glossy brown carapace covered only his torso, exposing his hairless, muscular limbs. He looked like some kind of arthropod superhero.

We heard a car start outside and screech away. Davison stood and stared at the front door, his antennae bobbing forlornly.

"Davison, why are you wearing my costume?"

"Was in my closet."

"You didn't hook the extra set of arms on." I set my notes aside and stood up to adjust the costume properly. "They're not just supposed to hang. There's a loop you attach to your wrists. Like this. See? Now when you move your own arms, the other two move with them."

"Aw, that's cool." Davison waived his arms.

"It seems like she didn't appreciate the costume."

"But it was funny, Dad. Cause look." He spread all four of his arms out and waggled them again, as if to say, see?

"What's funny to some people doesn't always work for other people." Donnie shrugged.

"Aw man. Now what? I gotta go kiss up, huh?"

"Davison, language." Donnie frowned.

"Sorry. I gotta go *suck* up, I mean." He sighed and adjusted his carapace. "Eh, Dad, you said you wanna talk to me? Guess I get some time now."

"It's about Randy Randolph," Donnie said. I watched Davison's face for any sign of guilt, but I saw only confusion.

"Did you hear anything about it?" Donnie asked.

"About what?"

Donnie looked at me. "Molly, do you want to tell him?"

I placed my pencil in the textbook to save my place, and briefly related the morning's events.

"Nah," Davison said, with as much delight as disbelief. "You saw 'em wheeling 'em out?"

"We saw a zipped-up body bag. According to Detective Medeiros, it was Randolph."

"Stupid to bench press without a spotter. Four hundred pounds?"

"Right. Two hundred pounds on each side. Remember, it was exactly the weight he told you he could press."

"I remember. Liar. No way he could press that much. Two hundred each side is more than four hundred pounds, too. 'Cause the bar by itself weighs forty-five pounds. Eh, I didn't have nothing to do with it."

"I'm glad to hear it." Donnie looked relieved.

"Between us, though? Baga had it coming."

"Go change into normal clothes," Donnie said. "There's still a lot of your organic pemmican left if you're hungry."

Davison turned and plodded away down the hall.

"That really is a good costume," I said to Donnie.

"Whoever constructed it actually went to the trouble of making a segmented abdomen. It's very realistic."

"You want it back now?"

I thought about it for a moment.

"And wipe down inside of that costume with rubbing alcohol before you put it away," I called out after Davison. "Other people have to wear it."

CHAPTER THIRTY-FIVE

It was the end of the workday, and I was relaxing in the back seat of Donnie's car while he braved the traffic. Davison and I had both caught a ride into town with Donnie that morning. I thought I'd give carpooling a try. Gas wasn't getting any cheaper and my Thunderbird got eleven miles to the gallon. Every trip between Mahina town and Donnie's house out in Kuewa cost me real money.

Davison had tagged along at the last minute, hoping to find Crystal at work and patch things up with her.

"It's nice to be a passenger," I said, as we idled on the single road out of town, stuck in the remains of Mahina's evening rush hour. "I can relax and look out the window."

"At what?" Davison groused from the passenger seat. "All the brake lights in front of us?"

Apparently, things hadn't gone as planned with

Crystal.

"Donnie, how did your restaurant inspection go today?" I asked. "I'll bet you got a perfect score. It's my favorite thing about Donnie's Drive-Inn, you know. It's always sparkling clean."

"You mean the food isn't your favorite thing about it?" He caught my guilty expression in the rear view mirror and smiled. "I know it's not really your taste, all the fried meat and the big scoops of rice."

The traffic began to flow again, and I saw what the problem had been. One car had been waiting to make a left turn onto a small side street. Mahina's planners (assuming there had been planners at some point) apparently didn't believe in left turn lanes.

"I'm still not used to getting rice *and* macaroni salad on the same plate," I said.

"It's not just the Drive-Inn. Every place with plate lunches does it. Merrie Musubis, all those guys."

"It's how come everyone getting so fat now, with diabetes an' da kine," Davison said. "All the rice an' mac salad an' soda. Killing people."

"Are you saying I'm killing people with the food I serve at the Drive-Inn?" Donnie asked.

"Nah. Just handing 'em the loaded gun."

"Just because you're in a bad mood, Davison, you don't have to take it out on everyone."

"So what happened with the inspection?" I asked.

"We passed, with a ninety-nine."

"Not a hundred?"

"It was Norris this time."

"Oh, the one you were telling me about? Never

smiles?"

"He won't give anyone a perfect score. I think he wants to look like he has high standards. Anyway, ninety-nine is good enough. We can keep our green placard. So it was a good day. How about you?"

"Class was fine. I'm a little worried about Lars Suzuki. My extra chatty student. I think you met him at the Halloween party."

"The one who wore his pants really long?"

"Yes, him. Today in class, he was contributing a lot to the discussion, which was fine, but then he got up, walked to the front of the room, stood next to me, and started lecturing the other students. I had to tell him to sit back down."

"Do you think he's dangerous?" Donnie asked.

"No, but his behavior's odd. I think I might send in a referral to the counseling center. Oh, and I got some bad news today."

Donnie slowed down and moved over to the grassy shoulder.

"I'm not sure it's so bad you need to stop driving," I said.

A police cruiser screamed by, lights pulsing.

"Sorry." Donnie moved back onto the road. "What's your bad news?"

"You already know one of my department members voted against my tenure package."

"But you told me you meet the criteria."

"Right. Or so I thought. Well, you know the senior faculty in my college. Apparently, last year they got together and voted to increase the requirements to get tenure. And they were supposed to send out a notice, but someone forgot. So, even though Hanson Harrison hasn't published anything except letters to the editor in the last three decades, and Rodge Cowper's never written a blessed thing as far as I can tell, I apparently have to clear this new bar. It's amazing how people love to have high standards as long as they're applied to someone else."

"But you have a lot of publications, don't you?"

"Well, I thought I had enough, but now, with the new rules, it's kind of a squeaker. It turns out being a co-investigator on a Federal grant gives me *just* enough points to meet our brand-new benchmark."

"How come we're pulling over again?" Davison grumped.

Two yellow fire engines zipped past us, sirens wailing.

"What kind of unlucky person has a fire in the middle of rainy weather like this?" I looked after the emergency vehicles.

"Could be a grease fire," Donnie said. "Or an electrical fire. Water only makes those worse."

"Molly," Davison said. "You get tenure, it's a sweet deal, ah? Guaranteed job for life?"

"It's not a guaranteed job for life, but it *does* mean you get some form of due process. So at least they can't fire you without making up a reason first."

Donnie pulled slowly back out onto the road.

"And you know what's really infuriating? Hanson freakin' Harrison *who voted for the new guidelines* decided to vote against my tenure bid anyway. Because he doesn't like the way I approach my research, even though my research got me onto a grant, the presence of which ensures that I meet the guidelines *he voted for*—gah, this is making my head hurt."

"This Hanson Harrison seems to have it in for you," Donnie said. "What'd you do to him?"

"Nothing. He's been difficult from the minute I was appointed chair. At our first department meeting, he started blathering on about how everyone in our department should start using some teaching method he liked, and according to him, I, as the new department chair, was supposed to come up with the money to send everyone to this expensive training. So then Larry Schneider claimed the method had been totally discredited, and no one should be using it at all, much less spending taxpayer money on it. So I said, 'Look, if you want me to get money for something, you'll have to help me make a case to the administration. Back up your claims with evidence, just like we always tell our students.' So Harrison started huffing and puffing about how we're living in a postmodern world now, and my empiricism was outdated and misguided. Meaning, basically, he didn't want to have to justify his demand for the money. So I told him, 'Look, Hanson, you can't just come in here like, I'm Silverback McGreybeard and everyone has to do what I say because I've been teaching here for a hundred years. If you want something, you need to do your homework just like everyone else.'"

"Well," Donnie said carefully, "whatever the outcome of this tenure application, I'm here for you. We're in this together."

"I appreciate it," I said. "Thank you."

Donnie slowed down and signaled a left turn. Now we were the ones backing up traffic. We had no choice. There was no other way onto his street, and the highway didn't have a left turn lane. A space cleared in the oncoming traffic, and Donnie gunned his Lexus through.

"Anyone smell smoke?" Davison asked.

"This is where all the fire trucks were headed." I said. "Your street. I mean *our* street."

We pulled up behind the line of emergency vehicles, which surrounded the smoldering ruin that had been Donnie's house.

CHAPTER THIRTY-SIX

Donnie's home was a blackened heap. The gorgeous living room with its hardwood floors, the paintings, the lithographs, the quarter-sawn oak side table with the jaw-droppingly expensive jade green bud vase, the wine collection, and the designer aloha shirts in now-discontinued patterns—all crushed under the remains of the charred metal roof.

Donnie climbed out of the driver's seat and stood, one hand braced on the roof of his car, watching yellow-jacketed firemen finish hosing down the already sodden ruins. The rain had subsided to a mist. The wet smell of burned wood filled the air.

I went around the car and quietly stood next to Donnie. Davison got out of the car and waded directly into the rubble. Surprisingly, no one stopped him. Far down the street, past the fire trucks and police cars, my turquoise and white Thunderbird sat where I'd parked it, apparently still intact.

I couldn't imagine what Donnie was feeling. I remembered how upset I had been when my office chair broke and I found out I'd have to pay for the replacement out of my own pocket. Iker Legazpi, my sweet-natured colleague in the accounting department, had tried to put things in perspective for me with a section of the Beatitudes.

Do not store up for yourselves treasures on earth, where moths and vermin destroy, and where thieves break in and steal.

On many occasions, Iker told me, he had found comfort in these verses. Iker had never volunteered much information about his background, and I didn't pry. He'd apparently grown up in one of those remote but highly-contested corners of Europe, where ancient blood feuds came blazing into the twenty-first century armed with high tech weaponry.

But store up for yourselves treasures in heaven, where moths and vermin do not destroy, and where thieves do not break in and steal.

At the time, Iker's little sermon had simply made me feel petty for complaining about my chair. But now, I saw what he meant. Getting attached to earthly things was a recipe for heartbreak. All of the fine, beautiful objects Donnie had been collecting over the decades had been lost in an instant, devoured by an irreversible exothermic reaction. Even the celebrated Ettore Sottsass sofa, with its clean lines and black and gunmetal fabrics, was somewhere under the collapsed roof, now a waterlogged, smoke-reeking glob of toxic waste.

Ka`imi Medeiros walked up and placed his hand on Donnie's shoulder. Donnie blinked, as if coming back from somewhere else.

"Was anyone hurt?" Donnie asked.

"No," Medeiros said, and then spotted Davison.

"Eh," he shouted. "Davison."

Davison looked up, and Medeiros motioned with his head: *Get back here.* Davison hitched his backpack onto his shoulder and trudged back in our direction.

"I just wanted to look see if there was any stuff I could save," he said.

"You find anything?" Donnie asked.

"Jus' small kine."

"You gotta stay out of there until we can get the fire investigators in. Donnie, you have insurance, ah?"

Donnie nodded. "Neighbors are okay?"

"Yeah, good thing you get three acre lots. Neighbors called in, reported an explosion. They said they felt their houses shaking, and some of them get debris flying into their yards. No actual damage to the neighbors' property, but by the time the firefighters arrived, your structure was fully involved. No saving it. Professor Barda, who knows you're still working on the biotech grant?"

"What?" Donnie stared at me. "I thought you put it on hold."

"That's correct. We *announced* we put it on hold. But then at that donor dinner, Randy Randolph insisted he wanted us to hear his side of the story, and Victor Santiago, our marketing guy, made it clear we should humor him."

"Who was present during the conversation?" Medeiros asked.

"Me, Pat, Emma, Randy Randolph, Victor Santiago. Wait, that's only five."

"Me," Davison said. "Ho Molly, you get absent-minded, ah?"

"Right, of course. Davison was there."

"Who else might know about this?" Medeiros asked. "That you didn't discontinue your research?"

"Let's see. Today, after I found out about my department's tenure requirements changing, I sent a message to Marshall Dixon and copied the chancellor, and my dean, and a few of the other administrators. I assured them even though I had to keep a low profile, I was still working on the grant as an active investigator. I wanted to make sure they knew I qualified for tenure according to the new standards set by my department."

"I want you to send me a copy of the email, with the distribution list," Medeiros said.

"You have email?"

"It's on our website," he said. "Mahina PD. Look under Contact Us."

"Wish I'd known that sooner."

"Where did the fire start?" Donnie's voice was flat.

"Hard to say," Medeiros said. "Looks like most of the damage is near the front of the house. A blast of this magnitude, we'd look for a propane explosion, but then the origin would usually be from the back of the house or the kitchen, not the front."

Donnie looked at Davison. "Unless propane tanks were sitting on the front porch, because someone forgot to bring them in."

Davison looked down at his feet.

"Do propane tanks explode on their own?" I asked.

"No," Medeiros said. "A propane tank would have to be subjected to extreme heat in order to get the liquid to boiling point. The fire would have to come first. Our investigator will be looking for an accelerant."

"What does that mean?" Davison asked.

Donnie took a deep breath. "It means someone set the fire on purpose.

CHAPTER THIRTY-SEVEN

"You all have somewhere you can stay tonight?" Detective Medeiros asked.

We must have looked pathetic, Donnie, Davison, and me, standing out in the drizzle, staring at the smoking remains of Donnie's house.

"I have my place in town," I said. "It's much too small for three people, but we could get Davison a hotel room. He's traveling back to the East Coast in a couple of days so it would only be—"

"Molly." Donnie looked aghast.

"What?"

Obviously, we needed to have a private discussion.

"Could you excuse us for a moment?" I said to Detective Medeiros. "Donnie, can you come help me check on my car?"

We gave the fire trucks and police cars a wide berth, walking in the middle of the road. Fortunately,

Donnie's street doesn't get much traffic.

"Donnie, this is terrible. I'm so sorry for what happened. I can't even imagine what you must be feeling right now. But please don't take it out on me. What did I do?"

"Davison just saw his house burned to the ground," Donnie said. "The house he grew up in. In a few days, he's going back to the East Coast, as far away as he can be from his family without leaving the United States. And you want to kick him out and put him in a hotel room?"

Kick him out? Which meant, in his mind, Davison had a rightful place in my house to begin with. This was a great example of how people entered arguments with completely different assumptions.

"I suppose it is still your house, Molly. And I can't tell you what to do."

"You can't tell me what to do, *but…?*"

We reached my car. It looked unharmed. The waxed turquoise and white paint gleamed dully in the sooty twilight. I pulled out my keys and unlocked the driver's side door.

"Molly? What are you doing?"

"Sorry, I just want to see if the smoke smell got into my upholstery. Hmm. Maybe a little. Sorry, what were you saying?"

I closed the door and faced him. I expected him to look angry, but his face was expressionless.

"Now that you've made sure your *car* is okay, maybe we can talk about the fact that our *son* just lost his childhood home and has nowhere to stay tonight."

"You're being unnecessarily sarcastic. All I was thinking was my place is so small. *You* don't even like to stay there."

"That's not true."

"Well, maybe I'm making the assumption because the last time you stayed over you said, quote, 'Your place is too small.' And it's true. There's only one bathroom. Of course I don't want to be the wicked stepmother who throws poor little Davison out into the snow. But where's he going to sleep? Tell me. Where?"

"In the guest room."

"Guest room? I don't have a…wait, are you talking about the *storage* room?"

The storage room contained all of the still-sealed boxes left over from my move from the mainland, along with what I called my "skinny" closet, filled with the clothes I would be able to fit into someday.

"There isn't enough room in there for an entire person," I said.

"Not the way it is now. We'll have to move all those boxes. I think if we stack them along one wall, we'll clear enough room for a cot."

"I don't have a cot."

"We can pick one up on the way over. We'll need to stop and buy some extra clothes for Davison and me too."

"Great. All taken care of, then."

Medeiros was still standing by the Lexus when Donnie and I returned. Davison was in animated conversation with one of the young firemen, who leaned against the truck, arms folded, smoking a cigarette.

"Are they allowed to smoke?" I asked no one in particular.

"You got a camera?" Medeiros asked. "Might want to take pictures of the damage for your insurance company."

"I'll use the tablet," I volunteered. "It has a really good built-in camera."

On the slim chance the fire had anything to do with our biotech research (although I sure hoped it didn't), it would be good to have the photos in the same place as all of our other documents. I opened my bag and groped around.

"Stay back, though," Medeiros cautioned.

"Definitely." I already wasn't comfortable breathing in the smoky air and wasn't particularly inclined to get any closer to the source.

"Where's the tablet?" I said. "It's not here."

"You got a cell phone?" Medeiros asked.

"Sure. Yes. But the tablet. I don't remember leaving it at my office. I must have left it…"

Medeiros followed my gaze to the charred wreckage of the house.

"If you left it in the house, might as well add it to your insurance claim," Medeiros said. "Gotta assume everything in there's a loss. Anything that didn't burn is gonna have smoke and water damage."

My heart sank as I remembered slipping the heavy case into the drawer of the night table on my side of

Donnie's bed.

I was not looking forward to telling our grants administrator I'd let an expensive piece of university equipment get destroyed in a fire. Maybe there was some way I could put off reporting the loss until after my tenure decision was made, just to be on the safe side. I took out my cell phone and snapped a few photos of the gutted house, and then took pictures of the undamaged houses on either side and across the street. The neat gravel-and-greenery yards indicated an old Japanese neighborhood, established Mahina families whose ancestors had arrived three or four generations earlier from Hiroshima or Osaka. No rotting cars on gone-to-seed lawns here. No blue tarps thrown over rusted-out roofs. This was a very different kind of neighborhood from the one Donnie had grown up in.

"That should be enough pictures for your insurance," Medeiros said. "Donnie, might as well take your wife an' son home. Nothing more to do here."

"So Donnie, you want to head up to the house with Davison? I can stop by the store and pick up a cot and some extra clothes for you."

Donnie shook his head.

"Let me do it. I know our sizes."

I reached out and squeezed his hand. It was trembling.

"Okay. In that case, I'll take my car back and start getting the guest room ready for Davison. Take your time. I'll see you two at home."

I stood up on tiptoe, and gently pulled Donnie's shoulder down so I could kiss him on the cheek. He pulled me into a hug, and then kept hugging me, and didn't let go for a long time.

As I walked back to my car, I started to feel a little better. Letting Davison stay with us was a selfless good deed, a *mitzvah*, as Emma might say. It's how you start storing up treasure in Heaven, right? And anyway, it was only for a couple of days.

CHAPTER THIRTY-EIGHT

As I drove to town, reality started to sink in. Donnie's house was gone. Everything he'd worked to build had been destroyed. And someone had done it on purpose.

I put my phone on speaker and called Emma.

"This better be good," she said. "We were just sitting down to dinner."

"A little late for dinner, isn't it?"

"It took a while for the pizza guy to get here."

"Emma, Donnie's house burned down."

"Donnie's *house* burned down? What hap—wait. Hang on a sec."

I heard Emma's voice offstage. "Yoshi, she doesn't need a lecture about fire safety right now, okay? Molly." Emma was back now. "How terrible. What happened? You think Davison left a cigarette burning somewhere?"

"Davison doesn't smoke. He quit. He's mister

my-body-is-a-temple now, remember? Oh, shoot, that's right. I'm probably going to have to go out and buy him grass-fed kale now or whatever it is that he eats."

"Is he staying at your house?" Emma asked.

"Yes. They're coming over tonight."

"With just one bathroom for three of you? And where's he gonna sleep? Oh, I know. You can put Davison up in a hotel."

"I already lost that battle."

"And Donnie's gonna be staying there? You better move your shoes outta your oven before he actually tries to use it to bake something."

"Shoot, I completely forgot about the oven. Emma, do you think we're safe staying in my house?"

"What do you mean safe? You mean you're afraid you might end up killing each other?"

"No. I'm afraid whoever burned down Donnie's house might come after me next. On Donnie's whole street, just his house burned. And not just charred. It looked like a bomb went off."

"Well, we've publicly announced we've stopped work on the grant. So no one should be coming after *us*. This must have to do with something Donnie's involved in. Or Davison."

"Well…" I said.

"Well what?"

"You know my tenure package is making its way up the chain of command, right? And being an investigator on a major grant is the one thing that'll definitely tip the scales in my favor. So I might have sent an email to Marshall Dixon and a few of the other administrators."

"Which other administrators? Never mind. Doesn't matter. You're telling me you think the call is coming from inside the house? One of our own administrators will go to any lengths to silence you?"

"I don't know. I don't *know*. Believe me, I realize how insane it sounds." I had almost reached the Mahina city limit when brake lights flared to life in front of me. I hit my brakes, causing the back end of my Thunderbird to swing out.

"Well, what about me?" Emma said. "Nothing's happened to me, and I'm the one doing the actual *science* on this thing."

"I'm going to ignore your insulting remark. Maybe you should be careful, too."

"Careful how? What should I be doing, exactly?"

I sighed. "I don't know."

"Molly, this obviously doesn't have anything to do with our research. Weren't you telling me Donnie was disappearing and not telling you where he was going? What ever happened with that? Any pattern to it?" I could hear Emma move her hand over the receiver. "Just a minute, Yoshi. This is important."

"Let's see. I think it's usually been on Wednesday evenings, now that I think of it."

"Tomorrow is Wednesday. Since he's staying with you, it'll be easier to keep tabs on him."

I was heading toward my house now. The silhouettes of overgrown mango trees loomed on either side of the dark street.

"I'm almost home, pulling up now."

"Anyone firebomb your house?" Emma asked.

"No damage at all. Everything looks fine."

"Great. I'm gonna eat my pizza now before it gets cold."

I pulled into the freshly-painted carport. Donnie would have to park behind me, blocking me in.

"Tell Yoshi hello for me," I said. "Oh, tell him one of my students showed up to class wearing a t-shirt with his kraken design. It was the white on a navy blue background. It looked good."

By the time Donnie and Davison got back to my house, I had cleared the shoes out of my oven, moved the pantyhose out of my freezer, and dumped all of the "skinny" clothes from my spare room closet into big black trash bags. Then I'd stuffed all of the shoes and pantyhose and bags of clothing into the spacious trunk of my Thunderbird.

I led Donnie and Davison to the "guest" room. Donnie directed Davison to start stacking boxes against one wall, then went over and opened my cleared-out skinny closet.

"Are you going to need these boxes?" Donnie peered at the top shelf.

"The boxes. I forgot about those."

I had divided the silver pieces between two boxes, hoisted them up onto the closet shelf with great effort (and a near shoulder sprain), and then forgotten about them. Of course, Donnie was tall enough to see them right away.

"Is this what Al Konishi's guys found?" Donnie asked. "When they were fixing your wall?"

"It's just old teapots an' li'dat," Davison remarked.

"I'll take them to my bedroom. *Our* bedroom."

"Let me do it." Donnie easily took down the cardboard box, then the wooden soap box, and carried them out.

While Donnie and Davison rearranged the guest room, I opened the cardboard box to have another look at my little treasures. Inside were the silver plated serving items and the folded up newspaper pages Konishi Construction had found during the repair job. Maybe I'd polish the items and put them in my kitchen, where they'd get some use. I could worry about it later. Right now, I needed to get dinner ready for the three of us.

I was in the kitchen, setting out paper plates, when the doorbell rang.

"Are you expecting someone?" Donnie called from the guest room.

"I hope this isn't against anyone's religion," I called back. "I sent out for pizza."

CHAPTER THIRTY-NINE

When I woke up Wednesday morning, Donnie had already left for work. I rushed to the bathroom, but unfortunately, I was too late. Light shone from under the closed door, and I heard the subdued roar of the fan. I made myself a cup of coffee, then went back to the bedroom to lay out my clothes for that day. A button-front white silk blouse. Black pencil skirt. *No, not this skirt, it's too tight around the hips. Maybe I should move it to the skinny closet. These charcoal gray trousers would work. But they have the bulky button and zipper in front. They show through the white silk blouse. Maybe a different shirt would work better. This red knit, with the ruching across the belly? No. The ruching hides the bulky zipper, but the weather forecast said it would be in the high eighties today, and this particular color shows armpit stains visible from the International Space Station.*

Donnie wonders why I can't just go into my closet and grab any old top and bottom to wear together. He has no idea.

When I was nearly finished picking out my ensemble, I heard the bathroom door open. I pulled on a robe and rushed out to see Davison, wearing only grey cutoff sweatpants, pushing the bathroom door back and forth in a fanning motion.

"You might wanna light a match before you go in there." He started back toward the guest room.

My bladder was aching, but I realized this might be my only chance to get information from him about Donnie's Wednesday night plans.

"Davison, would you like a cup of coffee?"

He looked confused.

"What? Oh, sure. Really?"

"Of course. I always show hospitality to my guests."

Davison seated himself at my kitchen counter. I pulled out my beloved sixteen ounce Chicken Boy coffee cup, brewed a large portion of coffee into it, and handed it to him.

"Eh, Molly. Hope you don't think I'm a guest. We're family, ah?"

He was giving me the sad eyebrows again. Great. I guess I said the wrong thing again, and now Davison will complain to Donnie, and Donnie will be all disappointed in me and my maternal inadequacy.

"Of course we're family. Drink your coffee."

"Never slept over at your house before." He pushed the heel of his hand up his face, as if to wipe away the remnants of sleep.

"Certainly not."

"Kind of a trip." He grinned. "Sleeping over at my teacher's house. 'Cause you was my teacher, ah?"

"Yes, I was. So. Today is Wednesday. Anyone have any special plans for the day?"

"Nothing special. Maybe go work out."

Davison gulped his coffee, holding the mug close to his face like a baby bottle. His slurping noises weren't making my aching bladder feel any better. I just had to hold out for another minute or so to see what information I could worm out of him before he was off doing whatever occupied his days.

"Hey, so what about your dad? What's he up to?"

Davison gave a one-shoulder shrug. The two-shoulder kind apparently cost too much effort.

"How about tonight?" I persisted. "Do you happen to know if your father has any plans for tonight?"

Davison set his coffee cup down. "How come you don't ask him? I dunno nothing."

"Look, Detective Medeiros said it looked like the fire was set on purpose. Remember?"

Davison nodded.

"Now, I was assuming someone was trying to intimidate me because of this biotech research, but no one's come after Emma Nakamura, and she's the other investigator on the grant."

"But Professor Nakamura's doing all the real science, ah?"

"Whatever. The point is it looks like Emma and I were not the target. So that leaves your father. He might be involved with something that's put us all in danger."

"You should just ask him, then."

I squeezed my eyes shut, and took a deep, cleansing breath, just as I'd learned in yoga class.

"If your father is in the crosshairs of some nutjob for some reason, then this little house, where we're all staying, is the next logical target. We were lucky last time. No one was home, and no one got hurt. But what if we're not so fortunate next time?"

"Eh, Molly. This coffee taste good, ah? I can get some more?"

I snatched the mug from his outstretched hand. "Davison, this is serious. Where is your father going on Wednesday nights? Where?"

"Chill. I dunno. I think maybe he said he was gonna go up to the college."

Now I knew where, but I still didn't know what. All kinds of groups used the classrooms as meeting spaces in the off-hours. The rental income provided a much-needed infusion to our frail budget. It wasn't like Donnie to get involved with a group of extremists, but then again, how well did I really know my husband? We'd only gotten married during the summer, and we were in the fall semester, barely at midterms.

"Do you know where at the college?" I asked. "Which room?"

"Shoot, I dunno. Eh, so how about that coffee?"

I couldn't continue this conversation any longer.

"Here you go." I banged the empty mug back down on the counter in front of him. "Coffee machine's over there."

"But Molly, I—"

I couldn't hear the rest of his sentence through the closed bathroom door.

CHAPTER FORTY

"You want me to keep you company while you spy on your husband?"

"Shh," I whispered. "I didn't need everyone in the cafeteria to hear. But yes, Emma. I need your help with this."

Emma picked up the stub of her Spam musubi from the cafeteria tray and popped it in her mouth.

"So it's tonight?" She looked at my tray. "Hey, you're not eating your burger. How come?"

"It's raw inside."

"So? Aren't you always complaining that you can't fit into the clothes in your skinny closet? A good dose of salmonella would fix you right up."

Emma thought the whole idea of my skinny closet was silly. According to her, I should have given away my too-small clothes long ago, and kept only the items that fit. That might have made sense for someone who didn't own a single Lilli Ann suit, and whose typical outfit was nondescript jeans and a five-year-old t-shirt from the annual meeting of the American Phytopathological Society.

"You ever find the tablet? The one we bought with the grant money?"

"You don't have to keep reminding me. No. I looked in my office. The more I think about it, the more sure I am that I left it at Donnie's house."

"Well, something weird's going on with it. Someone's adding new pictures to our photo stream."

"Photo stream? What are you talking about?"

"Come on Molly, what century are you living in? Whenever someone takes a picture, records an interview, whatever, it's automatically backed up onto a remote server."

"From our tablet?"

"Yes, dummy. So all the stuff you recorded, like at that biotech forum? It's all backed up and retrievable."

"It is? Great."

"I thought you knew."

"I didn't know. Was there some kind of online account you never told me about when you set up the tablet?"

"Oh. Yeah, I guess so. Remind me to get you the login information. Not now, though. I don't have it here."

"So you're saying new pictures have been appearing, *after* the fire?"

"Yup."

"Like what kinds of pictures?"

"Young guys, without their shirts on, doing muscle poses."

"Sounds like some kind of scam. We need to report it to IT. Can you do it since you have all the login information?"

"Sure, Molly. I'll get right on it."

"So back to my plan. Donnie's going to be on campus, so we can coincidentally happen to walk by. It won't look suspicious because we both work here."

"So you think we should be sneaking around here at *night*? That's never gonna not look suspicious. Why don't you call Detective Medeiros if you think Donnie's in trouble? He said he wants us to let him know about anything new."

"I don't have anything concrete to tell him. After tonight, we might, though. What could Donnie be mixed up with that would make someone want to burn his house down?"

"Who knows? Man, I'm still starving. I had a hard workout today. Here, let me see that." She grabbed my half-eaten, undercooked hamburger.

While she was devouring it, I explained my plan: I would go home after work as usual, where I'd cook dinner. (At this, Emma briefly choked on the burger). Right after dinner, I would say I needed to go grocery shopping. Donnie would tell me he had work to do and would see me at home later. I would drive about a block uphill and wait for him to leave, then follow him to campus. Emma would wait at her office for my text.

Emma swallowed the last of the burger. "Wait, wait, wait." She waved her hand vigorously. "You're gonna *cook*?"

"I'm going to do a slow cooker pork roast," I said.

"Doesn't Davison need all his meat to be organic and shade grown or something?"

"He ate half an extra-large pizza last night. I think he'll be fine."

I rushed home after lunch to start dinner. I rinsed off a five-pound pork butt, stuck it in the slow cooker, showered it liberally with steak seasoning, put the cover in place, and turned the temperature to "auto." Then I knocked the old, pebbly rice out of the rice cooker, rinsed out the inner container, and started a new batch. Both the meat and the rice would be ready by dinnertime. If I was feeling ambitious, I could even stop off to buy a couple of heads of lettuce this evening on the way home and round out the meal with a nice salad.

My dinner wasn't as elegant as one of Donnie's productions, but the pork was tasty, and the rice unobjectionable. I served the meal on my fanciest dinnerware, bright red and yellow vintage plates with whimsically mismatched utensils, all of which I'd purchased from the Salvation Army. Emma had volunteered to test the red plates for radioactivity and lead, but I told her I'd rather not know.

Davison looked like he was going to make a comment about the food, but Donnie shot him a silencing glare, and Davison ended up wolfing down a pile of salad, followed by three consecutive servings of pork and rice. I was too nervous to eat much.

After dinner, I excused myself to go "grocery shopping," ducked out, and waited in my parking spot a block away.

Half an hour later, I stood in the dark outside the Language Arts building, a two-story concrete structure with classrooms on the ground level and the English Department faculty offices on the second floor. Pat's old office was up there, along with what was probably the world's oldest working coffee vending machine. ("Working" in the sense that it accepted money and in return dispensed a hot liquid that looked like coffee but tasted like chocolate and chicken broth.)

"This building is creepy at night." Emma's voice in the dark made me jump about ten feet.

"Oh good." I clutched my chest. "It's you. I know. This building is *oppressive.*"

The Language Arts Building, constructed during the energy-conscious Brutalist revival of the 1970s, was a severe-looking block of raw concrete. Mahina's soggy climate endowed it with a perpetually tear-stained look.

"I can imagine Marcel Breuer shaking his head at the sight of this building, going, 'Dude, that's bleak'."

"Who's he? Some architect of hideous buildings?"

"Pretty much. He's the one who designed the

Hubert H. Humphrey building in D.C. It houses Health and Human Services. Ironic, because the mere sight of it makes you want to kill yourself."

Light glowed through the vertical strip of glass embedded in the door of Language Arts 124, the room into which I had watched Donnie disappear.

Emma and I tiptoed up to the source of the light. Emma peeked through the narrow glass window and then pulled back.

"Donnie's in there," she whispered.

"Anyone with him? I don't want to stick my face in the window."

"I don't see anyone except him."

"He's been coming to campus every week to sit in an empty classroom by himself?"

"Hold on." Emma ducked under the window and moved to the other side, then peered in again.

"Nicole Nixon," Emma hissed.

"From the English Department?"

"Uh-huh. Hey, she divorced what's-his-name, didn't she?"

"It's just the two of them? Donnie and Nicole?"

"Looks like it."

We scuttled away and ducked into the first-floor bathroom. The stall doors were missing from the stalls, and the dividers were covered with graffiti.

"Holy deferred maintenance." Emma glanced around. "This looks like something right out of that cop show Yoshi likes."

"Which one?"

"The one with a lot of swearing and people

getting shot and beat up. It's supposed to be 'gritty.' Molly, you okay?"

"He's having an *affair*." I blinked rapidly. "He's been coming here every Wednesday night for a rendezvous with Nicole Nixon. This whole time, he's been sneaking out—"

"Are you crying?"

I snatched a brown paper towel from the wall dispenser and dabbed it under my eyes. "I am not crying."

"So what does this have to do with his house getting burned down? You still think his life is in danger?"

"Yes, I do. Because I'm going to kill him."

"Whoa, Molly. Slow down."

"I have to see for myself."

Emma shrugged and followed me back to the classroom door. I was about to peek through the glass when my phone exploded with a burst of choral sound.

"Run," Emma hissed, unnecessarily. We were already fleeing at top speed toward the parking lot.

"Hello?" I panted as we slowed to a walk.

"Professor Barda? This is Ka'imi Medeiros, of the Mahina Police Department. I called your husband, but he doesn't seem to be picking up."

"Detective Medeiros. Yes, Donnie is apparently busy right now. Is there any news about the fire?"

"It seems the fire started on your front porch. According to the investigator, the accelerant was a large piece of cardboard or papier-mâché. Any idea what it might be?"

"The fire was started with something made of papier-mâché?"

"A piñata?" Emma suggested.

"Why would someone burn a piñata on Donnie's front porch?"

"Professor Barda?" Medeiros' voice squawked on my phone.

"Sorry Detective. I don't know. I have no idea what it might have been, or who would have wanted to burn down our house. Did you find anything else?"

"Just it's a good thing your husband's insurance is paid up. Not much salvageable."

"Any way we can help the investigation?"

"No, unless you remember something else."

Emma and I plodded glumly to her car.

"Donnie's having an affair." I regretted saying it aloud. I hated hearing the words.

"You don't know for sure. I mean, they weren't doing anything. It looked like they were just talking."

"Should I confront him? Should I wait until he tips his hand? Emma, what should I do? What would *you* do if it were Yoshi?"

She touched the door handle to unlock it.

"What would *I* do? I'd kill him."

CHAPTER FORTY-ONE

On the way home from campus, I stopped by Nishioka Drugs and bought a birthday card for Davison. He might not have been my favorite person in the whole world, but no one was going to accuse *me* of being a thoughtless, un-maternal birthday-forgetter.

When I got home, Davison was in my living room, bare feet on my coffee table, watching something on his phone.

"Eh, Molly, you been watching the feed?"

"Sorry. I don't know what feed it is I should be watching. Davison, people *eat* off of that table."

Davison pulled his feet off the coffee table and placed them on the floor.

"Come on, Molly. I know you not *that* old. The Mahina State news feed online. They send out announcements, what's going on and stuff. It used to be so junk an' boring, but now it's funny. Mister

Flanagan's doing it now, is why. Listen to this: Mahina State Slogan Contest. Now in the lead: Mahina State, Not as Bad as Everyone Says."

"I hope he doesn't get in trouble." I went into my little office (a tiny space, which originally served as a telephone nook adjacent to the main living area), set down my bag, started up my computer and navigated to my course website.

"Eh Molly, you looking at the feed now?" Davison called from my couch.

"No. I'm going to try to get caught up on my grading."

He was quiet for a few seconds and then,

"Eh Molly, what's this mean?"

"Can I look at it later?" I called out, but he was already walking his phone over to me.

"Try look."

The official Mahina State feed, tagged #AlohaState, showed a muscled, shirtless man working under the hood of a classic Mustang, his glistening brown arms covered with triangular Polynesian tattoos.

"It looks like a plug for our automotive repair program," I said.

"What's this mean, right here?" Davison pointed.

"I have no idea." I turned back to my computer and pulled up the course assignment page. "You'll have to ask Pat."

As soon as Davison was back on the couch, I pulled my phone out of my bag.

Are you trying to get fired? I texted Pat.

I didn't get a response. He was probably back up the mountain already. I sure wouldn't want to live off the grid, far from modern conveniences like county water and reliable phone service, but Pat really loved his place. It occurred to me that if Pat was really attached to the place, he might have killed Randy Randolph for it, but I quickly dismissed the idea.

I tried to tune out the TV noise (Davison had turned on some kind of sporting event) and pulled up the list of uploaded papers from the Intro to Business Management class. This week's assignment had been a gimme—or so I'd assumed. I'd asked my Intro students to find and describe an instance of an unsuccessful product launch from an otherwise successful company. I thought it would be an easy, fun project. Back in class, we'd have fun picking apart Colgate frozen dinners, McDonald's hotels, and Smith & Wesson bicycles.

Unfortunately, fewer than half my students had done the assignment. Well, as Emma liked to say, "You can lead your students to water, but then you have to restrain yourself from holding their heads under the surface until they stop struggling." On the bright side, tonight's grading workload was half of what I'd thought it would be.

I was interrupted by my ringing phone.

"Is Donnie there?" Emma's voice squawked on my speaker.

"Dad's not home," Davison bellowed over the sound of cheering on my television. I considered telling him to turn it off, but if I did, he'd just grump around the house, complaining about how bored he was and pestering me to drive him somewhere.

"Let me take you off speaker. No, Donnie's not here. What's up? Do you need to talk to him?"

"No, I want to talk *about* him, so I gotta make sure he's not standing right there. Molly, I've been thinking about it, and I've decided Donnie is not having an affair."

"Looks like I took you off speaker just in time."

"I know, not a lot of privacy in your little house, ah? I dunno how you can stand it. Anyways, if Donnie was really screwing around on you, he'd be sneaking out to a hotel all secret, not sitting in a classroom where everyone could see him."

"I hope you're right,"

"I *am* right. Seriously, think about it. What are him and Nicole Nixon gonna do in an unlocked classroom, where anyone could walk in? I mean, I *guess* if they *really* wanted to they could bring in a blanket and—"

"Emma, have you been watching the Mahina State feed?"

"Nah. Why would I? I get enough propaganda in my email."

"Well, you should take a look. I think Pat's livened things up a little."

I heard quiet clicking, and then a whoop of laughter.

"Well, they did want to get people talking about Mahina State." Emma chuckled. "Remember what

Pat was telling us at that donor dinner? He said his new boss wanted him to be his quote 'edgy' self."

"I'm not sure they really *meant* it." I lowered my voice, annoyed because I was unable to have a private conversation in my own home. "I hope Victor Santiago doesn't clap him into the iron maiden over this. I sure wouldn't want to get crosswise with the guy."

"Victor seems okay. I don't think he's so scary."

I heard the bathroom door close and lock, followed by the sound of water running. Davison had decided to take a shower, which meant I was shut out of my own bathroom for the foreseeable future, but on the plus side, I could speak in a normal voice again without being overheard.

"You don't think Victor Santiago is scary? *You're* the one who said he looked like the Grand Inquisitor."

"That wasn't me. It was Pat. I think you're both racially biased."

"Oh no, I remember. *You* were the one who said he had a devil beard."

"To describe is neither to endorse nor to condemn."

"Really."

"You think Victor looks scary 'cause he's not all-American white bread, like you and Pat. Have you ever noticed in the movies? The bad guy's always brown."

"That's not true. A lot of Hollywood villains are blonde Aryan types. Besides, I am not biased. My own husband is swarthy."

"And you think *he's* a bad guy."

"Only because he's having an affair with Nicole Nixon."

"Anyway, Donnie's not swarthy."

"What? Of course he is."

"No, he's not. He's totally smooth."

That stumped me.

"Emma, what do you think swarthy means?"

"It means hairy."

"It does not. It means dark-skinned. Why would I say Donnie's hairy?"

"I don't know why you'd say it 'cause it isn't true."

"I *know* it isn't true."

"Geez Molly, you don't hafta shout."

"All I'm saying is *hairy* is not at all the same thing as *swarthy*. Donnie is *swarthy*. He is not *hairy*, and I am *not shout—*"

I heard Davison emerge from the bathroom. At least he'd kept his shower short this time. The last time he was in there so long, he'd emptied out my entire hot water tank.

"Whoa. I just scrolled to the last thing on Pat's feed."

"The shirtless guy working on the car?" I confirmed.

"Come for the open admissions, *stay for the rough trade?*"

"I know. I texted him and asked if he's trying to get fired."

"He's pushing it. Hey, so are you gonna ask Donnie what he was doing on campus with Nicole or what?"

"I'm not up to any kind of confrontation right now. I think I'll wait until Davison's gone back to school before I decide how I want to deal with this."

"So you're just gonna simmer and stew while Donnie tries to guess how come you're so grumpy?"

"Something like that. Emma I have to go. It's my call waiting. Pat's calling me back."

"Okay. Ask him what he was thinking, and then call me back and tell me."

CHAPTER FORTY-TWO

When I woke up the next morning, Donnie had already left for work. The door to my spare room was closed, so I assumed Davison was still asleep. I showered and dressed. As I walked out the door, I propped Davison's birthday card on the coffee maker. I had gotten Donnie to sign it, too, and he'd seemed pleasantly surprised I'd remembered to buy something. Davison would wake up on his twenty-first birthday in an empty house, stranded without a car, and fresh from a breakup (which was his own stupid fault), but at least he'd have a cheerful card with a puppy on it.

Donnie and I hadn't had much to say to each other last night. I wasn't, to use Emma's words, simmering and stewing exactly, but Donnie's secret rendezvous with an attractive, divorced English professor had made me feel a little…pensive.

In any event, my thoughts were occupied with the

previous evening's conversation with Pat. His friend, Jeffrey the antique dealer, had found some very interesting information about the contents of my wooden soap box. It seemed that there might be hope for my career after all. But I had to play it exactly right.

As soon as I got to my office, I sent a file from my phone to the department printer, then called Marshall Dixon's office for an appointment. I was pleasantly surprised when the secretary told me Dixon would be able to see me that morning.

I arrived ten minutes early, checked in with the secretary, and then walked the twenty echoing paces across the polished floor to the waiting couch. (I could never recall the secretary's name. All I remembered about her was she always seemed miserably cold.) I felt inside my bag to make sure that I had brought the manila folder containing my printout. Five minutes later, irrationally, I checked again.

At last I was in Marshall Dixon's office, seated on the other side of her vast koa wood desk.

"I'm here to plead my case," I said. "For tenure."

"Your contract does give you the right to request a discussion of the process with members of the administration. Although any questions you may have had should have been answered during the orientation session."

"The grant Emma Nakamura and I got, investigating attitudes toward biotech? I really thought it would help my case. A grant should earn me extra research points toward being qualified for promotion and tenure, according to my college's guidelines. But in spite of my objectively meeting the guidelines, I received a negative vote from one member of my department."

Dixon nodded blandly, giving nothing away.

"I know how important it is for a candidate to have unanimous support from the department. I know the other committees in the decision chain don't look favorably on mixed votes. I'm hoping you—your support would counter any ambiguity or doubt."

"I'm sympathetic, but overriding the faculty is something only done as a last resort. At Mahina State, we respect faculty governance."

It sounded like the campus wide committee had already voted against me. I wasn't surprised. Once Hanson Harrison raised "concerns" about my research, everyone on the subsequent committees had to fall in line or risk looking naive or non-rigorous. And Dixon wasn't going to stick out her neck contradicting the faculty if there wasn't something in it for her.

Well, I might as well go for broke. I had nothing to lose.

"I see what you're saying. I certainly wouldn't ask you to expend political capital on my behalf. That's a lot to ask. Oh. Something else I wanted to get your input on."

I drew the folder out of my bag, placed it on the glimmering wood surface, and opened it to display the page I had printed out earlier.

"What's this?" Marshall drew the folder to her side of the vast desk. She studied the paper. Her only reaction was the lifting of her eyebrows.

"This cartoon ran on the front page of a mainland newspaper in 1893. The Brockton Bugle. Times have certainly changed. To modern eyes, this is extremely offensive. I mean, a half-naked Queen Liliuokalani, trying to pawn her crown? Goodness."

"And what does this have to do with—" I could see the light dawn before Marshall finished the sentence. "That's Mary Pfaff's signature."

"The Beatrix Potter of Hawaii," I agreed.

"Where's the original?"

"*I* have the original newspaper page. According to an antiques expert who researched it, it's likely the only copy in existence. What you're looking at is a photograph I took on my phone."

Marshall met my gaze. "Mary Pfaff's granddaughter, Dorothy, has been a great friend to Mahina State."

"I know. Thanks to her generosity, we have a whole library wing dedicated to Mary Pfaff. And I heard scholarships are being planned. One or two endowed chairs. Maybe even a naming opportunity. The Mary Pfaff College of Fine Arts. This relationship has been a *wonderful* thing for Mahina State. I'm a big Alice Mongoose fan myself."

Marshall didn't ask, "What do you want?" Her even gaze posed the question silently.

"I love working at Mahina State. I enjoy teaching,

helping our students succeed, and I have so many wonderful colleagues. Not to mention, I've put down roots here. My husband, Donnie, would never leave the Drive-Inn, so I don't have the option of moving away. And there aren't a lot of other employment opportunities outside of the university for someone with a Ph.D. in literature and creative writing. If I don't get tenure, the only thing I can do here in Mahina is maybe a little freelance writing."

"The *County Courier* would be fortunate to have someone of your qualifications," Marshall said.

"Unfortunately, the *County Courier* isn't looking for new writers. I've been in discussion with one of the airline magazines." I was improvising here, but again, what did I have to lose? "They're interested in running a piece on the legacy of Mary Pfaff. They think the accidental discovery of this cartoon would be a fascinating sidebar. This could generate a lot of buzz. And of course, Mahina State University has such a close relationship with Mary Pfaff's estate they'll certainly be part of the story too."

I hoped Marshall wouldn't call my bluff. Mary's granddaughter, Dorothy, had seemed so sweet and frail when I met her at the wretched Halloween party. There was no way I could bring myself to expose her to the embarrassment this awful cartoon would cause.

I narrowed my eyes a little, to try to make myself look more ruthless. In case there was any doubt in Marshall's mind that I Meant Business.

Marshall gazed at me for an unnervingly long

moment.

"And if you were to be awarded tenure?" she asked, finally.

"I were to be awarded tenure? I would celebrate by making a gift of this historically significant artifact to Mahina State University. Our library would probably want to archive it, to keep it safe, away from light and the elements. And of course, I would focus on my teaching, and my scholarly publishing. I *certainly* wouldn't be interested in writing any stories for airline magazines. I mean, I wouldn't have time."

"You'd donate the original?"

"Yes. *And* delete any electronic copies."

"May I keep this?" she asked.

"Of course."

I didn't want to take back the folder anyway. I was shaking so hard, I was sure it would start rattling in my hand.

CHAPTER FORTY-THREE

My afternoon classes went by in a blur. It's not every day I attempt to extort my administration into giving me tenure. I would never make it as a professional blackmailer.

I came home to find Donnie sitting on my couch, pressing the buttons on my television's remote control.

"Oh, Molly. There you are. I can't figure out your system."

"That remote controls live TV," I said. "Anything else has to connect from the computer in my office. What are you trying to do, exactly?"

"I thought we could watch a movie tonight." He stood up, came over to where I had seated myself at the computer and handed me a disk whose label indicated it was the property of the university library.

"You want to watch *Henry the Fifth*?"

"It's a classic. I don't think you and I have ever

seen a movie together."

"You know what? I think you're right. We haven't."

"I know you don't like movie theaters."

"I don't?"

"You said you can't relax and enjoy yourself because you always imagine there are ukus in the upholstery."

"No, I said it about airplanes. But now that you mention it, movie theaters probably have lice living inside the seats, too. You're right. I guess if I had a choice, I'd rather watch a movie in my own house."

"Good. Let's do it. I picked up some sushi and wine on the way home."

"This sounds really nice," I said suspiciously. "Is this to celebrate Davison's birthday? Is *he* going to watch with us?"

Donnie grinned happily, pulled me up from my computer chair and clasped me in a tight hug. "You're a great mom," he murmured into my hair, then pulled back to beam at me. "It was so nice of you to pick up a birthday card for him. I asked him if he wanted to do anything special with us, but it looks like he made plans to catch up with some old friends."

"When is he coming back? Are we going to have to get up and let him in at three in the morning?"

"No." Donnie smiled proudly. "I made him a copy of my key."

"Oh good. Davison has a copy of my house key now. So you just came home with a movie to watch?"

"Two. A double feature. I got *Becket,* too, another classic. Go ahead. Show me how this works so I don't have to bother you next time."

He watched me insert the disk into the tray.

"So we have sushi and wine and classic movies, just you and me? It sounds wonderful."

Too good to be true, even. Most likely the product of a guilty conscience. Well. I could spend the rest of the evening grilling him about his motivation. Or I could put off arguing until later, and enjoy the evening.

I had seen *Henry the Fifth* long ago, the 1944 Technicolor version with Laurence Olivier. What I wasn't prepared for was how much my attention span had deteriorated in the intervening years. The scenes seemed intolerably long, the dialog wordy, the pace glacial. This was probably the fault of social media. We were all getting so used to tiny morsels of information flying by. I'd have to remember to remind Pat how his new occupation as Mahina State's Social Media Czar was helping to destroy civilization.

I dozed off a couple of times, lulled as much by the wine as by the film. Every so often, a soft buzzing from Donnie's side of the couch signaled he, too, had succumbed. Donnie and I both perked up for the famous scene of King Henry in disguise, mingling with his men on the eve of battle.

"This is like the show where bosses go undercover to see what their employees are really like, when they think they're not being watched,"

Donnie said.

"I wonder if you could do that. Probably not. People at the Drive-Inn see you every day."

"I could put on glasses, like Clark Kent." Donnie grinned.

"Or you could wear the cockroach costume. Oh, sorry."

The cockroach costume was gone, along with everything else in Donnie's house. Now I'd reminded him of the fire. *Nice going, Molly.*

Donnie chuckled. "Nah. Norris the health inspector would have a heart attack seeing a giant cockroach in the kitchen."

He placed his arm around me and squeezed. "This is nice. Hey, I forgot to ask. Any news on your tenure thing?"

"Oh, I think things are going to be okay."

"I'm glad to hear it."

Was it just that morning that I'd been in Marshall Dixon's office, calmly threatening the reputation of one of Mahina State's most generous benefactors for the sake of my own job security?

"How about you?" I asked. "Anything going on?"

"No. Oh, there is something. I almost forgot."

"Yes?"

"Davison finally confirmed his flight for tomorrow morning. I'll take off from work to drive him. It would be nice if you could come along, too, to see him off."

"I don't think I have any meetings until tomorrow afternoon. Okay, I guess I can come with you."

Conversation having thus petered out, we turned our attention back to the Technicolor Battle of Agincourt.

I was ready to pack it in after *Henry the Fifth*, but Donnie insisted on watching *Becket* as well.

"It's a good example of miscommunication," Donnie said. "When Henry the Second says, 'Will no one rid me of this turbulent priest,' he's just thinking out loud, 'I wish I didn't have to deal with this troublemaker,' and the four knights take him at his word."

"I don't think it's miscommunication. Isn't this how businesses get their dirty work done? You don't tell your store managers, force your employees to punch out and make them work extra hours for free. You just give them store targets, and let *them* worry about how to meet them. Or say you have—Victor Santiago."

"Victor Santiago? Your marketing person?"

"Yes. Marshall thought Primo Nordmann was a troublemaker, with all of his protesting against biotechnology and insulting one of our potential donors on his website. She probably said something to Santiago like, 'will no one rid me of this turbulent eco-warrior?' And he went and took care of it for her."

"You think Santiago is so serious about his job he'd kill someone to make his boss happy?"

"It wasn't just commitment to his job. He's infatuated with Marshall Dixon."

"How do you know?"

"The way he looks at her."

"The way he *looks* at her? That doesn't exactly prove—"

"Santiago is the killer. Let's call Detective Medeiros."

Donnie gave me a look.

"Fine. *I'll* call Detective Medeiros. Oh, better yet, I'll email him."

"Molly, why don't you sleep on it? I've heard you say it's a good idea to give your unconscious a chance to work things out. Maybe it's the best thing to do in this case."

"You're right." I scooted closer to Donnie and rested my head on his shoulder. I knew Victor Santiago had a motive, but Donnie had a point. It would be a good idea to wait until I had some actual evidence.

CHAPTER FORTY-FOUR

I pulled up to the curb in front of Emma's house, a neatly landscaped split-level in the deepest suburbs of Upper Mahina. I wasn't supposed to call, knock or ring the doorbell, which would risk waking Yoshi, and I wasn't allowed to park on her concrete driveway lest I stain it with my Thunderbird's chronic oil leak. I waited at the curb and texted her while I idled the engine. I could have shut it off, but starting up again wasn't a 100% proposition.

Five minutes later, Emma came out, dressed for our yoga workout and carrying a travel mug.

She plumped into the passenger seat and handed me her coffee. I held it for her while she buckled in.

"You gotta get some cup holders in this thing."

"They didn't have cup holders in 1959."

"What did people do? Didn't they drink coffee?" She took her cup back from me.

"Not in their cars. I think they smoked instead.

Hey, did you ever talk to IT about those pictures coming up on our photostream?"

"Not yet."

I pulled out of Emma's cul-de-sac to the main road. The Cruise-O-Matic transmission bucked into second gear. Fortunately, Emma's travel mug had the lid in place.

"Emma, aren't you worried about security? If someone else has access to our account—"

"Hey, we got some new pictures," Emma interrupted. "Wanna see?"

"No."

"I'll bring 'em up on my phone."

She stuck her phone in front of my face. The screen was filled with a scrawny brown male torso, his articulated abs adorned with swirling script tattoos.

"Please don't do that while I'm driving. Hey, can you can search their faces online, maybe identify who hacked into our account?"

"They aren't showing their faces. It's just abs and biceps, a few lats, and delts. Anyway, they don't look like hackers to me."

"Really? Why not? You think these guys can't be hackers because they're lean and fit, and hackers are pasty and pudgy?"

"Well, yeah."

"Aha. Who's stereotyping *now*? Listen, I'm going to talk to IT today if you won't. What if some political group does a Freedom of Information Act request on the university's records and these body parts pop up? How is *that* going to look?"

"Oh, all right. Fine. Man, you've been grouchy lately."

"No I haven't."

"I don't blame you, crowded into that tiny house with Donnie and Davison. When's your beloved stepson leaving anyway?"

"His flight is later today. After that, it's just going to be Donnie and me in my teeny house. Oh no, I hate this left turn."

I swiveled my head left and right looking in vain for a break in the morning traffic. I finally managed to zoom through as the yellow light changed to red.

"Yeah, it'd be better if there was a left turn arrow. Or even a left turn *lane*, 'cause I can tell you're stressing out about all the cars stuck behind you."

"I *know*. Tell it to the city planners. You're preaching to the choir here. Do we even have city planners in Mahina?"

"So what's going on down at Donnie's place? When's he gonna start rebuilding?"

"The police and the insurance company are still investigating," I said. "It's a little more complicated than when the tree fell onto my house. Whatever fueled the fire would normally have burned itself out without causing much damage."

"Right, the piñata?"

"Whatever it was. But because of the propane tanks, the heat caused what is called a BLEVE. Boiling Liquid Expanding Vapor Explosion. That's why it looked like a bomb went off. They still don't know what, or who, started the fire in the first place."

"How come you had propane tanks sitting in your entryway? Guy drop 'em off that day?"

"Actually, the tanks had been sitting there for a while. I heard Donnie ask Davison to bring them in. A couple of times."

"Oh man. I sure wouldn't want to be Davison right now. I bet *he's* feeling the love from his dad. Hey, what about Nicole Nixon's ex-husband Scott? Do you think he started the fire? 'Cause he wants Nicole back? And she's having these secret nighttime meetings with your husband?"

"Scott Nixon's still on the mainland, as far as I know. And I thought you were convinced Donnie *wasn't* having an affair with Nicole Nixon."

"Maybe we should ask around at the yoga studio."

"Oh Emma, really? It's are-you-freaking-kidding-me-o'clock in the morning, and I just want to have a nice, energizing, low-impact workout. I don't want to do any investigating right now."

"What's wrong? You have a rough night?"

"Not at all. I had a perfectly delightful night."

I told Emma about the movies Donnie brought home, along with the sushi and the wine.

"It sounds amazing. All the things you like. Alcohol, sushi, and some dusty old movies. Man, I wish Yoshi would plan a nice evening for me instead of sitting around the house like a fungus."

"We watched *Becket*."

"That means nothing to me. Sorry."

"It's okay. What do you think of this? Victor Santiago is good at his job, and takes it seriously. Not only that, he's in love with Marshall Dixon. One day, Marshall remarks her life would be a lot easier without Primo Nordmann buzzing around antagonizing her important donors."

"And Victor Santiago uses his swordcraft to make her wish come true." Emma finished my sentence.

"Exactly. What do you think?"

"Perfect, except we don't have any, what's it called? Oh yeah, *proof*."

"Killjoy."

"Hey, speaking of administration, any news on your tenure application?"

"In fact there is, but you can't tell anyone."

"Ooh, is this gonna be scandalous?"

"Kind of. The *good* news is it looks like I have Vice President Marshall Dixon's support for my tenure bid."

"Great. So what's the bad news?"

"It's a long story." I told Emma all about how I'd used Mary Pfaff's editorial cartoon to get Marshall Dixon on my side, finishing my narrative just as I pulled into the strip mall parking lot. "You still want to associate with me?"

"You know, Molly, I'm impressed. Most of the time you seem like kind of a *schlemiel*, but once in a while, you manage to grow a spine."

"You're not horrified?"

Emma and I climbed out of opposite sides of the Thunderbird, pulled out our workout bags, and started inside.

"You're learning to play their game." She socked my shoulder. "Good for you. You tell Donnie?"

"No, Donnie's kind of old-fashioned. He wants to think of me as Innocent and Pure. I don't think he wants to know about my Machiavellian maneuvering."

"Yeah. Sounds fair. He doesn't seem to have any problem keeping things from *you*."

CHAPTER FORTY-FIVE

I walked through the front door of the Laughing Lotus yoga studio anticipating a serene warmup of gentle stretches and sighing background music, followed by a low impact but rigorous workout, with the scent of smoldering joss sticks drifting in from the meditation room. I was not expecting Sharla to intercept us the minute we were past the reception desk, physically blocking our progress and accosting me with cries of, "Hey, you. Business professor."

Sharla held a worn wooden box. It had a slit carved into the top, and was fastened shut with a small brass padlock. The sides of the box were decoupaged with mandalas, Tibetan suns, and yin-yang symbols.

"She's talking to you," Emma said.

"Hi, Sharla. Guilty as charged. What's up? Isn't that the money box?"

It turned out Sharla wanted to get some free

business consulting from me. Money continued to disappear from the Laughing Lotus, and could I step into her office for just a minute to talk about it? Emma managed to slip away to the class, leaving me to deal with the assertive Bostonian by myself.

"Sharla." I followed her to the back. "Loss prevention isn't really my specialty. And Heaven knows, I'm not an accountant. Why not just get rid of the box, and make sure people pay at the front desk?"

She paused at a door and produced a ring of keys. "We can't do that."

"I understand. You want to have an honor system. It conveys an atmosphere of trust."

Sharla opened the door and waved me inside. Her office didn't particularly look like it belonged in a yoga studio. With its putty-colored file cabinets and its secondhand faux-walnut-and-chrome desk, it could've fit right in at an insurance agent's, a real estate office, or any small business. The stale cigarette stench and the small black plastic notched ashtray on Sharla's desk gave the office a retro feel.

"I can't afford to cover the front desk all the time. But sure, what you said about having trust? That too."

"Sharla, this is really not my specialty at all. I can ask around when I get into the office today—"

"Tell you what, hon. Gimme a half hour right now, and I'll trade you for a free class session, any time you want."

"A half hour? Sharla, you said a minute. And I

don't need a free class session. I've already pre-paid for six months of classes."

"I'll stick an extra week on the end of your contract. You could really help me out here, Molly. Me and my sister. I love Sharon to death, but honest to—she can be such an airhead sometimes."

I wasn't even sure the Laughing Lotus was going to be in business six months from now, but I couldn't bring myself to tell Sharla no. Emma was right. I really could be a *schlemiel* sometimes.

Sharla closed the door, sat down, and lighted a cigarette. She caught my expression, rolled her eyes, and stubbed it out in the ashtray. "Here's the thing, I think it's an inside job. I don't think it's someone who's just wandering in off the street. It's happening too regularly. Gotta be an employee or a regular customer."

"Have you notified the police? I know they'd rather handle these things themselves. I get the feeling they don't care for amateurs doing police work."

"I don't have anything to tell the police."

"Do you even have a suspect?"

"I haven't narrowed it down to just one."

I wondered whether her sister Sharon was the likely thief, and if so, whether Sharla was hoping to prove it was really someone else. People say they want to know the truth, but they're not always happy when they get it.

"I'm thinking of setting up some kinda surveillance," she said. "Like a computer with a camera in it. You know how I can get started with something like that? I wanna buy something high quality enough that it's not gonna break, but I don't wanna get ripped off."

"I thought you said you don't want to pay someone to watch the counter. A surveillance system is probably going to be even more expensive."

This kind of hit a nerve with me. At Mahina State, we never had enough money to replace faculty members who left, yet our administration could always find funding for some new computer system to automate advising or grading.

"Since you asked my opinion, Sharla, I don't like the idea of replacing people with computers."

"I'd rather deal with a computer than a person. A computer's not gonna call in sick when it's a nice day out, or come in and steal my money out from under my nose, or freak out and have a big hissy fit when I accidentally call it the wrong name."

"Computers can crash, or get hacked. If you don't have anyone you trust, maybe you and Sharon should split desk duty and keep the money box in sight at all times. In my opinion…what do you mean a hissy fit? Who had a hissy fit?"

"Oh." Sharla massaged her sun-browned forehead with one hand. "Princess Crystal Phoenix does *not* answer to her real name."

"What's her real name?"

"Christine Roach. Which she *hates*, FYI. I accidentally called her by her name one time, and man. I thought her head was gonna explode."

"Crystal is working under an assumed name?"

"It's not too unusual. I see it a lot in this business. People go through some hard times, they find yoga, and they reinvent themselves. It's a good thing, mostly. Like Primo Nordmann. Primo wasn't his real name either."

"I know. When he was my student, I knew him as Harold. So how do you know peoples' real names?"

"I do a background check on all our employ—contractors."

"Right. You'd need the social security number for taxes, worker's comp, all of that."

"What? Oh, yeah, sure." Sharla picked her stubbed-out cigarette from the ashtray and put it down again.

"Well, as a customer of your yoga studio, I'm happy all of your instructors have passed rigorous background checks."

"Don't get too excited. Ten bucks an hour, you're not exactly getting Mary Poppins."

Sharla finally freed me, but of course, the class was over.

"So, you have a good workout?" I asked Emma as we drove back to her house.

"*You* took long enough. I hope you got a big consulting contract out of it."

"Not exactly, but I have a pretty good idea who might have burned down Donnie's house."

I told Emma what Sharla had told me, how touchy Crystal Phoenix—nee Roach—was about her birth name.

"Oh, and Davison busted out that cock-a-roach costume. Crystal musta thought he found out her real name and was doing it on purpose to make fun of her."

"Exactly. How much you want to bet that the mysterious kindling substance on the front porch is a papier-mâché cockroach costume? I heard Donnie scolding Davison for forgetting to lock the door. I bet Crystal just walked right in when no one was at home."

"Well, we maybe didn't solve any murders this morning," Emma said, "but it looks like we figured out an arson. Should I call the police, or do you wanna do it?"

"Let me tell Donnie first."

Donnie was sitting at the kitchen counter when I got back to my house, drinking a cup of coffee and reading the latest copy of *Island Business*.

"Where's Davison? Aren't we taking him to the airport?"

"He wanted to get a workout in this morning. He's going to be sitting on that plane for hours."

"I have some interesting news for you. I think you'll be happy to hear it. Or at least relieved."

Donnie was not relieved, as it turned out, and certainly not happy. In his mind, I was trying to put the blame for the fire on his beloved son.

"It's not what I'm saying at all, Donnie. I'm blaming Crystal. She's the one who set the fire. At least, it's a possibility. The cockroach costume was an unfortunate coincidence. Who could have guessed Crystal's real last name was Roach? Or that she was so sensitive about it?"

Donnie removed his reading glasses. "You don't know what really happened. And the insurance company might try to say the fire was Davison's fault. Davison invited Crystal into our house. He did something to make her angry, and he forgot to bring the propane tanks in after I asked him to."

"What *are* you telling the insurance company?" I asked.

"I'm answering all of their questions truthfully." Donnie swiveled away from me and back to his magazine.

"So you don't want to tell Medeiros about this."

"There's nothing to tell him."

"We could ask him to test the burned patch where the fire started—"

Donnie swiveled back around to face me. "Molly, what would be the point? You want this young girl in prison for arson? And what if it wasn't her? What if your theory is wrong? Anyway, Davison's leaving today. If it really *was* Crystal, she's not going to bother us again."

I glanced up at my Felix the Cat wall clock. "Speaking of which, isn't Davison supposed to be here by now? When is his flight?"

"He's supposed to be back any minute."

"I thought he was looking forward to going back to school and seeing his friends again. He's not trying to miss his flight or anything, is he?" I pulled down a coffee mug from the cabinet and brewed myself a cup of coffee, not that I needed the caffeine. I was pretty worked up about Donnie's unfair and wet blanket-y dismissal of my brilliant sleuthing.

"Of course, he doesn't want to miss his flight. Relax. It's probably just taking him longer to walk back from the gym than he expected."

"I'm not comfortable waiting until the last minute. Donnie, maybe we should go down to the gym and get him. So he doesn't miss his plane. We can take my car. It's blocking yours in."

Donnie checked his watch. "Good idea. I'll get his bag and his boarding pass. We might have to go to the airport straight from there."

"Call the gym," I said as we buckled ourselves in. "Ask them to check on Davison, make sure he's okay."

"You think something's wrong?" Donnie asked.

"I don't have a good feeling about this."

CHAPTER FORTY-SIX

"No one's answering at Strongman," Donnie said. "Someone should be there. What do you think is going on?"

"I don't know." I wished the slowpoke drivers clogging up the road in front of me would get a move on. "This doesn't seem right. No one's answering the phone at the gym? Maybe you should call 911."

"I'm not sure it's necessary."

"Donnie, listen. Davison—"

"Whoa, careful. Want me to drive?"

"I am being careful. People should make up their minds what lane they want to be in. As I was saying, it's worrisome that Davison's so late. Since he's been away at that school, he's become a lot more, what's the word?"

Donnie said, "Responsible," at the same time I said, "Rigid."

"Exactly," I said. "*Responsible*. He has a plane to catch. He wouldn't just float off and lose track of time. Would he?"

"No. I'll try his phone."

Donnie dialed, and Davison's duffel bag started to ring from the back seat.

Strongman gym was in the middle of a block on a short one-way street. I pulled into one of the diagonal spots at the curb next to a battered black pickup truck with a spray-painted black roll bar over the bed.

The gym's weathered front door stood propped open. Donnie and I walked into an empty reception area. A small television on the front counter was tuned to a daytime talk show.

We walked past the counter into the main workout room. Mirrors on every wall displayed my reflection at different angles, most of which called unwelcome attention to my abdomen and thighs. Treadmills and machines in duplicate rows receded into the distance, reflecting infinitely in the mirrors like some dystopian mechanical army. I looked around wildly for Donnie and was relieved to find him next to me.

"Let's not get separated," I said. "He's not here. Now, what?"

"Maybe he's back in the weight room."

"Oh no."

"What do you mean, oh no?"

"Nothing."

Randy Randolph's death was foremost in my

mind. Heavy weights everywhere, no one around. I didn't like this. I followed Donnie around a corner, to the deserted weight room.

"You smell incense?" I actually thought it smelled like pot, but I didn't want Donnie to think I knew what pot smelled like.

"There's the back exit." Donnie pointed. "Someone's probably taking a smoke break."

Three shirtless young men stood in the narrow alley behind the Strongman gym. One of them was short and stocky, meaty arms folded across his broad chest. The second was tall, rangy and shirtless, a curtain of orange-bleached hair flopped across his forehead. His belly tattoo looked familiar for some reason.

The third was Davison. He didn't see us at first. He seemed to be concentrating on holding his thumb and forefinger to his mouth. At the sight of Donnie and me, he dropped something on the ground and started coughing uncontrollably.

"Davison," Donnie said in a level voice. "You're going to miss your plane."

Davison gulped. "Yes, sir."

"Isn't someone supposed to be at the front desk?" I asked Davison's sketchy friends.

"Sorry, Miss." The taller one ran his hand nervously over his tattooed stomach. "Didn't know you guys was coming by."

"We have your bags," Donnie said. "We have to hurry." Then to me, "Want me to drive?"

"Great idea." The last thing I needed was Donnie

breathing down my neck while my Thunderbird stalled out in the middle of traffic. I slid into the back and let Davison have the Death Seat. Donnie had some trouble starting the car. He flooded the engine and had to wait before starting it again. This didn't exactly improve his mood.

"Who were those two guys?" I asked.

"Those are the Balusteros brothers," Donnie said. "Davison's known them since small kid time."

I noticed Donnie hadn't greeted them, despite the longstanding acquaintance.

"Balusteros as in Balusteros World of Furniture?" I asked. "Where I bought my living room set?"

"Right," Donnie said. "They also own Balusteros Baby World, Strongman Gym, and Lucky Bail Bonds."

We drove in heavy silence, Donnie staring straight ahead. Of course, he was annoyed with Davison for wandering off and getting high with his friends when he was supposed to be catching his flight. But I suspected his irritation was intensified by the fact that Davison had (once again) made a bad impression on me.

"If it weren't for your mother, you would've missed your plane," Donnie said, finally.

"Who?" I wondered what Sherry had to do with this.

"You," Donnie said. "You had the presence of mind to go out and look for him. Davison, *you* hadn't even started walking back yet. You owe her a big thank you."

"It's okay," I said. "Let's just get him on his flight."

We pulled up to the curb of tiny Mahina Airport. Davison got out, then reached into his duffel bag and pulled something out. A rectangle of black glass. He went over to the driver's side window and handed it through to Donnie.

"What's this?" Donnie asked.

"I found it in the house. Still works."

"It's mine," I cried. "Davison, it's the tablet our grant paid for. I was *frantic* about losing this."

"Aw, now you can be happy, then." He grinned, his grouchiness dispelled by what he apparently thought was a humorous plot twist.

"Where did you get this?"

"Our house, after it wen' burn down."

"It still works?"

"Yeah, fireproof case, like you said."

"Were you taking pictures with it?" I demanded.

"Baron and Boyboy was going in one bodybuilding contest and needed high res photos for the entry," Davison said. "Eh, lucky I found the thing, ah?"

"Please don't ever do that again."

"Davison, I'm very disappointed you kept this from Molly," Donnie said. "You caused her unnecessary worry. You're lucky we don't have time to discuss this now."

Donnie and I got out, said our goodbyes, and watched Davison shamble into the little terminal. Donnie got back into the driver's seat, and I buckled into the passenger seat. I picked up the tablet, unlocked the screen and checked the files.

"Everything's here, and then some."

"Sorry about that. I had no idea. I really thought everything was destroyed in the fire."

"I'll tell Emma she made a good decision getting the upgraded case. Boy, am I glad to have this back. You have no idea what kind of paperwork we were in for, reporting destruction of grant-funded equipment. It would've been a nightmare."

"Davison didn't mean any harm. He didn't know it was yours. Anyway, you might not even have it back now if it weren't for him."

"Hm. I thought you might point that out."

I spent the ride home deleting the shirtless gym photos, most of which I could see were of Baron and Boyboy Balusteros, and a few of which I now recognized as Davison himself.

CHAPTER FORTY-SEVEN

With Davison gone, Donnie and I were able to settle into a pleasant routine in my little place. We spent a relaxing weekend *a deux*, and even took Monday off to enjoy some additional quality time together. Tuesday I was back to morning yoga.

Sharla sat at the front desk of the Laughing Lotus, talking on the phone. She smiled when I walked in and hurriedly ended her telephone conversation.

"Molly, I followed your advice. Worked like a charm."

"You're staffing the front desk full time?"

"Nah. I got a video camera and ran surveillance."

"Oh. That wasn't really what I—"

"Wasn't even two days. Caught her red-handed."

"Oh. A customer? An employee?"

"Crystal Phoenix, aka Chrissy Roach."

"So what did you do?"

"Fired her, of course. And made a report to the

police. We have her on video. Know how she did it? She took the chopsticks out of her hair and used them to fish the bills out through the slot. Hey, your class is starting. Better hurry. Listen, thanks again. You were a real help."

After an invigorating yoga session, I went back to campus and spent several eyeball-aching hours filling out my department's weekly reports for the Student Retention Office. Then I joined Emma for lunch in the campus cafeteria. The fare would never pass muster with Davison's whole-food crew—everything tasted like it came out of fifty-gallon drums shipped from some central warehouse in Kansas—but it was fatty and salty enough to be palatable. We had just found an empty table and settled in with our trays when my chatty student Lars Suzuki buzzed over to us.

"Hey, Professors. Real quick, you know my friend who works on the cruise ship? He says he has a couple reduced rate cabins on the Christmas cruise next month. If you're interested you gotta act fast."

We declined gently. Lars probably made some small commission on referrals like this, and I liked to support my students in their business endeavors when I could, but I couldn't see Donnie getting away from the Drive-Inn long enough to go on a cruise.

"Yeah, it's probably for the best," Lars said. "The ship that's out now? They have another stomach virus going around."

"Well, that sounds unpleasant," I said.

"Oh yeah, and they just lost one of their

passengers at Aloha Tower."

"How do you lose a passenger?" Emma asked.

"I dunno. Someone's in a lotta trouble, though."

Lars took his leave, and Emma made a face.

"It's the last place in the world I'd wanna spend Christmas. Floating around on some plague ship. Hey, sorry I couldn't make it to yoga this morning. What'd I miss?"

"Oh, turns out Crystal Phoenix was the one stealing the money. They caught her on video. Fired her."

"Whoa, Sharon an' Sharla don't mess around. Anyway, I'm sure Crystal's gonna be fine. Doesn't she have like, twenty other jobs? Hey, there's Pat. Finally."

"Where were you?" I asked him.

"Hikers found the body of a young woman at the bottom of a ravine," Pat said. "She was wearing a crystal around her neck on a leather string."

"I thought you stopped reporting for *Island Confidential*," Emma said.

"I'm not reporting this. I was just in a meeting with our legal team. The university owns the property where the accident took place."

"A crystal around her neck?" I asked. "Wait a second. Was it Crystal Phoenix?"

"The lawyers told us not to say anything about it."

"You know she just got fired from the yoga studio."

"Really? So she might've jumped on purpose. Hang on."

"What are you doing with your phone?" Emma demanded. "Texting the lawyers with the *good news* we might not be liable?"

"No one said it was *good news*," Pat muttered as he typed.

"It's so sad," I said. "I hate to think of someone in such despair they think they have no other way out."

"Hey, Pat," Emma said, "speaking of people getting fired, when are *you* gonna get canned?"

"Not me." Pat laughed as he finished his text and put his phone away. "In fact, I'm starting a new project. I'm going to be promoting the university's new Prison Education Project. We call it PEP."

"PEP?" Emma snorted. "Seriously? Aw, Molly, *your* phone's ringing now? Geez, they should build a Faraday cage around this cafeteria. Then people would be forced to actually talk to each other."

It was Marshall Dixon's secretary calling. I was to report to Dixon's office immediately.

"How did she know I'd be available?"

"The central scheduling system," Pat said. "It knows you don't have any classes or meetings right now."

"Well, wish me luck." I piled my napkins and utensils on the tray and picked up my bag.

"Whatever happens," Emma said, "don't *you* go jumping off a cliff, okay?"

"And thanks for the encouragement," I added.

CHAPTER FORTY-EIGHT

Marshall Dixon had called me in to notify me that I had been awarded tenure. That was the good news.

The bad news was it looked like I was going to continue in my assignment as Interim Department Chair for the foreseeable future.

"Yours is the last tenure-track position the College of Commerce is going to get for a while," Marshall explained. "If we lose you, we won't get a replacement. Unless this budget situation turns around. And no one realistically expects it to. At best, we'd be authorized to hire an adjunct on a semester-to-semester basis."

"Well, I certainly don't want to contradict the idea that I'm indispensable, but what about the other tenured members of the department?"

"A department chair needs to be someone with a minimum of successful personnel actions," Marshall said.

"You've only had one grievance filed against you," Victor Santiago added, "and you were cleared."

"Right. The cheese-eating incident."

Hanson Harrison and Larry Schneider, the department's two most senior professors, had been slapping each other with formal complaints and grievances since before I was born. And Rodge Cowper—well, he was the reason for the Rodge Cowper Rule, which specified when you had a student in your office, you had to keep your door open at a forty-five-degree angle or greater. Our HR department was rumored to have an entire file cabinet dedicated to Rodge Cowper.

And Dan Watanabe, who was smart, reasonable, and even-tempered, was currently acting as Interim Dean. So much for the other four members of the Management Department.

"So what about our grant?" I asked. "Primo Nordmann's murderer hasn't been caught. And they still haven't worked out what happened to Randy Randolph. We'll continue to keep it on hold?"

"Yes," Victor said. "Let's wait to see what develops. We'll touch bases later."

"I have tenure now?"

Marshall handed me an envelope.

"This is the letter confirming your tenure and promotion."

I opened the envelope and read the letter, then folded it back up and tucked it into my bag.

"Marshall mentioned you wanted to make a gift to

the university," Victor said.

"Yes. This is unrelated to my tenure bid, of course, and is simply a contribution to Mahina State University and its important mission."

"We are grateful for the support," Marshall said.

"I'll bring the document in tomorrow. Where should I drop it off?"

"With my secretary. She'll take care of it."

"May I say something?"

Victor and Marshall exchanged a look.

"Certainly," Marshall said.

I looked from Marshall to Victor, and back to Marshall. "So I really have tenure?"

"For all intensive purposes, yes," Victor said.

I took a deep breath.

"It's touch *base*. Not touch *bases*. The expression is touch *base*. It's from baseball. You can only touch one base at a time."

"But it's two people," Victor said. "That's why you say touching *bases*."

"No, I think she's right," Marshall said.

"And it's all intents and purposes, not all intensive purposes."

"Thank you, Molly." Marshall looked weary. "I see your English background will be very useful for all of us in the years ahead."

"Great. Thank you. Thank you." I stood up and shook Marshall's hand (firm, perfect handshake) and then Victor's (a little on the bone-crushing side. Maybe he didn't like being corrected.) I couldn't wait to tell Donnie the good news.

CHAPTER FORTY-NINE

I came back home after class that evening to find a police cruiser in front of my house. Inside, Donnie sat at the dining room table with Detective Ka`imi Medeiros.

"Detective," I said. "It's, uh, great to see you? Would you like a cup of coffee?"

He shook his head.

"It's about Davison," Donnie said. He looked tired and drawn. I think most of Donnie's prematurely gray hairs had Davison's name on them. Anyone's guess what Davison had done *this* time.

"Did you tell Detective Medeiros Davison left on Friday?" I set my bag down in my office nook and went into the kitchen for my usual glass of wine, but then, I thought better of it. I didn't want Medeiros to think I was a lush. While I was in the kitchen, I noticed a frosty ice bucket sitting on the counter. A foil-wrapped cork protruded from the top. Donnie had been planning to celebrate something. Was it some kind of anniversary? I couldn't think of anything. Whatever the occasion was supposed to be, this news about Davison had put a damper on it. I'd ask Donnie about the champagne after Medeiros was gone.

"Detective Medeiros wants you to call Davison," Donnie said.

"He's already back at school," I said. "On the mainland. It's six hours later there."

"I realize that," Medeiros said. "Usually goes better when they can talk to the mother."

I came out into the dining room and sat down next to Donnie.

"When you say 'the mother,' you mean me?"

"This is about Randy Randolph," Donnie said.

"Oh no."

Medeiros explained his men had spoken to witnesses who had observed hostile interaction between Davison Gonsalves and the victim. Furthermore, Davison had been seen in the vicinity of Randolph's apartment. I could see this was breaking Donnie's heart.

"I think it's too late to call the East Coast," I said, to buy Donnie some time. "Maybe tomorrow would be better?"

"Don't want to delay," Medeiros said. "Better to do it now."

"Does it have to be Molly?" Donnie asked. "Molly, Davison already knows you don't think very highly of him. This is going to be hard for him."

"What are you talking about? I'm very tolerant of Davison."

"He told me what happened with the paper, in your class," Donnie said.

"Ah. So he told you that he cheated? That he copied his entire paper from his friend and handed it in as his own?"

"He admitted he made a stupid mistake. And afterward, he could never get in your good books. He's tried, Molly. He really has."

I could tell this was new information for Detective Medeiros.

"Detective," I said, "this was before I knew Donnie. Davison was a student in my class, where he uploaded a completely plagiarized paper. To a *plagiarism detection website*. Come on, that's just insulting Geez. What a day. Did you hear about Crystal Phoenix?"

"What about her?" Donnie asked, although he didn't seem very interested.

"She's dead. A couple of hikers found her."

Medeiros gave me a wary look.

"Where did you get that information, Professor?"

I remembered Pat wasn't supposed to tell us anything.

"Oh, *everyone's* talking about it on campus. Mahina State is such a gossipy place."

"Professor, would you mind calling your stepson for us?"

I looked from Donnie to Detective Medeiros and back.

"I really don't feel comfortable calling him."

You can't make me. And why should I? I should be celebrating with my husband right now, not spending my precious time wringing a confession out of my prodigal stepson.

Medeiros regarded me with a steady, calculating gaze.

"There *was* a body," he said finally. "But it wasn't Crystal Phoenix. Or Christine Roach, which was her birth name."

"What?"

"The victim had Crystal Phoenix's ID on her, which is how come we thought it was her. But when her former employers came in for ID her, it wasn't the same girl."

"It wasn't Crystal? Who was it?"

"If I tell you, will you make the call?"

I had to hand it to Ka`imi Medeiros. He knew how to motivate me. I nodded yes.

"The victim's name was Alison Boyd. She had been teaching yoga aboard the cruise ship. She visited the Laughing Lotus yoga studio the day before her death and had met the owners. They recognized her."

"She must have had Crystal's ID, though?"

"We think she borrowed it to get *kama`aina* discount at the shops. Not supposed to do it, but lotta people do."

"So, what happened to her?"

"Probably just unfamiliar with the terrain. Big mistake to go out hiking by yourself here."

"So, probably an accident," I said.

"You ready to make the call, Professor?"

That was apparently the signal my stalling was over. Donnie gave me a faint nod as if to say, "Might as well get this over with." He looked truly miserable.

I wasn't so sure poor Alison Boyd really had gone out hiking by herself. If I was right, maybe Donnie's life wouldn't be ruined after all. I took my phone out of my bag and placed it on the table. The quilted turquoise case (chosen to match my Thunderbird's paint job) looked frivolous and out of place, its little rhinestones glinting irreverently.

Medeiros produced a device that looked like a shiny black pack of gum and plugged it into my phone.

"Both one party states," Medeiros said, in response to my questioning look. "Your consent is sufficient. Please make the call on speaker."

CHAPTER FIFTY

I switched on the speaker and dialed. Three rings, four rings—

"It's too late," I said. "He's already asleep."

As I said it, the line clicked.

"Eh, Molly?" It sounded like Davison had been woken from a sound sleep. "Where you?"

"I'm calling from Mahina, Um, sounds like you got back okay?"

"Mahina." Davison guffawed. "Aw, kinda far for one booty call, ah? How long's it gonna take you to get here?"

I rested my forehead in my hands.

"Davison, have you been drinking?"

"Nah, nah, nah. Just some margaritas is all."

"I don't think this is going to be a productive conversation," I said.

"Please," Medeiros mouthed.

"Molly." My phone squawked. "Who's there wit'

you?"

"Your father is right here, Davison. You're on speaker."

"Hey, buddy," Donnie said, without conviction.

"Aw, Dad. I was just kidding around wit' Molly, ah?"

Medeiros motioned to me to start talking.

"Hey, Davison? Remember Randy Randolph? The unpleasant man who ended up squashed to death in his home gym?"

"Yeah?" Davison sounded wary now.

"I remember Crystal mentioned he was a client. You must've talked about him with her."

"Aw, that girl was *psychic*."

"Do you mean *psychotic*?" I asked.

"Nah. What I said. Psychic. I told her how I almost got into it with Randolph, and she says, 'Don't worry about him. Karma's gonna get 'em. An' she was right."

"Did you ever talk to Crystal after that incident with the cockroach costume? When she stormed out of the house?"

"Nah."

"Do you know why Crystal was so angry about the costume?"

"'Cause young girls like her want things romantic an' perfect all the time an' can't appreciate when someone's just joking around."

"Her *real* name was Christine *Roach*. She didn't like her name, and she thought you were making fun of it."

Davison absorbed the information in silence, then slurred a few swear words.

"Language," Donnie mumbled halfheartedly.

"Okay, listen," I said. "They just found the body of a young woman. About Crystal's age, hair color, and build. She was wearing a crystal around her neck on a leather string."

"Aw, no. Crystal?"

"It wasn't Crystal."

There was no sound on the other end.

"Davison, are you there?" I said.

"Yeah?"

"I'm telling you this because you knew Crystal better than any of us. Now, did she ever tell you she changed her identity, went on the run, anything like that?"

"She told me her last name, Phoenix, meant something about a bird that dies an' gets reborn."

"Did she tell you whether she's ever been reborn, specifically?" I asked.

"I dunno."

"Crystal was caught stealing from her employer," I said. "She was fired, and the theft was reported to the police. If Crystal had committed a serious crime under another identity, she couldn't afford an encounter with law enforcement. She'd have to get away quickly, and throw the police off her trail."

I was talking to Medeiros now. The fact that Davison was on the line was incidental.

"Conveniently, a young woman fitting Crystal's description ends up dead, wearing Crystal's jewelry and carrying Crystal's ID. Obviously, this is supposed to make people think Crystal herself is dead. Shortly afterward, a passenger disappears from a cruise ship at Aloha Tower, the next major stop on the cruise ship route after Mahina."

Detective Medeiros perked up at this.

"One of my students has a friend who works on a cruise ship. Someone disembarked on Oahu and never returned to the ship. I'm *sure* the police will look into this, to find out if the missing passenger was, in fact, the ship's yoga instructor, Alison Boyd."

Medeiros took his small notebook out of the pocket of his aloha shirt and started to make notes. He didn't look happy about it, but to his credit, he did it.

"What do you want me to say?" Davison demanded. "If Crystal did something bad, let someone else snitch. I'm not gonna do it."

"Someone else?" I said. "Who? Randy Randolph, her former client? Primo Nordmann, her former coworker? The poor visiting yoga instructor who fell down a five hundred foot embankment, dressed as Crystal? *None of them can snitch, Davison.* You know why?"

Medeiros was making a palms-down motion at me. Either "that's enough" or "calm down."

"All right, I'll let you go," I said. "I know it's late, and you probably want to get to sleep."

"Eh, Molly," he mumbled. "It's *cold* out here, ah? Freezing my `okole* off. Maybe you could—"

I disconnected the call.

"We'll follow up on the missing cruise ship passenger." Medeiros plucked the eavesdropping device off my phone and tucked it into the pocket of his aloha shirt. I was annoyed. He didn't say thank you or anything like it. "You got anything else you want to tell me?"

I gave him Lars Suzuki's contact information.

"You think he'll talk to us?"

"Lars Suzuki? Oh, absolutely. He'll talk."

CHAPTER FIFTY-ONE

As soon as Medeiros left, I went for the wine. Donnie remained at the table, contemplating his folded hands.

"So that went as well as it could have." I brought my brimming *furikake* glass and sat back down next to him.

"I think you saved him, Molly," Donnie said quietly. "Thank you."

"You can thank me by telling him not to talk to me in that gross way."

"What gross thing did he say?"

"Doesn't matter," I sighed. I knew Donnie had a blind spot when it came to his beloved son. He apparently had a deaf spot, too. "Anyway, happier topic. I have some good news."

"I know you do." He smiled for the first time that evening. He stood up and went to the kitchen. I heard a loud *bang*, like a gunshot. Donnie returned to the table holding the smoking champagne bottle in one hand and two glasses in the other. They were the narrow kind that let the imbiber watch the little bubbles floating up to the surface.

"Real champagne glasses. Where did you get them?"

"Hagiwara's Specialty Liquors." Donnie was grinning. "Same place I got the champagne. Congratulations on earning tenure."

"Tenure *was* my big news. How did you know?"

"No secrets in Mahina." He set the glasses down on the table and poured. "This is a very gossipy place. Like you said."

"Donnie, listen. I have to tell you something. You'll probably think less of me, but, okay, come sit next to me."

I selected the picture gallery on my phone and pulled up the photo of the old cartoon. Donnie took out his reading glasses and peered at the screen.

"This was on a newspaper page wrapped around the teapot. In the box of old silver-plate."

"It's supposed to be Queen Liliuokalani?"

"The cartoonist was Mary Pfaff, the Beatrix Potter of Hawaii. And the grandmother of our most promising donor."

I described how I had used this embarrassing information to pressure Marshall Dixon into supporting my tenure bid.

"And that's how I got tenure," I said, when I had spun the whole sordid story. "Now you know your wife is a blackmailing fraud."

"You're not a fraud. Although the cartoon is, to use your word, gross."

"The cartoon saved my job. But it's kind of ruined Alice Mongoose for me."

"Was this before her children's books?"

"Yes. The overthrow was in 1893, right? I don't think the first Alice Mongoose book was printed until after World War 1."

"Mary Pfaff was young. Maybe the cartoon wasn't even her idea. Maybe she had to make some compromises to get her career started."

"Well, that's a thing that happens, yes."

"I don't think you need to throw away the old t-shirt you like. Or those Alice Mongoose refrigerator magnets."

"The socks, the earrings, my Alistair Rat alarm clock…" I pushed my wine aside and took a sip of champagne. It tasted dry and prickly.

"What *is* the appeal of Alice Mongoose for you? I always thought it was just popular in Hawaii. Did you get the books on the mainland?"

"I never heard of her until I moved here. You must've grown up with the stories, though."

"I think a lot of kids around here grew up with their parents reading the books to them. I didn't exactly have that kind of—I've seen the characters but I don't know the stories too well."

"Alice Mongoose is based on when the mongoose was brought in to Hawaii to get rid of the rats. But it didn't work out because the rats were nocturnal, so the mongoose were asleep when the rats were out and about."

"Uh huh. We learned about it in school."

"Exactly. So the story goes, Alice is supposed to find and kill rats, right? But Alice isn't cut out to be a killer. She wears pearls and gloves and a print dress and a little cloche hat, and she loves to sit down at a properly set table to a meal of eggs. When she eats, she picks up a whole egg in her little mongoose hands and nibbles on it. It's cute."

Donnie refilled my champagne glass. "And then?"

"So the first rat she meets is Alistair. She's heard all about how rats are vicious and aggressive, but Alistair is very polite and gentle and he wears a shiny little top hat, and they start to talk and he invites her to breakfast, which for him is dinner, because she's waking up at the same time he's going to bed. Or maybe it's the other way around. Anyway, they become good friends, and they have a series of adventures and little misunderstandings. They're kind of like Frog and Toad, have you ever read *Frog and Toad*?"

Donnie shook his head.

"There's this really touching illustration of when Alice first arrives on the Hamakua Coast. You see her from the back, standing on the bluff in her little print dress with her tiny steamer trunks and hatboxes piled next to her. The landscape is so vast, and she's so tiny, and she's holding one of her hatboxes in one hand and looking up at Mauna Kea. This is how good Mary Pfaff's illustrations are. You can see it in her little mongoose body, her posture, the mixture of trepidation and courage. It's such a sweet, innocent little world they live in, Alice Mongoose and Alistair Rat."

"Alice Mongoose finds herself in an unfamiliar situation." Donnie nodded. "But she makes the best of it, stays true to herself, and ends up finding friendship and happiness. I can see why you like her."

"Alice Mongoose never has to threaten anyone in order to keep her job. Oh, Donnie, you must be so disappointed in me. It's just, I didn't know what else to do."

"I'm not disappointed at all. Anyway, I already knew about it."

I set my half-full glass down and stared at my husband. He did, in fact, look completely unruffled.

"Everything I just told you? You already *knew*?"

"Well, I hadn't seen the cartoon before, but I heard about it." Donnie placed his hand on mine. "Look, Molly, sometimes in business you don't have the option of making the right decision. All you can do is make the less wrong decision. And that's what you did. You deserved tenure. The process wasn't working, and you did what you had to do."

"Oh my gosh. How many people know about this? Everyone must hate me."

Donnie laughed. "I don't think so. They appreciate you handling things discreetly. You didn't make a big fuss when things weren't going your way."

I exhaled with relief and drained my champagne

glass. "Hey, as long as we're being all honest and everything. Why were you sitting in an empty classroom with Nicole Nixon? And being so secretive about it?"

"Ah." He took a sip of champagne. "I didn't want to tell you right away in case it didn't work out."

"But now you will tell me, right?"

"I'm taking an English literature class."

"Really? A class with one student?"

"No, there's about twenty students."

"I happened to walk by the classroom Wednesday and it was just you in there with Nicole Nixon."

"That must've been the twelfth. All of us have been meeting with the teacher individually to talk about our annotated bibliographies."

"Is that why you were in the library?"

"Yes. I'm a registered Mahina State student now, with full library privileges. You have some good databases there. I wish I'd known about them earlier."

"The movies, then? Were they for the class, too? *Henry the Fifth*, and *Becket*?"

"Yes. They were homework. But it was fun to watch with you. Have you eaten?"

"No, I haven't. And I'm getting a little lightheaded from the champagne."

"I made some chicken cacciatore." Donnie got up. "I'll heat it up for us."

"Thank you. So, why are you taking an English literature class, of all things?"

"I don't like it when someone uses an expression,

or makes a reference, and I don't understand it. So I'm fixing that. Becoming a better-rounded person. How hungry are you? Should I heat up the whole thing?"

"Just one piece for me. I'm already well rounded enough."

CHAPTER FIFTY-TWO

The authorities caught up to Crystal Roach in Henderson, Nevada.

Crystal confessed she set the cockroach costume on fire on Donnie's front porch. She felt hurt, she lashed out, and she was terribly sorry, she said. She claimed she hadn't noticed the propane tanks and never would have dreamed a little fire could have done so much damage.

The cruise ship's records indicated Alison Boyd, the resident yoga instructor, disembarked at the Aloha Tower Cruise Ship Terminal and disappeared. In fact, it wasn't Alison who walked off the ship. It was Crystal. Poor Alison had walked off the cruise ship one stop earlier, in Mahina, and visited the new Laughing Lotus yoga studio. All Crystal had to do was take Alison for a walk in the woods, push her down a ravine, hike down after her, swap IDs, and fasten her distinctive necklace onto the victim.

Crystal swore Randy Randolph's death had been accidental. True, Randolph had been holding back on his payments, claiming he wasn't getting the results he wanted from her training, and he'd threatened to post negative reviews of her work online. To make matters worse, he had been inexcusably rude to poor Davison, who was practically still a child. But she insisted that she did not orchestrate Randy Randolph's tragic misadventure.

She did *not* wait until he was holding aloft his heaviest weight, and then pick up additional plates and slide them onto the bar, one after another, until Randolph's arms trembled and gave way. And she most certainly did not stand back and watch him die as he gasped for help, the bar slowly crushing his larynx. She claimed he must have tried to lift the heavy weight after their session had ended. She would not have allowed him to attempt it had she been there. She would never, she insisted, jeopardize a client's safety.

Crystal outright denied having anything to do with Primo Nordmann's dismemberment. Even though according to testimony from Laughing Lotus employees, Primo knew Crystal was stealing from the money box, and he'd threatened to tell Sharon and Sharla. And several members of Students for a Better World recalled Crystal and Primo going out together on a midnight "action" at Art Lam's papaya farm the night of the murder. The leather string holding the crystal pendant—the necklace that

Crystal had worn continuously until she'd placed it on Alison Boyd's body—had traces of Primo's blood. Thus, second-degree murder charges (for chopping up Primo) were added to arson (Donnie's house), negligent homicide (Randy Randolph), and first-degree murder (Alison Boyd).

In case you're wondering how I know all this, I got the details from Pat Flanagan. He's no longer working for Mahina State's Associate Vice President in Charge of Student Outreach and Community Relations. *Island Confidential* is back in business.

Pat announced this transition to Emma and me during one of our regular Sunday brunches at the Pair-O-Dice Bar and Grill. He claimed that he was tired of shilling for The Man and wanted nothing more than to return to honest and thoughtful journalism.

"You saying you didn't get fired cause of your PEP thing?" Emma looked skeptical.

"You were *fired*, Pat?"

"It was a mutual decision. I'm gonna get more coffee."

Pat got up to refill his Styrofoam cup with the Pair-O-Dice's watery brew.

"What happened?" I asked Emma.

"He did this social media blitz promoting the university's new Prison Education Project, you know, PEP. So this one post went viral."

"That's good, right?"

"Had a photo of the prison weight room with some of the guys, yeah? And the caption was,

'Hands off the cage meat, ladies'. Some people in the sociology department said it was disrespectful and complained to the chancellor."

Pat returned to our table.

"What are we talking about?"

"Nothing," Emma said.

"You told me you had some good news for me?" I asked.

"Oh yeah. My friend, Jeffrey couldn't believe your cartoon was really Mary Pfaff's handiwork."

"But it was signed. By Mary Pfaff."

"Well, he dug into it. Mary Pfaff's illustrations had become so popular, her editor at *The Brockton Bugle* started putting her signature on the work of other artists. Including that piece. Her editor was the main reason she quit and moved west. He was kind of a jerk."

"So someone way out in Minnesota went to the trouble to draw a cartoon about the overthrow of the Hawaiian Kingdom?"

"Sure. The overthrow was front page news in the U.S."

"Does this mean I can wear my Alice Mongoose t-shirt again?"

"With a clear conscience."

"That is good news. Thank you, Pat."

"Focusing on the *important* questions," Emma sighed. "Hey Molly, I drove by Donnie's place the other day. Doesn't look like there's any rebuilding going on. Insurance company stalling or what?"

"Oh. Donnie has decided not to rebuild his

house."

"How come?" Emma pressed.

"My place is a much better location for him. Just a few blocks from Donnie's Drive-Inn. So he decided to use the insurance payout to build us another bathroom."

"That actually seems like a good idea," Pat said. Emma nodded agreement.

Three months after that conversation, my house is unrecognizable. Gone is the little telephone nook and nearly every non-load-bearing wall. Instead, the living room, dining room, and kitchen are one vast entertaining space, with a lofty vaulted ceiling overhead. Donnie bought us a full set of proper tableware and moved my boxes and the contents of my "skinny" closet into a storage unit, ensuring we have both a guest room and a spare room available for visitors.

I'm thrilled, of course. How could I not be? This is a new adventure, this living together in close quarters, with no privacy or space of my own, sharing decisions instead of having things exactly the way I like them. I know I'll adjust brilliantly. Just like Alice Mongoose did.

As Emma has pointed out, invasive species are very adaptable.

ABOUT THE AUTHOR

Like Molly Barda, Frankie Bow teaches at a public university. Unlike her protagonist, she is blessed with delightful students, sane colleagues, a loving family, and a perfectly nice office chair. She believes if life isn't fair, at least it can be entertaining. Sign up for Frankie's newsletter and get a short Professor Molly story: http://bit.ly/Trust-Fall

ALICE MONGOOSE

"I would like to ask about the house next door," Alice said. "My name is Alice. I have just arrived in Hawaii."

"I am pleased to meet you," said the dapper little fellow. "My name is Alistair. I am just getting up. Do come in and have a bit of breakfast and a cup of tea."

Alice Mongoose and Alistair Rat in Hawaii by Mary Pfaff is now available in bookstores. Download the free e-book and sign up to get the latest news: http://bit.ly/AliceMongoose